"Join me for a bite.

It was a simple enough question, but for Laurel, it suddenly became complicated. "No, thanks," she answered, trying to sound casual. She took a step back. "I really can't tonight."

"What do I have to do to change your mind? It's just dinner between friends."

"We're not friends," Laurel said, wondering what he was playing at.

"I promise not to bite."

He didn't look much like a predator now, but the warning alarm kept sounding in her head. Earlier he'd looked like wicked temptation, danger and sin. Now with dark hair falling boyishly over his brow, the hard lines of his jaw relaxed, a slight evening shadow softening the sharp angles of his cheeks and chin, he looked sexier than any man had a right to. Their eyes met, his gaze holding her captive.

His charcoal brow lifted slightly. "Hungry?" he asked lightly.

"I—I was."

A flash of a satisfied smile touched his lips before he glanced down and opened the menu, releasing her from his silent hold.

Dear Reader,

Whether this is your first or a return visit to Luna Hermosa, New Mexico, and the Morente/Garrett families, welcome!

As natives of the Southwest, Luna Hermosa has been a wonderful place to visit every time we sit down to write. When we penned our first book in the Brothers of Rancho Piñtada series, *Sawyer's Special Delivery,* we knew two things. First, we wanted to write a family story about people with imperfect lives finding perfect love. And second, that story needed to take place in a town that was alive with the things that matter to us—community, friends, fun and familiarity.

Our second book in the series, *The Rancher's Second Chance,* gave us another chance to explore more of the town we created. Handsome Rafe Garrett and his lifelong love Julene Santiago also allowed us to visit an enchanting, fictional American Indian community.

In *What Makes a Family?* you'll meet the second gorgeous Morente brother, Cort, and his new "friend" Laurel Tanner. Cort is trying to rebuild his life. Laurel has left behind all that was safe and comfortable to her and moved to Luna Hermosa. She thinks her dreams of love and a family are over, and then she meets Cort....

Enjoy!

Nicole Foster

WHAT MAKES
A FAMILY?

NICOLE FOSTER

Silhouette

SPECIAL EDITION

Published by Silhouette Books

America's Publisher of Contemporary Romance

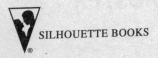

SILHOUETTE BOOKS

ISBN-13: 978-0-373-24853-7
ISBN-10: 0-373-24853-9

WHAT MAKES A FAMILY?

Visit Silhouette Books at www.eHarlequin.com

Printed in U.S.A.

NICOLE FOSTER

is the pseudonym for the writing team of Danette Fertig-Thompson and Annette Chartier-Warren. Both journalists, they met while working on the same newspaper, and started writing historical romance together after discovering a shared love of the Old West and happy endings. Their seventeen-year friendship has endured writer's block, numerous caffeine-and-chocolate deadlines and the joyous chaos of marriage and raising the five children between them. They love to hear from readers. Send a SASE for a bookmark to PMB 228, 8816 Manchester Rd., Brentwood, MO, 63144.

For Heidi,
As a daughter you are a treasure;
as a woman and friend you are a gift.

To my partner,
who has proved to me every day
for the last twenty-four years that family
isn't just the people to whom you're related.

Chapter One

I should have expected it, Cort Morente thought as he tried to avoid being caught up in the jostling, noisy mob on their way to the buses and waiting cars. *This is what you get when you decide to start the rest of your so-called life on a Monday.*

It was quitting time at Luna Hermosa Middle School and it looked to Cort as though every kid in the place was trying to get out the doors at once. Every kid except the skinny eleven-year-old boy who'd left him standing here in the midst of all this chaos looking stupid. And he didn't have a hope of finding him in this crowd.

"Don't say I didn't warn you." Alex Trejos, the middle-school principal, walked up to where Cort stood. Cort had known Alex since they'd gone to junior high here and he knew from Alex's smirk that he was enjoying himself way too much at Cort's expense. "I told you Tommy was skittish."

Cort cursed under his breath. "Yeah, but you didn't warn me he also kicks like a mule. If this is your idea of therapy, I think I'll go back to sitting alone in my apartment and feeling sorry for myself."

The only reason he was here was because he'd been doing largely that for longer than he cared to admit. And he didn't like what he was turning into—brooding, withdrawn, uncharacteristically short of patience and long on frustration. He was supposed to have been easing back into normal life after nearly two months in the hospital and then another nine months of intense physical therapy. The problem was he'd lost what had passed as normal life for him after one of the suspects in a drug case he'd been working on took offense at being investigated and decided to let Cort know it by attempting to make him part of the pavement. In the collision between Cort and the pickup truck, the truck had won. The doctors had told him he was lucky to be alive. Instead, it was his career with the sheriff's department that had died.

They'd put his right arm and shoulder back together, but the nerve damage was permanent, along with, it seemed, the headaches that at times laid him flat for hours. He'd never again be fit enough for any job at the sheriff's department other than riding a desk and he knew he wouldn't last a week at that before boredom drove him crazy. So for the last several months, he'd been dutifully going through the motions of therapy, recovering while his life fell down around him and he tried not to think about having to start the whole game over with a completely new set of rules.

When Alex called to ask him for a favor, he'd reluctantly agreed, not because he particularly wanted to do it but because it was doing *something*. He wasn't used to sitting around. Most of his ten years with the sheriff's department had been as part of the special-narcotics task force. He'd worked undercover a good amount of the time and had gotten addicted to the adrenaline-spiked cocktail made up of lack of sleep, regular infusions of caffeine and living on the edge. The withdrawal had been hell.

He suspected Alex knew that and had asked him to talk to

Tommy Lujan more as a distraction than because he thought Cort was the best person for the job.

Tommy had problems of his own. Abandoned by his mother when he was two, no idea who his father was, living for years with an abusive uncle who was now in prison for the foreseeable future, then bounced around foster homes from which he was always running away. The kid had never been in any real trouble but Alex was worried that unless someone could reach Tommy, befriend him, it was only a matter of time before things got worse.

Cort hadn't been confident about his ability to become any kind of mentor to Tommy. The only kids he was used to talking to were of the high-school dealer variety and his nephews—who at two and a half and eight months were still largely into monologues instead of dialogues—none of which had prepared him for an actual conversation with a kid. He'd planned to take Alex's advice and just talk to the kid. But the instant Tommy saw him the boy looked like he'd been confronted by the devil and bolted. When Cort made a grab for him, the kid had kicked him in the shin and had run out of Alex's office before either of them could stop him.

"I suppose you think this is funny?" he grumbled as Alex's smirk threatened to become a grin.

"Well, I gotta say, seeing big, bad Cort Morente outwitted by an eleven-year-old is pretty entertaining. And you have to admit, it's given you something else to think about." Alex turned serious. "I'm worried about Tommy, though. Despite everything, he's a good kid. I hate to think he's run off again. He doesn't have anywhere to go."

"So you don't have any idea where Tommy might hang out?" Maybe if he could find the kid, he could salvage something from what had so far proven to be a wasted day.

"No, but Laurel would." Seeing Cort's unspoken question, Alex said, "Laurel Tanner. Tommy's resource teacher. She works with the kids who need academic help and she knows him better than anyone. He likes her and if Tommy were going to confide in anyone, it would be Laurel."

Cort glanced around him. Most of the kids had left and the building looked empty. "Is she here?"

"Probably," Alex said over his shoulder as he started back inside. "Let me warn her about you first. She's new here and she's one of the best teachers I have. I don't want her running away, too."

Cort started to follow him when Alex pulled up short and looked toward the parking lot. "Wait, there she is. She must be coaching at the community center today. Hey, Laurel!"

Alex waved at a woman poised beside a battered-looking compact car, her hand on the open rear driver's-side door, apparently frozen in the motion of either retrieving or stowing something in the backseat.

At Alex's call she looked up and directly at Cort. In the seconds they stood watching each other, Cort had a brief impression of a tall, slender woman, pale honey-colored hair gilded by the late afternoon sun. Her expression reminded him of Tommy's just before the boy had run.

He started forward. She suddenly moved, waving quickly in his and Alex's direction then hurriedly getting in her car and driving off.

Frowning a little, Alex said, "I guess she thought I was just saying goodbye."

"Not likely," Cort muttered under his breath, instinctively knowing she, too, had taken off the moment she laid eyes on him. "Didn't you say she was doing some kind of coaching at the community center today?"

"Girls' basketball. But you just can't go chasing after her. Hey, Cort!"

But Cort was already halfway to where he'd parked his motorcycle, pulling on his gloves as he went. This time he was going to find out just what it was about him today that had everyone running in the opposite direction.

Laurel Tanner looked at the frightened boy hunched over

in the seat behind her, his face propped on skinny fists, and decided both of them were in a lot of trouble.

She'd been stunned to find Tommy hiding in the backseat of her car. She never locked it, figuring the chances of it getting stolen were slim since on a good day she had trouble starting it. But she never imagined one of her students would take advantage of that to use her backseat for a refuge.

Even more unnerving was the reason Tommy was hiding in the first place.

"You aren't gonna tell him where I am, are you?" Tommy asked for the umpteenth time since she'd found him cowering in her car and he'd begged her to help him escape from the man she'd seen with Alex. On a wild impulse she was starting to regret, now that she'd actually taken the time to think, she'd taken him and run.

Tommy had balked at going to the community center, but Laurel insisted. He couldn't hide in her car forever and she needed a place where she could talk to him without worrying about who might be listening. Her basketball class didn't start until four and she knew the center, particularly the snack-bar area where she was taking him, would be relatively empty for at least a half an hour. Even better, the snack bar overlooked the parking lot so Laurel could keep an eye on new arrivals.

"I'm not going to tell anyone," Laurel reassured him. The last thing Tommy had to worry about was her telling that man or anyone else that she'd helped him escape from school. She didn't even want to imagine the repercussions. "But you need to tell me why you ran away."

"I told you, because of him." Now seated in the backseat, Tommy began shredding the edge of a paper napkin. "He has something to do with my uncle's business." Tommy had been removed from his uncle's house nearly two years ago when his uncle was sent to jail. Laurel didn't know the whole story but whatever had happened to Tommy had left scars.

"Do you know him?" When Tommy answered with a sharp

shake of his head, Laurel asked gently, "Then how do you know he has something to do with your uncle?"

"You saw him. He looks like all the guys that used to come to my uncle's house. My uncle must have sent him."

Laurel didn't blame Tommy for being afraid of *him*. The man she'd glimpsed with Alex at school was big and intimidating, the all black he wore did nothing to soften her first impression. For the seconds they'd locked gazes, she'd felt as if he could see right through her and knew even before she did that she was going to run with Tommy.

She hesitated over what was potentially a taboo subject with the boy before saying, "I thought your uncle was in jail."

She could see Tommy looking at her in the rearview mirror. The expression in his dark eyes was a mix of fear and impatience. His hands clenched tightly as if he were trying to hold himself together. "He is. But that don't mean anything. I'll bet he could do stuff from jail."

Laurel knew she had to tread cautiously or Tommy would shut down. "What kind of stuff?"

"Just…things. Lots of things. I don't want to talk about him." He looked away from her again, his mouth drawn in a hard line, retreating into himself.

"Okay, you don't have to." Later at the community center she plotted how she might get Tommy to trust her again. To give herself time to think, she fished some change out of her purse and bought Tommy a soda from a vending machine. He accepted it wordlessly and they sat in silence as Laurel tried to decide what to do next.

She could be in serious trouble for running with Tommy, but she'd acted impulsively, out of an instinct to protect him. She didn't know what to think of his story now. Surely Alex wouldn't have allowed the kind of man Tommy feared into school, let alone let him talk to Tommy.

But Tommy was obviously frightened of the man and equally afraid of his uncle and what he imagined the man could still do to him.

This wasn't the first time Laurel wanted to reach out and do something to help Tommy. Since she'd come to Luna Hermosa two months before to accept the post as the middle-school resource teacher, she'd connected with the thin, quiet boy who spent most of his time alone. Maybe it was because of that, because both of them, by choice or circumstance, were isolated, unconnected to anyone else. And maybe part of it was because involving herself in someone's else's problems was becoming a habit, one of the things she did, like teaching basketball or spending hours running or hiking, to avoid going home where she was alone except for her ghosts and memories.

"Tommy, I'm sure Mr. Trejos wouldn't let anyone that meant to hurt you into school. And why would your uncle send someone like that to find you?"

Tommy looked up at her, an almost adult seriousness on his face. "You don't know my uncle. Nobody messes with him." He averted his eyes. "He told me he'd come back for me one day."

He looked so utterly lost that Laurel started to reach across the table to touch him, to assure him his uncle, no matter what he'd threatened, couldn't hurt him anymore. But at that moment a slight sound caught her attention and Laurel turned to look over her shoulder just as Tommy's glance shot up.

The man from the school was there.

Laurel fleetingly gave herself a mental kick for letting her focus on Tommy cause her to miss the man's arrival.

Tommy didn't take time to think. He immediately jerked up and out of his chair and scrambled for the door. The man made a move as if to step in Tommy's path, but Laurel moved faster. Putting herself between Tommy and his pursuer, she grabbed handfuls of the man's leather jacket just above the elbow, preventing him from chasing after the boy.

He made a frustrated noise that sounded suspiciously like a curse and grasped her shoulders as if he intended to put her aside to go after Tommy. When it became clear Tommy's head start made that impossible, he fixed her with a dark glare that made it obvious he wasn't too happy having her practically in his arms and in his way.

An odd nervous quiver plucked at Laurel's insides. Fear. It had to be fear. He was the man chasing Tommy, he was holding her and he looked dangerous. So she called it fear, even though she suspected any other woman would say it was because he looked like the star of a wicked fantasy. One that involved black leather, slow heat and a wild ride.

But she told herself it was the way he looked at her now, slowly assessing, as if committing every detail of her, inside and out, to memory. That and he made her feel small, almost petite. At five feet eight inches that rarely happened to her. This man, though, had to be over six foot and from his build, spent a good portion of his time working out.

This close she could see his eyes were a deep brown, almost black. But they gave her no clue what he was thinking when he looked at her, though she doubted she inspired any fantasies for him. She'd changed before leaving school into baggy gray sweats, her hair hastily pulled into a ponytail, with only the barest trace of makeup on her face.

She noticed his scent of leather and wind, so close now as he held her between his hands, seemingly distracted for a moment by his study of her. Her skin prickled with a sudden awareness immediately followed by a flash of irritation. What was wrong with her? She'd never felt this way around a man, so unsettled, uneasy. She didn't understand it when she should be thinking of him as an adversary, if not the enemy. And she definitely didn't like it.

She wanted peace and she wasn't going to find it with dark, wicked-looking strangers who could start her pulse thrumming and her nerves quivering with just a look and a touch.

Realizing she was making herself a willing captive by still clutching his jacket, Laurel let go at the same time he dropped his hands. She took a few steps back then stopped, not at all sure she wanted to confront him. Yet she was certain he wasn't about to let her run away again.

He eyed her up and down. "My guess is you're Laurel Tanner," he said wryly, bringing a flush to her face.

She could hardly deny it since Alex must have told him who she was. "Yes, I am." Laurel stopped herself from looking away from that steady gaze. She refused to back down even though he didn't have to say a word to be daunting. All in all, the situation couldn't get a whole lot worse so before she could tell herself it was a bad idea, she blurted out, "Why are you chasing Tommy?"

Laurel could have sworn she saw a flash of amusement in his eyes. "I'm not exactly chasing him."

He reached as if to retrieve something from an inside jacket pocket then stopped. He frowned, shrugging it off when she looked at him questioningly. "Some habits are hard to break. I used to be a cop. I'm Cort Morente. I know you saw me with Alex. Alex and I are old friends and he told me a little about the trouble Tommy was having and asked me if I'd talk to him. Alex thought I might be able to help."

"Oh…you—I thought…" Laurel inwardly groaned. *No, the problem is I didn't think. And what I think is now I'm really in trouble. Taking a kid from school and running. Just great.*

He smiled, slow and easy, and this time the amusement was definite. "I think I have a pretty good idea of what you thought. Here!" Reaching around her, he pulled out a chair for her, waiting until she'd dropped into it before taking a seat across from her. "Just for the record, I'm not a bad guy trying to snatch Tommy. Although obviously both you and he had other ideas. Maybe I need to work on my image."

"It's not that, exactly," Laurel said. Studying him more closely, without the distractions created by her overactive imagination, he didn't look as threatening, especially when he smiled and she heard the dry humor threading that deep, dark voice of his. And she recognized the lines of tension on his face and the shadows in his eyes. They were almost identical to the ones she saw in her mirror every morning. He looked as if he hadn't gotten a good night's sleep in a long while, as if he had to contend with his own ghosts.

Her perception of him shifted, softening at the edges.

"Tommy thinks you're involved in whatever his uncle's business was. He said you looked like the guys that used to come to his uncle's house."

"Yeah, so I heard," he told her, making Laurel realize he'd overheard at least part of her conversation with Tommy.

"That's why he ran away. He's afraid of you."

"Is that why you ran with him?"

He smiled a little and Laurel couldn't quite meet his eyes. "I...he—I was worried about him." Looking back up at him she said in a rush, "You don't exactly look the part of the hero in all this."

"Guess not," he countered with a rueful smile. "Look, I used to be part of the narcotics task force and I worked a lot of undercover. I haven't quite kicked the habit of dressing the part."

The trace of bitterness in his voice stirred her curiosity but, too used to deflecting well-meaning inquiries about her own private demons, she didn't pursue it.

"Tell me about Tommy. Alex said you know him better than anyone at school."

"Not just at school. I'm not sure Tommy has anyone he's close to, maybe never has had. I've not been here long myself, I just started in August and Tommy's one of my resource students." She looked down at her hands, picking at the napkin Tommy had been shredding. "He stood out from the beginning because he's so withdrawn. He hardly ever talks to any of the other kids. It took me a while to get him to say more than two words at a time to me."

She didn't add that she'd finally broken through to Tommy when she discovered his writing talent. Her gentle encouragement and frequent praise caused him to start hanging around after school, with the excuse of asking her questions or to show her something he'd written. Laurel suspected it had more to do with him being lonely.

She'd asked him several times to come to the community center and try one of the after-school activities. He did once in a while, but always just to watch, never to take part or interact with the other kids.

"He's alone and from what I gather, to call his home life broken would be a compliment. It's hard when you don't have anyone to confide in, to share yourself with," she said, almost to herself. "You're so isolated. It feels like you don't belong anywhere…" Laurel trailed off, realizing she'd been talking about more than Tommy and that Cort was looking at her oddly, a slight frown between his eyes.

"It sounds like you understand him pretty well," he said slowly.

A call of "Mrs. Tanner!" saved Laurel from trying to come up with an answer. A long-legged girl in shorts and an oversized sweatshirt poked her head in the door. "It's after four. Are we gonna have practice today?"

Laurel glanced at her watch. She was five minutes late. She'd completely spaced out about practice. "Sure, I'll be right there. You guys go ahead and start warming up."

Cort stood up with her. "Does your husband approve of these extracurricular activities of yours?" he asked with a slight smile. "You know, the ones that involve helping kids escape from school?"

He was teasing her but for a moment, Laurel froze. He caught it and she forced herself to relax though she felt anything but at ease. "I'm divorced," she said shortly. "I'm sorry, I have to go. I have a class. About Tommy…" She didn't want to leave it like this when there was so much more she wanted to say, wanted to know.

Cort pulled a pair of sunglasses from his pocket and shoved them on. "I'd like another shot at talking to Tommy, but I'm probably going to need your help first convincing him I'm not one of his uncle's buddies. Maybe we can talk again later, when you've got more time."

Laurel hesitated. "Maybe."

"I'll be in touch then." With a nod, he turned and left her.

Laurel waited and a minute later, she saw him heading toward the parking lot. Something kept her there, watching, as he strode to where a silver-and-black motorcycle was parked. He moved with the confidence of a man comfortable with his size and strength, hard muscle flexing underneath his jacket. Pausing for a moment by the bike, he looked back in her direction, as if sensing her watching him.

Then he shook his head and pulled on his gloves and helmet before mounting the bike, gunning the engine and roaring away from the center.

When she couldn't see him, Laurel finally made herself move. She headed for the gym, not sure what she thought about Cort Morente, what she felt. The only thing she was certain of was that nothing about him was simple or easy.

After only a few minutes with him, she sensed he could be a threat to the fragile peace she'd worked so hard to find. The peace that she guarded so fiercely.

Chapter Two

Food, then sleep was all Laurel wanted. Her fledgling team had just given her a workout that left her breathless. As usual on Mondays, Wednesdays and Fridays after her marathon sessions coaching middle-school girls who had more energy than she could ever remember having, too tired to cook, she stopped at the diner that was on her way home.

Still a little sweaty from chasing kids up and down the court, Laurel parked her car in front of the diner. She paused to fan her jacket and sweatshirt in the breeze a little, then yanked her scrunchie out and shoved her wild hair back into a ponytail. She knew she looked faded and rumpled in her gray sweats. But it wasn't as if any of the regulars at the diner cared what she looked like. They never even noticed the school-weary teacher eating in solitude.

Of course, Nova Vargas noticed the minute Laurel yanked open the heavy door to the squat, sun-baked adobe diner. It was flat-roofed dried desert mud on the outside, pure Route 66, fifties-era diner inside. Tempting aromas of fried chicken, chili and apple pie drew her quickly to the waitress, despite the *tsk-tsk* look on Nova's perfectly painted face. Slender, sassy, her pink waitress' garb hemmed inches shorter than the other women's, Nova knew how to use her body and her smile to win enough in tips to make her minimum-wage job worth keeping.

"I keep telling you you'll never get a life if you go around looking like yesterday's laundry," she chided, shaking her head as she waved a menu Laurel's way.

Smoothing her ratty jacket with the palms of her hands in a vain attempt to look more presentable, Laurel shrugged. "You're not going to kick me out because I don't meet the dress code are you?" As if on cue, her stomach let out a loud, very unfeminine growl. "Have mercy, I'm starving," Laurel pleaded.

Nova's cherry red lips twisted in what could only be called a pretty grimace. "Of course not. You always look like that. I like you and I don't really care. But tonight, you will."

Before Laurel could make sense of the comment, Nova turned, motioning Laurel to follow. Instead of leading Laurel to her usual table by the side window, she took her past tables laid with red-checked plastic tablecloths, where sat the usual mixture of families and senior citizens, to a table at the back of the diner. Except for the occasional screech of a bored toddler or the raised voice of someone trying to communicate with an elderly partner, people spoke quietly. Laurel rarely saw twentysomethings like herself at this diner. The cool crowd obviously had cooler places to go.

Largely because she was too tired to talk to anyone anyway—even if there had been someone there to talk to—Laurel didn't object to sitting where high-backed red-and-black booths lined the walls of a narrow room, making people who sat in them essentially invisible to other patrons.

Stopping in front of the last booth in the corner, Nova set the menu on the table. "Here she is."

Confused, Laurel stepped around Nova and saw a now familiar set of dark eyes. But something else about him wasn't familiar. Gone was the black-on-black leather biker look, replaced by a white T-shirt and faded jeans. Still, her stomach clenched and this time it wasn't hunger. In fact, her appetite momentarily vanished, replaced by the fight or flight instinct.

Make that the flight part only. She had no reason for it other than she'd gotten into the habit of keeping people at arm's length, unwilling to trust anyone beyond more than a casual friendship.

Cort watched her, a hint of a smile lifting the corners of his lips. "Join me for a bite?" he asked, his deep, relaxed voice a foil for the intensity of his gaze.

It was a simple enough query, but for Laurel, it suddenly became complicated, involving conversation with a man who rattled her and potential questions she didn't want to answer. "No, thanks," she answered, trying to sound casual. She took a step back. "I really can't tonight."

"Don't tell me you've got a better offer."

"Oh, come on, Laurel, keep the poor guy company. Can't you see he's all alone?" Nova toyed with the shoulder of Cort's T-shirt, her long red nails glistening. "Of course, you have no one to blame but yourself for that."

"Hadn't you better get back to your other admiring customers?" Cort lifted Nova's fingers from his shirt smiling at her exaggerated pout. "Mr. Padilla over there looks like he's about to storm over here and belt me for keeping you all to myself."

"Fine. Flag me when you're ready to order." With a toss of her long ponytail, Nova whirled around and cat-walked her way back to the other part of the restaurant.

Cort turned his attention back to Laurel. "Well? What do I have to do to change your mind? I promise I'm not here to dig for all your deep dark secrets. It's just dinner between friends."

"We're not friends," Laurel said, wondering what he was playing at. "We're barely acquaintances."

"Tonight I'd like to change that." Her skepticism must have shown clearly on her face because he held up his hands in a gesture of surrender. "Okay, you win, I confess. I want to talk to you about Tommy. This seemed as good a place as any to do it."

"I suppose…" She started to consider staying when a reality check hit her. "Wait, how did you know this is where I'd be tonight?"

Cort waved a hand over the table, urging her to slide into the booth opposite him. "If you'd just sit down, I'd explain. Besides, I can't believe you're not hungry after basketball practice with those kids. Just watching them today made me tired."

"You were there?"

"For a while. Another of Alex's ideas to get me out of the house."

She didn't understand the comment but recognized the note of exasperation in his voice. It echoed her own every time someone had tried to offer her advice about fixing everything wrong in her life.

It made her hesitate and consider saying yes to his invitation. But reason warred against instinct, her mind telling her to turn and walk away, something else inside her drawing her to him with magnetic force. Not for the first time since she'd left her small hometown and moved away from everything she'd ever known to everything she didn't, Laurel felt completely out of her element. She had no experience with men like Cort Morente who looked like a living, breathing invitation to bed.

Sometimes she envied women like Nova, comfortable with their sensuality and not hesitant to let it show, confident in their ability to hold a man's attention. That had never been her. Her ex-husband, Scott, had bluntly reminded her of that day he'd walked out the door. *You're great at being a friend, Laurie. But you're lousy at being a woman,* Scott had said.

She doubted Cort cared. *It's Tommy, he wants to know about Tommy,* she reminded herself. Surely she could do this to help Tommy. It might turn out to be a waste of time but she had nothing to lose by trying. So she pasted on a smile, hoping it covered her sudden and unwelcome attack of nerves, and slid in opposite him. "Okay, what the heck. It's getting late. I have to eat and I still have papers to grade."

"That's the spirit. I promise not to bite."

He didn't look much like a predator now, but the warning alarm kept sounding in Laurel's head. Earlier he'd looked like wicked temptation, danger and sin; now, dark hair falling boyishly over his brow, the hard lines of his jaw relaxed, a slight evening shadow softening the sharp angles of his cheeks and chin, he looked sexier than any man had a right to.

He leaned forward, his biceps flexing beneath the taut short-sleeved shirt. Their eyes met, his capturing hers. He held her a moment, dangling her off the edge of a cliff.

She hung there, helpless to break the gaze and pull herself back to safety.

His charcoal brow lifted slightly. "Hungry?" he asked lightly.

A flash of a satisfied smile touched his lips as he glanced down and opened the menu, releasing her from his silent hold.

She fell back into reality, dropped from an invisible height she'd never experienced and didn't understand. A little stunned, a lot confused by what she'd just felt, she stumbled. "I'm starving."

"I'd imagine so," he said, his eyes roaming over her face and hair. "You look like those kids gave you quite a workout."

Where was a rock to crawl under when you needed one? "I didn't plan on having company for dinner. I'm sorry if I look like a drowned rat."

"Did I say that?" His voice fell a notch lower. "Not at all. You look flushed with exertion, healthy. Beautiful, actually," he added, lifting his hand to brush her cheek gently with the back of his knuckles. "There's nothing like a little exercise to bring color to a woman's face."

Trying to ignore the blush that was about to make the flush in her cheeks look pale by comparison, Laurel was beginning to feel like a ping-pong ball he could bat at will from one end of an emotion to another. She had to get a grip. Find her footing before she fell completely.

The problem was it had been a long time since she'd felt in control of anything in her life. Her inability to keep up with his banter emphasized how much she felt a stranger in a strange place—a stranger to herself—hesitant, off balance.

Her cheek still warm from his touch, she distracted herself, fiddling with a loose strand of hair at her ear. She had to change the subject and try to get an upper hand on this conversation. Her sensibilities were slipping away faster than the scrunchie from her ponytail.

"So, I've accepted your invitation but you haven't told me how you found me here tonight."

Cort leaned back in the booth. "I used to be a detective," he said with a shrug. "I haven't been off the job so long that I've forgotten how to track someone down, Laurel." Her name rolled off his tongue like warm brandy, almost exotic sounding when he said it in that deep voice with its hint of an accent. "It didn't exactly take an IQ over sixty to find you. From what I know about you so far, one thing's for sure. You're a creature of habit."

She knew that but she'd never admitted it to anyone and he certainly wasn't going to be the first person she confessed her secret frustration to over what she considered an unattractive trait. "You make me sound incredibly boring," she muttered, thinking that's probably exactly what she was, at least to a man like him.

"Not at all," Cort said, at the same time twisting to get more comfortable in the tight booth. The breadth of his shoulders made the process awkward. "When you don't have a clue where you're going, predictable sounds pretty good."

"You don't strike me as the kind of person who gets lost easily," she countered lightly.

"Not easily, but lately, it feels like permanently." He shifted his shoulders as if uncomfortable with whatever weight he carried there then seemed to make an effort to smile. "Hey, you said you were starving. You haven't even looked at the menu. But then you'd be having the regular, wouldn't you?"

"Very funny. Just wave Nova back over here, please. I'm sure you'll have better luck getting her attention than I will."

Cort rubbed the shadow of stubble on his jaw, his eyes almost dancing with challenge. "Nova and I went out in high school. I remember wasting a lot of class time, dreaming of ways to get a look at her tattoo." He grinned as Laurel squirmed inwardly and couldn't help but wonder exactly where Nova's tattoo was. "It was a good time, nothing more."

"Is that so? Well, I think you'd better speak for yourself. The way she looks at you, I think she's still waiting for the class reunion." The remark slipped out unchecked and she wanted to kick herself. What was the matter with her?

"We've had one or two of those, but we're just friends. Does it matter?"

"Not at all. It's neither here nor there to me," she said, trying to sound flippant while banishing an utterly ridiculous twinge of jealousy. She put it down to her lingering issues with Scott. He'd left her for a woman like Nova—dark, vivacious and beautiful, who made her feel bland and colorless by comparison. "I was just making an observation."

Nova returned to set out a basket of chips and a bowl of salsa, put a bottle of beer in front of Cort and to take their orders. As Cort had guessed, she quoted Laurel's usual double cheeseburger, fries and a glass of milk.

"Don't you want green chili on your burger?" Cort asked.

"I've never had that."

Nova rolled her eyes and twisted her pencil between her fingers. "She ain't from around these parts," she teased, an exaggerated twang dripping off her words.

"Bring her some on the side." Nova's eyes began to twinkle. "Mild, Nova, not hot. And bring me a couple of enchiladas and a tamale with red sauce, please."

Nova bent toward him, sliding her eyes to Laurel and back. "Are you sure that's all you want, Cort?"

"For now," Cort said but his smile was for Laurel. "Just

make sure Laurel's chili is mild, or I'll have something to say about it."

"Hmm…" Nova winked at Laurel. "I think we might be out of mild chili tonight."

When Nova had left, Cort turned to Laurel. "Time you had our New Mexican baptism by fire. But we'll make it a small fire the first time. I'll taste it first, in case Nova tries to pull a fast one."

Laurel took a chip and dipped it into the salsa. "I'd say that's a given."

"She's all meow and no claws."

"I thought so, too, until tonight." Darn, she was doing it again, letting some absurd instinctive feminine competition make her say stupid things. The problem was she'd forgotten this wasn't a date, she wasn't competing with Nova for his attention; he wanted her help with Tommy, nothing else.

"So," she said, trying to turn the focus of the conversation back to Tommy, "since you didn't come here tonight for the pleasure of my company—"

"Who says?"

"Oh, please. You wouldn't be here if you didn't want my help with Tommy," she said.

"I don't know about that." Cort started to pick up his beer bottle and as he did, Laurel noticed the slight tremor in his hand that made the bottle slip in his fingers and rattle against the table. "Damn," he muttered, scowling, and letting go, he deliberately reached out with his left hand instead.

When he realized she'd seen, he glanced away, taking a long drink before looking back at her with a tight smile. "Despite the months of torture they insisted on calling therapy, I haven't quite got the hang of having to be ambidextrous yet."

"Months?" she repeated, a little taken aback, then quickly tried to retract the question. "I'm sorry, I didn't mean to pry."

"It's okay. It's not as if the whole town doesn't know about it anyway." His eyes fixed again on the beer bottle as he toyed with the neck of it. "I told you I used to be a cop. About a year ago, one of the local bad guys tried to stop one of my investigations by running me over with his truck. The doctors put me back together but they couldn't fix everything. Since I can't count on my right arm to work all the time, I lost my job and now I'm in the market for a new life." He paused, his expression hard. "You know one of the worst things about it? Everyone asking me what I'm going to do now. Reminding me I need to pick up the pieces and move on. Like a little duct tape and wishful thinking is going to make it all right again."

He was silent for a few moments then smiled ruefully. "Now I'm the one who's sorry. I think that fell under the category of too much information."

"No, it's all right," Laurel said quietly.

"Yeah, well, I'm sure you had better things to do tonight than listen to my bout of self-pity. I think I'm in danger of turning into the pathetic guy who dumps his sad life story on any unsuspecting stranger who even pretends to listen."

The self-mocking laughter in his eyes and tugging at the corner of his mouth made Laurel laugh, too. "*Pathetic* is the last word I'd use for you."

"What's the first?"

Several sprang immediately to mind and Laurel felt her face grow hot. "I'd have to give that one some thought. And by the way, I wasn't pretending to listen." This time she was the one to look away. "I'm sorry about what happened. Believe me, I understand having to give everything up and start over." She said the last so quietly she doubted he'd heard her until she caught him watching her.

For several suspended seconds they looked at each other and although Cort didn't say anything, his confessions to her and a strong sense he would empathize without pity or judgment compelled her to answer the questions in his eyes. Fixing her gaze on a scuff in the table, she tried to tell it as if it were someone else's story and not her reality.

"I grew up in a small town in Montana and until a year ago, I thought I'd be there forever. I had a teaching job I loved, I married my high-school sweetheart—we were going to have a baby. I thought I had everything I'd ever wanted. But you can never trust that what you have is real, that it's going to last, can you?"

"Not always," Cort said softly.

"I couldn't. I lost my baby and afterward..." She paused, not willing or able to tell him the worst of her pain. It was still a raw wound that hadn't begun to heal. "Afterward my husband became distant. I convinced myself it was just grief and disappointment and that in time we'd be close again. When he wouldn't talk to me, I began confiding in a woman I thought was a good friend. She was so sympathetic and understanding. But she used what I told her to get close to my husband. I trusted them both. I believed they cared about me. It was all a lie. He left me for her. They're expecting twins." It used to hurt saying it, remembering, so much she couldn't breathe sometimes. But this time, Laurel drew in a deep breath and found, with a little twinge of surprise that although the familiar ache was there, it didn't paralyze her as it once had. "I'm not like you, I couldn't take people telling me I needed to move on with my life anymore. I ran.

"And here I am." She forced herself to look up and meet his eyes again and to put a lightness into her voice she didn't feel in an attempt to cover her sudden awkwardness. She'd spilled her story out in that moment of sympathy between them and was now beginning to regret it. What had convinced her she could trust him? She'd thought she'd hardened herself against trusting anyone ever again and yet here she was, pouring out her heart to a man she scarcely knew.

"I'm the pathetic one," she said.

She didn't realize she'd said it out loud until Cort laughed. He reached over and touched his hand to hers. "Not pathetic. Just a little lost. And I understand, too." Sobering, he lightly gripped her hand. "I'm sorry about what happened. It took a lot of courage for you to come to a place full of strangers and start over."

Laurel denied him with a sharp shake of her head. "I told you, I ran. I convinced myself then I was being bold and daring for once in my life, coming here and starting over. But it was a lie. And it's easier with strangers. They don't know. I don't have to wonder who I can trust."

"Because you don't trust anybody?" Letting go of her hand, Cort leaned back in his seat again, his expression unreadable.

Fortunately for Laurel at that moment Nova arrived with their food, giving her a reprieve from answering.

"Enjoy." She turned to Cort then glanced over to Laurel. "But not too much."

"That's all we need for now, thanks," Cort returned with a brief flash of that smile Laurel was sure had made more than a few female hearts beat a little faster.

Nova let out a little sigh then buzzed away.

The smell of freshly fried potatoes, chili, cheese and a juicy burger filled the space between them. Hunger temporarily overcoming the uncomfortable tension between them, Laurel started to chomp into her burger like a starving woman, drawing a smile from Cort.

"Wait, here try a little green chili," he said after tasting it.

Midbite, Laurel stopped and reluctantly let Cort add the chili to her burger. When she took another huge bite and chewed, a look of surprised pleasure spread over her face. "Oh, this is fantastic," she said when she'd finished.

"Consider yourself baptized. We'll knock it up a notch next time."

Laurel looked up from her burger. "Next time?"

His expression shuttered and abruptly he became all business. "Yeah, well, I wanted to get your advice about Tommy, but let's just forget it, okay? You obviously don't want to and it's not that important. I'm sure I can muddle through on my own."

He focused on his own food, obviously dismissing the topic and any idea they might work together to help Tommy.

Laurel couldn't blame him since she'd thrown up enough

signs warning him away. But her concern for Tommy was stronger than her determination not to get too close to anyone.

"Really?" Laurel put down her burger and looked hard at him. "So you went to all this trouble to track me down, convince me to have dinner with you, just because it's not that important? Come on, Mr. Morente—"

"You know, it's against the rules to be so formal with someone who's told you his secrets and then introduced you to the delights of green chili."

"Fine. Cort. I never said I wasn't interested in helping you."

"No, but you've gone out of your way to warn me to keep my distance. I got the message. Although it's got to be pretty obvious that at this point in my life, when I can't even figure out what I'm going to do about me, that I'm not looking to get involved with anyone. Especially someone like you. And, no," he went on before she could respond, "it's not because I don't think you're attractive. I do. And if things were different…" He let the sentence die. "But your life is as about as screwed up as mine right now and neither of us needs any more complications."

"No…but what we could use is a friend."

Whatever he might have said had obviously been erased by surprise and instead Cort just stared at her. Laurel couldn't blame him; she'd surprised herself saying it. "And so could Tommy," she added. "So if you're willing to put up with my paranoia, I'll overlook your crankiness and maybe together we can come up with a way to help him."

Studying her for a few moments as if he were seriously considering her offer, he finally said, "Maybe."

"Maybe? Listen, I—" she started to argue then noticed the smile playing with his mouth. "You're going to make me work for this, aren't you?"

"Hey, I'm cranky, remember?"

"I think I'll change that to *provoking,*" she said.

"You know, calling me names isn't a very good way to persuade me to do what you want."

"I can give her a few better ideas," Nova said, coming up to the table and making a miserable attempt to hide her curiosity. Ignoring Cort's scowl, she smiled and asked, "Dessert? Coffee? Which in your case, Laurel, would be the same thing considering all the honey and cream you dump in it."

"Coffee, please," Laurel said, trying to pretend she hadn't heard Nova's provocative comment. "If you're through playing hard to get…" She began when Nova left to get her brew.

Cort laughed and the approval his eyes aimed at her simultaneously flushed Laurel with warmth and made her question what crazy impulse had convinced her she could look at him and think, *friend only.* "Not one of my better efforts, I guess. Okay, you're on. At least with you on my side, I might get to actually talk to Tommy without risking another bruised shin."

As he was telling her about his first encounter with Tommy, Laurel listened and laughed, but with only half her attention on what he was actually saying. Another part of her mind was busy fighting against a surge of panic, urging her to run again.

If she hadn't wanted to help Tommy, she would have seriously considered running. Because no matter what they both said, and what they both vowed to avoid, Laurel had a bad feeling that she was going to have a hard time keeping Cort Morente at arm's length.

Except she had to, because letting him become anything more than a friend would be a mistake she couldn't afford to make.

Chapter Three

Cort pounded down the sidelines of the basketball court, his body telling him that despite getting back to regular workouts, it had been way too long since he'd done any real running. Before he'd been laid up, he'd played basketball several times a month, but it hadn't prepared him for keeping pace with twenty kids who didn't have the words *slow* or *time out* in their vocabulary. As he ran, his eyes darted back and forth from Tommy, hunched in a corner on the top row of the bleachers, to the antics of the boys' team he'd started coaching that day.

Frustrated with the team's complete lack of strategy and inability to consistently make even basic shots, he blew his whistle and motioned the boys over to talk to them. He used the brief reprieve as the group shuffled over to try to catch his breath, figuring that doubling over and gasping for air wasn't going to earn him any points with these kids.

"Okay, guys," he began, looking into the skeptical eyes of the group of middle-school boys gathered around him, "I know you don't know me and I don't know you, yet. But I'm getting the picture watching you play today that we need to do some serious work on team strategy."

"Coach Armijo never talks about stuff like that," a tall, skinny boy with a spotty face spoke up.

It wasn't the first time Cort had heard that. He realized, as the new guy, he was on trial with the team and so he curbed his irritation. After just one practice with this rowdy group of preteens, he was beginning to have a serious appreciation for Laurel's job in the classroom. Anyone who could spend six or seven hours a day with a roomful of middle schoolers and still keep her sanity and her smile was something special.

He'd agreed to take on this volunteer duty three days ago at Alex's prodding, half amused and half exasperated at his friend's persistent but none too subtle efforts to push him back into real life. But he probably would have told Alex no thanks this time if it hadn't been for Tommy.

One of the things Laurel had told him about the boy during their dinner the other night was that Tommy often hung around the community center when she coached the girls' team. Cort hoped by showing Tommy that he didn't have anything to do with his uncle that Tommy might be more willing to trust him.

"I'm sure Coach Armijo talks about the things he thinks are important," he told the kids. His regular basketball games had been with Jorge Armijo, Alex and a few of the deputies, and he had a pretty good idea of Jorge's strategy—all muscle and no finesse. "But he and I are going to be taking turns coaching from now on, so I'll be working with you on things I think you need to work on."

A few murmured grumbles circulated through the group, but no one protested out loud.

"So, for now, let's go back out there and work on free throws and lay ups. You're missing easy shots way too often. We'll tackle strategies next time."

Another boy waved a hand in the air. "Can we quit a few minutes early today? It's *Día de los Muertos*."

Cort had forgotten about that. He could still remember

being twelve—barely—and looking forward to the first days of November and the *Día de los Muertos* celebrations. "Tell you what," he said. "You guys make fifty consecutive foul shots and we'll call it quits."

A round of "Awesome!", "Sweet!" and "All right!" swept through the team as they turned and ran back to line up at the free-throw line.

Cort stayed on the sideline, glancing from his team to the other side of the gym where Laurel now stood, her team huddled around her.

He watched as the group broke up and went back to the game, and couldn't deny that knowing he would be seeing her regularly now, dashing up and down the other end of the court, ponytail flying, her long, slender legs moving with the graceful ease of a natural athlete, was a bonus he hadn't counted on.

But watching her was as far as he intended to go.

He admitted to himself he'd felt an almost instant—and disconcerting—attraction from the first time they'd met and she'd practically thrown herself into his arms to protect Tommy. Maybe it had something to do with their shared struggle to start over with a new set of priorities. Maybe it was the way she looked at him, all her feelings in those big blue eyes of hers; the way she defended Tommy, her heart on her sleeve. Or maybe it was just a natural reaction to a woman he found beautiful despite those god-awful gray sweats she seemed to like so much.

Whatever it was, Cort was sure the feeling was one-sided. He'd gotten that message loud and clear at dinner when she'd told him about her losses and the way she'd been betrayed by her ex-husband and her friend. He realized the only reason she'd told him so many personal things was to warn him away. She'd made it clear the last thing she wanted was to get close to anyone. And he'd meant it when he'd told her the last thing he needed was to get involved with someone as emotionally vulnerable as Laurel or anyone period, for that matter.

They'd keep it friendly while they worked together to help Tommy and that would be the extent of it.

He had this uneasy feeling, though, that keeping it strictly friendly was going to be a lot harder than he expected.

"Forty-nine, fifty! That's it!" several boys shouted at Cort in unison. "Can we go now?"

"Good job." Cort nodded toward the gym doors. "You guys are outta here. Good practice. See you next week."

As the boys ran to gather up bags and coats and head for the door, Cort lazily dribbled the ball around, making a few outside shots while watching Laurel finish her practice. He was glad his shoulder was handling the motions much better than he'd expected. It was obvious the girls liked her and he began to see why. Her face beaming, she clapped and jumped up and down cheering for the shortest team member who'd finally made her first basket of the day, before handing out praise all around.

"Okay, that's it for today," she said at last, "go get some water and your stuff and then meet out front."

Cort took the chance to make his way through the sea of mostly brown heads to Laurel now bent over a girl sitting on the floor, her knee elevated, Laurel feeling it for injury. Two other girls stood nearby, watching as Laurel gingerly probed their friend's knee.

He came up behind her and leaned over her shoulder for a better look. "Is she okay?"

Laurel started, her expression flustered when she glanced up and recognized him. "Oh, um—hi. I didn't know you were still here."

"I wanted to talk to you for a minute, when you're finished," Cort said, flashing a smile at the girls who were eyeing him and giggling as they exchanged quick whispers.

Laurel, on the other hand, did her best not to look at him. "How does it feel, Stephanie?" she asked the girl sitting in front of her.

"Fine." The girl wriggled to her feet. She gave Cort a quick look then asked, "Mrs. Tanner, I'm thirsty, can I go now? It doesn't hurt anymore. Really."

"Sure, just take it easy for the next week or so. Promise?"

"I will," the girl shouted back over her shoulder as she and her friends ran off, still giggling, to join the other kids.

Getting to her feet, Laurel finally looked back at him. "So how was your first day coaching? You looked like you were holding your own."

"That's because you missed me holding the stitch in my side. Much more of this and I'm gonna need therapy again."

"That bad?" she said, half laughing, but with a touch of concern in her voice. "Maybe you overdid it."

"It beats staring at the walls," Cort said shortly. He didn't quite bank the annoyance in his voice but nearly a year of people telling him to take things slow and easy was beginning to fray his nerves.

Laurel bit her lip to keep from smiling.

"I'm getting tired of being treated like I'm going to fall apart at any given second," he grumbled.

She did smile at that. "So do you want me to sympathize with your pain or tell you to stop whining?"

That made him smile back. "How come I can never have it both ways?"

"Sorry, you have to pick one. Oh, this stupid thing—" A thick swathe of hair drooped over her temple and Laurel yanked the band out of her hair and then made an attempt to gather the heavy mass together again and tie it back into a messy ponytail.

Cort smiled, amused. "That thing doesn't seem to do its job too well."

"I know." She sighed, giving up. "My hair is so heavy, it just keeps sliding out. I should cut it short and then I wouldn't always be fussing with it."

Her hair fell straight and smooth over her back and shoulders, tempting him to find out whether or not it was as silken as it looked.

"You have great hair. Don't ever cut it." The words slid out before he caught them.

Laurel looked at him uncertainly then smiled a little. "It's a disaster, but thanks. I don't actually get around to going to a salon very often anyhow." Seeming to need an excuse to move away from him, she lunged out to grab an errant basketball about to roll under a bleacher.

"Have you played before?" she asked when she returned ball in hand, holding it as if to create a barrier between them. Her eyes kept sliding away from him, never fixed on his for more than a moment. "I was watching you and you made some good shots."

Cort found it interesting she'd been watching him since she now appeared determined not to, but answered casually, "My brother Sawyer and I both played in high school, and I used to get together regularly with Alex and Jorge for a game in the evenings."

"Your brother? You mean, there are more of you?"

"Only one of me. But I've got four brothers," he said, not bothering to go any further in explaining his complicated family situation. Deliberately steering the subject away from a topic he wanted to avoid at the moment, he glanced up at Tommy, still sitting in the stands, intently watching them. "You must have convinced him I'm not the bad guy."

She followed his glance. "I told him you didn't have anything to do with his uncle and that you just wanted to talk to him. I guess he believed me or he wouldn't still be here now."

"Maybe I could talk him into shooting a few hoops with me," Cort said.

"Good luck. You're going to need it with Tommy. He doesn't trust most people." She looked him up and down. "At least your coaching sweats are a lot less intimidating than the leather. That'll help."

"You mean, none of your fantasies involve black leather and chains?" Cort teased, unable to resist. "Now I'm disappointed. Want me to share a few of mine?"

She stared at him as if she couldn't decide whether to run or accept his offer, then quickly averted her eyes. "I—ah, no thanks. I have enough in my head without adding that."

"Oh, come on, you have to be fearless once in a while."

"Not today." In a nervous gesture, she wet her lips with the tip of her tongue, drawing Cort's eyes to her mouth. "Weren't you going to ask Tommy to play ball?"

"Yeah, sure," Cort said absently, realizing then he was looking at her mouth instead of focusing on Tommy.

Laurel frowned a little and hurriedly turned to set the ball aside before making another effort to subdue her hair. "I really wish he would join in once in a while. He's so lonely."

"Like you?"

"No," she bristled, "not like me. And we're talking about *Tommy.*"

Her quick jump to defensiveness pricked at a place deep in Cort's chest. "Right, so we are." And right she was, Cort reminded himself. Why did he keep letting himself get distracted? Normally, he had no trouble keeping his focus; it was one of his strengths that had made him good at his job.

But every time he was within ten feet of Laurel Tanner his brains scrambled and he got sidetracked into places he didn't need to be. It was getting annoying. "So do you make it a habit of getting this involved with all your students?" he asked, this time working at keeping his tone casual.

"I care about all of them. But I told you the other night Tommy is special. He's a great kid, with a lot of potential, but he deliberately isolates himself. I'm worried that he's carrying around so much pain and fear inside that one day it's going to crush him."

She rubbed her hands over her arms as if the thought chilled her. Before he could stop himself, Cort reached out and touched her hand. "Not if I can help it."

"Not if *we* can help it," she said firmly. "Here," she said, and picked up a ball and pushed it into his hands. "Take your best shot with Tommy. I've got to make sure all the kids get to their rides."

"Wait," he said, stopping her as she made to turn and leave. "I could use your help." When she looked at him doubtfully, he added, "You're the kid expert. I was hoping you could give me an idea of the best way to approach Tommy. Obviously, I didn't do too well the first time."

"That wasn't your fault," she said, unbending in the face of his appeal. "You couldn't have known Tommy would assume you had something to do with his uncle. And you just need more practice talking with kids. I thought you did a good job coaching today. You're really patient with the boys." She flushed a little as they both realized it was an admission she'd been watching him but Cort kept silent, not wanting to go out of his way to fluster her any more than he already had. Glancing at Tommy, she lowered her voice, "Why don't you ask Tommy to try to make a basket? When I was trying to get him to open up about his writing, I more or less challenged him to prove he could do it. His pride wouldn't let that pass without showing me he could."

"Thanks, I'll give it a shot."

"Don't thank me until you see how it works," she said, heading for the door.

When she disappeared, he glanced up to where Tommy was, seeing the boy start to make his way down the bleachers. Jogging up a few steps, Cort met him at the bottom.

"Hey, don't leave yet. It's okay," he said, trying his best to sound reassuring. "I wanted to talk to you for a minute."

Tommy ducked his head, his mess of dark brown hair falling forward. "I gotta go."

"Sure, in a minute, but could you show me one thing first?"

Slowly, Tommy raised suspicious eyes. "I don't have nothin' to show you."

"I meant with the basketball."

"I don't play."

Cort dribbled the ball a minute then passed it to Tommy. His reflexes quick, the boy caught it easily. "How do you know if you've never tried?"

Tommy dropped the ball deliberately. "I just know, that's all. Like I said, I gotta go." He turned away but Cort stopped him with a firm hand on his shoulder.

"Prove to me you can't play and I'll stop annoying you, okay?"

The look on Tommy's face told Cort he was considering the challenge. Over the kid's shoulder, Cort saw Laurel come back in the gym. Seeing Cort with Tommy, she hesitated, then sat down on the edge of the bleachers, watching them.

Cort picked up the ball and tossed it to Tommy, hiding a smile when the boy caught it again. "There's no one here but you and me and Mrs. Tanner. So what've you got to lose by proving to me you can't make a basket? It'll get me off your case."

"But if I do it, you won't leave me alone."

"But if you don't, I will." It was a gamble, but Cort sensed Laurel was right. Beneath all the sulky protest, the boy had pride. And he crossed his fingers that pride would win out over Tommy's fear of Cort's interest in him.

Finally, with every appearance of wanting to be anywhere else, Tommy dribbled the ball a few times, moving over toward the basket. He stopped, looked back at Laurel. She nodded, smiled, gesturing for him to go ahead and try.

Tommy looked hard at Cort. He dribbled a few more times, chewing at his lower lip, obviously arguing with himself over what to do.

Cort found himself holding his breath. If, deep down, Tommy truly wanted help, wanted to connect with someone, he would risk this moment of trust and take a chance on Cort, especially now that Laurel had promised him Cort only wanted to help him. Tommy would want to prove his masculine worth, prove he wasn't afraid, while at the same time, tell both Cort and Laurel he needed someone.

Bouncing the ball several more times, Tommy then stopped, seeming to come to a decision and abruptly shot it straight up, out and into the basket.

"Great shot," Cort called to him. He looked back at Laurel to find her coming up to them, smiling, her eyes suspiciously bright.

"That was terrific Tommy," Laurel said. "I knew you could do it."

Tommy shuffled up to them and Cort put a hand on his shoulder. "You should think about joining the team."

Tommy shrugged. "Maybe." He handed the ball to Cort. "I gotta go now. I wanna go to the festival tonight."

"Is that the one all the girls were talking about?" Laurel asked. "What is it again?"

"It's just *Día de los Muertos*, that's all." Tommy glanced at Cort as if expecting him to explain it.

"Day of the Dead," Cort said. "It's a Mexican festival, held right after Halloween the first two days in November. Everyone celebrates the reunion of the dead with their families. You'd probably call it All Saints' Day and All Souls' Day."

Laurel raised a brow. "Interesting. I'd like to see that. It's not something we ever celebrated in Barker's Creek. That's the town in Montana where I grew up," she added when Tommy looked confused. "Tommy, does your foster mother know you're going?"

Tommy stared fixedly at the floor. "Yeah, sure. She can't go. She's got the little kids to take care of. So she said I could go by myself."

Cort knew he was lying. He also knew that accusing Tommy of sneaking out wasn't going to get him anywhere with the kid. "Hey, I was going to go, too. And Mrs. Tanner hasn't ever been. Why don't Mrs. Tanner and I give you a ride home—"

"That's not my home," Tommy interrupted with a touch of belligerence, still refusing to look up.

"Fine, I'll give you a ride to your foster mother's house, we'll tell her where you'll be and then we'll all go together. It'll be better than hanging out alone." Mentally he crossed his fingers that Laurel didn't have other plans and that she'd forgive him for including her in his impromptu invitation. Having her along would ease the situation in more ways than one.

Tommy looked up at him and Cort could see the conflict

in his eyes between wanting to believe Cort's interest in him was real and lasting and the pain of too many past disappointments and broken promises. Finally he backed away, shaking his head. "No. I can't. I mean, I'm not supposed to—" He broke off, his lips pressed tightly together.

"That's okay," Cort said gently. "Maybe next time."

"Yeah, okay, whatever."

"Sure I can't give you a ride anyway?"

Tommy hesitated then half turned away. "Yeah. I gotta go," he muttered, and sprinted for the door.

"Damn." Cort shoved a hand through his hair, frustrated. "I handled that real well."

"Yes, you did," Laurel said softly. She touched his shoulder, drawing his eyes to hers. "You connected with him. It'll be a little easier next time."

"I'll have to take your word for that. I don't feel like I made much progress."

"You just have to be patient. Nothing with Tommy is going to happen quickly."

"Apparently not," he said with a small smile. Studying her a moment, Cort decided to take another risk and hoped he'd have better luck with her than he'd had with Tommy. "You know, just because Tommy ditched us doesn't mean we can't still go tonight. I don't think it's against the rules for a friend to introduce you to one of the local customs."

He could see the same conflict in her eyes as he'd seen in Tommy's.

"Come on," he coaxed, "it'll be fun. Besides you can help me out by changing the subject every time someone starts asking me what I'm doing with myself these days."

Laurel rolled her eyes but smiled as if she couldn't help herself. "I don't think you need my help. But I would like to go and going with a friend sounds more appealing than going alone." She put a slight emphasis on the word *friend*. "I need to go home and change first. Tell me, what's the proper attire for a festival of the dead?"

"Black leather?" Cort suggested, trying his best to look innocent.

"Does my body look dead to you?"

"Never say never. I'll make a convert out of you yet."

"You won't live that long," she said, her blush at odds with her quick bantering comeback.

Cort let that one go. "Give me your address. I'll pick you up in an hour."

"Only if you promise you'll be driving something other than that motorcycle of yours."

"You ruin all my fun. Okay, I promise," he said, laughing when she flashed a glare at him.

Chapter Four

Laurel had hurried home and changed into comfy jeans, a plain blue sweater and a heavy fleece-lined jacket before Cort picked her up—as promised without the motorcycle, but in an almost respectable looking Jeep.

From the moment she saw him, though, she began to question her decision to accept his invitation. He smiled and she felt off balance again. He touched her arm helping her into the vehicle and she flushed, unnerved by the sensation. The last time she'd dated anyone, she'd been a teenager, and that had been movie, pizza and high-school football games with Scott. All her dates after that had been with Scott: nice, easy-going, familiar, without the edge of sexual tension and her worrying about how she looked and what to say.

This is not a date, she firmly reminded herself. Surely she could spend a few hours with a friend—*a tall, dark, sexy, drop-dead gorgeous, very male friend with an affinity for black leather, who could rattle her just by saying hello*—without acting like a gawky, teenager.

The town square was only minutes from her house and the festival was well underway when they arrived. People were pouring in from all sides of the plaza, making the square a sea of dark heads and bright clothing. She was glad to have Cort at her side. She hardly knew anyone in town and she wasn't the type of outgoing person who could make friends easily.

As she and Cort strolled around the plaza on narrow cobbled streets lined with compact adobe shops and restaurants, the sound of a cheery mariachi band greeted them. The autumn air was crisp and fresh, laced with tempting aromas of homemade tamales, fried bread and pungent spices still foreign to her nostrils.

Festively dressed families and revelers mingled, with much of the conversation in Spanish. For Laurel, still working to improve her command of the language beyond the bare basics, that and everything else unfamiliar, intensified her feeling of being alone, an outsider, pretending to belong.

As fascinating as this festival was, a pang of missing home, missing her town's fall apple-picking festival and parade stabbed at her heart. From as far back as she could remember, she'd gone with her family and friends and later with Scott to the traditional celebration that was all about apples, bobbing for them, juggling them, slicing them up for pies, covering them in caramel, tossing them softball-style into baskets for prizes. Looking around her now, she felt like an alien at this event. It wasn't simple. Apples were simple. Who wouldn't understand apples? But the revelers at this occasion had a lot more going on than apples.

She continued to walk, lost in her thoughts, until Cort suddenly wrapped his arm around her waist and pulled her against his side.

"Why did you do that?" she blurted out before looking down to a piece of painted wood lying in her path. "Oh, I see."

"I thought you might not want to wind up with your nose on the street," he said, setting her away from him. He bent down, picked up the splintered wood with the painted face of a spiritlike creature on it and dropped it in a nearby trash can.

"Thanks. I guess I was looking everywhere but where I was walking."

"You were about a thousand miles away, too."

"I'm sorry. It's just that I've never seen anything like this. I was thinking about our fall apple festival back home. It's a little different than this."

Cort laughed, a rich melodic sound that somehow comforted her. "I'm not surprised. *Día de los Muertos* is hardly a common tradition in the states, except in a few parts of the Southwest."

As he led her around to the booths that had been set up in the plaza, he pointed out things of interest. Mostly he let her soak in the experience on her own. At the moment, she appreciated that. She was feeling so out of her element that she needed a little space to get her footing. She didn't know him well enough yet to second-guess his thoughts, but the way he always seemed to keep one eye on her made her suspect he sensed her awkwardness. And he was doing a pretty good job of it. Probably left over from the detective in him, she decided. Nothing personal, just habit.

Her attention shifted then to a band's lively music that rang out from a stand at the center of the plaza on an elevated gazebo decorated with bright balloons, paper flowers and papier-mâché figurines. "Are those skeletons?" she asked Cort. She looked again at the skeletons of all sizes placed in various positions all around the square.

Cort grinned at her frown. "It seems creepy, but all of this represents the souls of the dead who come back to visit living relatives and eat, drink and be merry for a day, just as they did when they were alive. It's actually a very happy event but it's strange if you haven't grown up with it."

Laurel agreed wholeheartedly with that. "It takes some getting used to."

Several couples danced on the brick patio area beneath the gazebo, while children played all around them, weaving in and out between couples, squealing, laughing and teasing each other. Everyone but her seemed oblivious to the dancing bone figures looming above them.

"Would you like to dance?" Cort asked, offering his hand.

"Me? Oh, no, I don't dance. I mean, I do—or I have—but I'm awful."

"No one's awful. It just takes the right partner. Come on."

She stepped back. "No, really, I'll embarrass you. Those people out there know what they're doing. I'm a klutz."

"Sorry, that one won't work. I've seen you on the basketball court. Come on, they're starting a slow one."

A slow song was less intimidating, but then again, it did involve being in Cort's arms and that made it more daunting.

"If you're going to live here, you have to learn to dance," he said, his voice soft seduction.

He took her hand in his and with a little tug led her to the dance area in front of the gazebo. There he skillfully pulled her to him and began to move in perfect rhythm to the Latin beat. His right hand pressed lightly at the small of her back, his fingers splayed out to help guide her. His left palm cradled her hand, his hold confident and firm yet not harsh. Instead of pulling her hard against him as she'd half expected, he kept a small space between their bodies. Though only his hands touched her, she felt his warmth and strength with every step. He gave her confidence and within moments, she began to relax.

"You make this so easy. It's fun when all I have to do is follow you. I see why you like it so much."

Cort eased a fraction of an inch closer. "Then I definitely have to teach you to rumba."

When the song ended, he eased her down into a dramatic dip, which surprisingly she handled without skipping a beat. Laughing, she stood again and impulsively threw her arms around his neck. "Thank you! I've never danced like that."

"If you thank me like that again, I'll teach you a lot more than the rumba."

Embarrassed, she pulled away. "Sorry, I got carried away."

Cort reached down with the pad of his thumb to brush a wild

strand of hair that had caught on her lip. "Don't apologize. I'm glad to know you can get carried away once in a while."

The intensity of his gaze and the low rumble of his voice brought a blush to her already warm cheeks. She ducked and turned away, glancing at the shimmering rays of the setting sun. "It's going to be dark soon," she said, ignoring his insinuation.

"The lights at night are beautiful," he said as she felt him move close in behind her. "They're strung all through the trees."

Before she could decide how she felt about his nearness, Cort suddenly stepped back and smiled, waving a hand in greeting.

Two couples were walking toward them, and Laurel knew at once from the strong resemblance at least one of the men was related to Cort. "Okay, you told us you weren't coming." He gave Laurel a quick, assessing glance. "Looks like somebody changed your mind."

"She's prettier than you," Cort said with a laugh. He introduced her to the foursome and their children. "Laurel, this is my sister-in-law, Maya, and my brother, Sawyer," he said, indicating the man who shared his thick black hair, deep, dark eyes and chiseled bone structure. "The little guy with candy all over his fingers is Joey and the bundle somewhere in that blanket is Nico, our family's newest addition. And this is my brother, Rafe, and his wife, Jule."

Returning the group's smiles and greetings, Laurel darted a look among the three men, a little confused because Rafe, though tall, broad-shouldered and dark like his brothers, was obviously American Indian.

"Wait til you meet Josh," Rafe said, smiling a little as he caught her glance. "He doesn't look like anybody."

"Josh is the baby and the only blonde in the group," Cort explained. "We're pretty sure he was switched at birth."

Laurel remembered Cort telling her he had four brothers and she wondered why the fourth wasn't mentioned. But it didn't seem right to ask.

"Laurel just moved here a couple of months ago from

Montana," Cort was saying. "I thought I'd introduce her to one of the local customs."

"You had to pick the weirdest one," Jule said with a laugh. She turned to Laurel, her dark smiling eyes holding a touch of concern. "I hope this isn't making you uncomfortable."

"No, it's fine. Well, maybe a little," Laurel relented at skeptical looks she got from everyone in the group. "But I think I'm catching on."

"What brings you to Luna Hermosa?" Sawyer asked, glancing between her and Cort. Laurel got the impression he was trying to figure out how they'd ended up here together but didn't want to make her uncomfortable by asking. "You're a long way from Montana."

Don't I know it. She pushed back a pang of homesickness and forced a smile. "Oh, I just wanted a change. There was a teaching position in my area open at the middle school here so I took it."

"She's been giving me a few lessons on how to talk to kids without scaring them into running away," Cort said. He winked at Laurel, his voice threaded with laughter as he invited her to share his joke.

Laurel instead found herself jumping to his defense. "I don't think you need me to teach you that. You did a great job today coaching the boy's team."

"Cort's coaching a bunch of kids?" Sawyer exchanged an amused glance with Rafe. "This I gotta see."

"Maybe it's some new kind of therapy," Rafe added.

"He's trying to help Tommy. Tommy's one of my students and he really needs a friend," Laurel spoke up before Cort could answer his brothers' teasing. "He actually got Tommy to pick up the ball today and make a basket. It's the first time anyone's gotten him to do that, even me."

Sawyer looked at Cort. "So, you're out of that cell you call an apartment, you're doing amazing things with kids and you've got a date, all on the same night. I'm impressed."

"Oh, stop already," Maya admonished lightly. A small

muffled noise drew her attention away from her husband. She bent to the stroller and picked up the edge of the handwoven baby blanket, showing Laurel the face of her tiny sleeping angel. Laurel's heart went to her throat, choking back words. "Still sleeping. We got lucky," Maya said softly. "He decided to take his nap early."

"He's precious," Laurel managed to whisper at the same time she was banking tears. "They both are."

She blinked hard, hoping no one noticed, but Cort took her hand, squeezing lightly, and she knew someone had. She held on to him, needing his comfort more than she cared about the glances they were getting.

Joey squealed excitedly as two young boys ran by, dragging brightly colored balloons behind them, thankfully drawing everyone's attention away from her and Cort. Laurel looked again at the adorable baby. He appeared to be about eight months old. While Joey had inherited his mop of red hair from his mom, Nico, with his fuzzy dark hair and olive skin favored his dad. Envy mixed with a jolt of loss jabbed at Laurel's heart. Her baby would have been a toddler now, the child she so often imagined in her dreams—

Ruthlessly, she pushed the vision away, her attention quickly and thankfully drawn to Joey, who was struggling to get a sticky piece of candy off of his fingers and the fur of the stuffed buffalo he was gripping tightly.

"What's that he's eating?" She glanced up to Maya. "It looks like a bone."

Maya smiled and nodded to the variety of odd candies displayed in the booth in front of them. Laurel realized all of the sweets were in the shapes of skulls and skeletons. "Okay. Those are—different," she murmured.

Maya grimaced as she plucked the sucker out of Joey's fist. "I think that's enough for you, little guy."

"No, Buff'lo wants more," Joey started to protest until his dad picked him up and swung him high over his head for a moment, to Joey's obvious delight.

"Buffalo's gonna get sick if he eats any more candy. You just ask your Uncle Rafe. His buffalos only eat grass."

"Sounds like mine are deprived," Rafe put in the same time Joey blurted out, "Yuck!" and everyone laughed.

Shaking her head and smiling at her husband and son, Maya turned back to Laurel. "Today's the day we remember the children in our families who've died. We call them little angels and we decorate their graves with toys and pretty balloons."

Laurel's heart twisted. Coming here had been a bad idea after all. It was getting harder to keep her emotions in check. Though she tried, she had trouble believing a celebration like this could help anyone cope with the loss of a child. Nothing, it seemed, could ever heal that empty, painful place in her heart, the ache for the baby she'd never held. For the children she'd never have.

"Laurel, are you all right?" Maya asked, reaching out to lightly touch her hand. "You look pale all of the sudden. Is this too much for you?"

Laurel struggled to bury the sadness flooding her. "No, I'm fine. It's just…I think I should get something to eat. I coach the girls' team and I played hard with them today. Usually by now I'm at the diner with a burger in hand."

Maya looked unconvinced and Laurel felt a little exposed at the keen way the other woman studied her.

"If I were you, I'd grab dinner before my wife decides you need some kind of foul tasting weed tea," Sawyer said lightly, although he was looking at her with a slight frown of concern. "Maya practices alternative medicine and she's the best there is. But I speak from experience when I say her remedies are never something you want seconds of."

Maya slid her hand up his arm and slipped him a teasing smile. "Hmm…you never say that about the massage therapy."

"Think I'd rather have her remedies than yours," Rafe told Sawyer and then looked at Jule.

Jule laughed, drawing a smile from Rafe. "Was that a hint?"

"Sawyer's a paramedic," Maya explained to Laurel. She

glanced at her husband. "And I think you're making Laurel nervous. She knows her body and I'm sure she's just hungry, like she says."

She looked at Laurel as she said it, and from the tone of her voice and the knowing expression in her eyes, Laurel knew Maya didn't believe it, but that she also wasn't about to press Laurel for any other explanation.

"I'm falling down on my job as tour guide," Cort said. "Let's go find you some dinner. You guys want to join us?"

Sawyer cuddled a messy Joey a little closer as his son nestled against his shoulder. "We'll have to take a rain check. We need to get this little guy home and give him a bath."

"We need to get going, too," Rafe said, pulling Jule close. "Have to stop in and check on Jule's parents and then do the night rounds at the ranch."

They exchanged their goodbyes and as the flame of light in the west died down to a coral glow, Laurel and Cort found booths selling food and drink and sat down side by side to eat at one of the picnic tables that had been set out for the festival.

"You okay?" he asked, reaching over to touch her hand.

The gentleness in his touch and tone started Laurel's eyes prickling again. "I—"

"Hey, look who's here."

Both she and Cort looked up to see Alex coming their ay. He was part of a group of about a dozen people, most of whom Laurel recognized from school.

"I didn't expect to see you here," Alex said as she and Cort stood up to meet them. She could almost hear him add, *especially with him,* as he nodded a greeting to Cort. "Now I know what it takes to get Cort out of his apartment." He didn't look particularly pleased at the idea.

Neither did the attractive woman at his elbow who alternated between trying to catch Cort's eye and giving Laurel looks that would have frozen fire. Laurel had met Trina Hernandez, the middle school's music teacher, but she'd never gotten past exchanging more than a few words with her. "I've missed seeing you around," Trina said to Cort. "If you had told me you were coming tonight, we could have all come together."

Cort's smile came as easily as his shift closer to Laurel and his reach for her hand. "Laurel's new to all this. I thought it might be easier if her first introduction was a little more personal."

Laurel looked up at Cort and immediately knew from the glint in his eyes he was sending a message to both Trina and Alex that said, *not interested* and *hands off.* She didn't know whether to be annoyed or flattered. Not wanting to make unnecessary waves with her boss or a coworker, she started to pull her hand away. But Cort held fast, lacing his fingers with hers.

"Some of the kids at practice today mentioned the festival and I was curious," she said.

"You might have been better off coming with us," Alex said. "You won't learn much from my old amigo here. The last few times Cort was here it was late and in his leather and chains disguise and with people I wouldn't want to meet on a dark street corner. Lately, he's been in hibernation. I was beginning to think you'd forgotten how to be you," he added to Cort.

"Lucky I found someone to drag me back into the real world," Cort said, a slight edge to his voice.

She might not have known him long, but Laurel recognized the signs he was getting irritated and silently cursed Alex. He was baiting Cort and Laurel knew she was the reason. Since she'd started teaching in Luna Hermosa, Alex had seemed to make it his mission to tease and flatter her into coming out of her shell, as he called it. The trouble was, Alex had no idea how carefully constructed that shell was and that Laurel had no intention of leaving it. Especially not for him.

Cort, on the other hand, seemed to know precisely how thick her shell was. Somehow, he could be sensitive to it and at the same time treat it with utter disregard, leaving her too befuddled to be self-protective with him.

Alex turned to Laurel. "I hear you've been giving Cort a few lessons on how to talk to kids without getting bruised."

"He's doing fine without me," she said. "You should have

seen him with Tommy today. He actually got Tommy to open up a little bit. It took me weeks."

"Really. That's amazing," Alex said, but with a tightness to his voice that dampened his show of enthusiasm. Not for the first time, Laurel got the impression Alex made everything between himself and Cort a competition and Cort's small success with Tommy was definitely a mark in his opponent's favor.

"I don't think it's amazing at all," Trina said. "I'm sure you're wonderful with children, Cort."

Cort let go of Laurel's hand and slid his arm around her shoulders. "Actually, I have no idea what I'm doing, but I'm counting on Laurel to teach me."

Trina's brilliant smile slipped. She didn't get a chance to comment as the rest of the group moved in and Cort was drawn into conversation with three or four others. Alex suggested they go for a beer and Cort, with a quick, "be right back," moved away from her, leaving Laurel alone with Trina and several other women. They wasted no time in questioning her about dating Cort, the only still-available Morente brother.

Laurel tried to brush them off and minimize their relationship, but they seemed insistent on making more out of it than it was. "Honestly, we're just friends. We haven't known each other that long."

"Is that so? Maybe you should tell him that," Trina shot back. "You should know Cort's not exactly the marrying type. He and Nova Vargas are lovers from way back. Cort was engaged once, but that didn't work out and he and Nova picked up where they'd left off in high school. Or did he forget to mention that?"

"Oh, come on, Trina," one of the other women countered, "That's been over for years."

"It didn't look over the last time I saw them together."

"Which was when?" the other woman scoffed. "Two, three years ago? You're just jealous because you haven't been able to get him into bed."

"Who says I haven't?" Trina demanded.

"Oh, in your dreams, girl."

"You wish," a second echoed.

Truth or not, the words hit Laurel like a punch in the gut. She'd assumed from what he'd said that Cort wasn't involved with anyone. But then, she'd also assumed her husband was faithful until she found out he'd been bedding her close friend. She'd trusted Scott. Did she trust Cort? Did she have any right to make a judgment one way or another about him? Yes. And no. She had no right to assume trust, but she had trusted him. Until now.

"Cort is single. He can do as he pleases," she said as lightly as possible.

Trina gave her a nasty smile. "Well, I'm sure you've got no idea of what might please him."

"Give it a rest, Trina," another woman said. "Let's get back to the gazebo. We're wasting the music. Are you coming, Laurel?"

When Laurel murmured something about having to get home, the other women drifted off, laughing and chattering. Laurel started to walk away, trying to figure out how she'd get back to her house on her own when a hand on her shoulder stopped her.

"What's wrong?" Cort asked, setting two beers and a plate piled high with burritos on the table.

"I want to leave. Where's Alex? If you don't want to go, I'm sure he'll give me a ride."

"Alex left with the rest of them. I think he might have given up on you, for a while at least."

"Why? What did you say to him?"

"I told him we were going out," he said matter-of-factly.

"You what?"

"Hey, I was just trying to help. I figured you didn't need the hassle of having to keep telling him no."

"I think you're the one I should be telling no. Why didn't you ask Nova to come with you tonight?"

"Nova?" He stared at her in confusion. "What's she got to do with this? I told you we were just friends."

"Do you sleep with all your friends or is she special?" Laurel threw back at him.

Cort shook his head as if he hadn't heard correctly. "What did you say?"

"You heard me. Trina told me you and Nova are lovers."

"And you believed her?"

"I don't know what to believe. I don't know you at all. Maybe Nova does. Or Trina. She claims to be one of your friends, too."

"Trina is a—" He added something in Spanish that Laurel couldn't translate, but the way he spit the words out gave her a pretty good idea of what he meant. Shoving a hand through his hair, Cort looked as if he wanted to say something, stopped and then said, "Will you at least sit down and eat a burrito with me?"

Laurel eyed the tempting plate, her stomach letting her know she was way overdue for a meal. Reluctantly, she sat down.

Cort set her beer and burrito in front of her, but instead of sitting next to her, this time he walked around the table and sat opposite her. "I want you to look in my eyes so you can see I'm not lying when I tell you this. Nova and I were lovers, but it's been over for a long time. She's a good friend. That's it. And I have never, will never, don't ever want to sleep with Trina Hernandez. And she knows it. Which is why when she saw us together tonight, she went out of her way to make up a few lies to screw things up between us."

Laurel wanted to believe him. But she'd been slammed the whole evening with reminders of her past and now yesterday and today were mixed up, messing up her ability to judge. She took her first bite, barely tasting it. "Thanks for the burrito," she mumbled, trying to focus on her food instead of Cort.

"Well? Do you believe me?"

"I don't know. I need—I need to think about it."

She looked up from her plate and noticed that a huge orange hunter's moon had risen behind the bare trees that lined the plaza. A few scattered lanterns had been lit and most of the children were gone from the crowd.

Darkness was settling in lending an eerie air to the festival now, as candles sprung to light here and there, illuminating carvings of skulls and skeletons painted white. Little white lights dotted the barren trees casting random patterns of shadows on the cobblestones and brick walkways. A new band started up, mostly acoustic guitars, playing a haunting Spanish ballad. The air turned rapidly chilly, sharp against the bare skin of her face and hands.

"You're cold," Cort said as they finished their meal. "We should go. When it gets late, a different crowd shows up. You don't want to be here."

Taking his word for it she let him lead her back to his Jeep.

Before he opened the door for her, he hesitated, looking down at her, his expression unreadable in the darkness.

"Cort—"

"It's okay," he murmured, and very gently, pulled her into his arms.

Laurel didn't resist, sliding her arms around him and resting her head against his heart. For a moment they stood there, pressed close in the darkness. It felt right. She wanted to stay there and not think about anything but how good it was to be held by him.

Abruptly an image of them together at the diner, Cort bantering with Nova, Nova's fingers on his shoulder, pushed into her thoughts. With it came a memory of Scott and Karen. Karen, another dark and beautiful woman, her hand caressing Scott's shoulder as they told her they were lovers.

She pushed away from Cort, hugging her arms to her to ward off a chill that came from inside. "Don't. I can't. It's too soon."

"Too soon for what? To believe I'm telling the truth?"

"I don't know what's true or who I can trust anymore." In the feather-white moonlight, she saw his flinch, knew she'd hurt him by not saying she believed him. It hurt her and she just stopped herself from reaching out again, this time to be the one to offer comfort and assurances. "I'm sorry. I just…I need time."

Cort lifted his hand and slowly drew his fingertips down her cheek. He leaned forward and her breath caught on a sigh that sounded like longing. Instead of bringing him closer, it stopped him.

"You can trust me," he said softly.

Yes. But she never said the word.

Only whispered it in her heart.

Chapter Five

She awoke abruptly in the cold and the dark, her head pounding, her face wet with tears. Running a trembling hand over her hair, Laurel glanced at the clock. Four-thirty. Hours before daylight but she knew she wouldn't go back to sleep. She never did.

The counselor had told her that the dreams—nightmares, Laurel called them—were her mind's way of trying to cope with her losses and that eventually, when she put the past behind her, they would stop. But it had been over two years and Laurel was beginning to think eventually meant a lifetime.

The dreams were always the same. She was in the sunlight, carrying her baby, happy and laughing, when Scott came and took the baby from her. He would smile a little, ignoring her pleading and tears as he walked away, leaving her alone in an empty place.

She was still there because although she was alone, at least she was where she could never be hurt again, where she never had to feel anything too deeply, where there were no emotions that could cut or wound. She told herself she could live with the loneliness.

And then Cort Morente had come into her life and for some reason he made her recognize the loneliness as an ache that never went away, something that hurt her more than she admitted.

Getting out of bed, she wrapped herself in a worn flannel robe, pulled on a fat pair of socks and went to the kitchen to make coffee. She didn't want to think about Cort. She suspected he, along with the weirdness at the festival, was the reason she'd had the dream again. But he was there, in her head, refusing to be banished and in the end she gave up.

Slowly she stirred a generous amount of cream and honey into her mug of coffee, remembering last night, and the same confusing mix of feelings came tumbling back.

Part of her remembered with pleasure how she'd liked being with Cort and the way he'd taken care to make her a part of the festivities and his group of family and friends. It was the first time since she'd come to Luna Hermosa that she hadn't quite so keenly felt like an outsider, in a place she didn't belong. If she were honest, she felt more comfortable with him than she had with anyone since the loss of her baby and her divorce, maybe because she knew he understood too well what it meant to have your life ripped apart, to have to struggle to find yourself again.

Those feelings were good but she didn't know if she could trust them. Trina's declaration that Cort and Nova were lovers still bothered her. Her reasonable side believed him when he denied it; knew Trina had said it out of spite. But her newer, hesitant, vulnerable side warned her against trusting someone who could hurt her again.

She told herself it was ridiculous because their only reason for being together at all was Tommy and once that was settled, she'd probably never see him again.

The problem was she instinctively knew he had that power to hurt her because she couldn't ignore the connection between them. To complicate things, he attracted her, in a basic woman to man way that had nothing to do with reason or logic.

She didn't need a man like Cort upsetting her life and making her want things she couldn't have.

Finishing her coffee, Laurel decided to go running. The exercise would be good for her, would help her clear her head and focus on ridding herself of the lingering dream and her pointless thinking about Cort.

But as she stepped out into the cool, silvery dawn twenty minutes later and started off toward the park, Laurel couldn't stop herself from wondering what he was doing now and whether he felt even a little of the crazy, mixed up emotions she did whenever they were in the same room.

Lost in thought, Cort realized he'd just sat through an entire light change at the main intersection in town and was now stuck again at a red. He was trying to figure out what it was about Laurel Tanner that messed with his head and whether or not she felt even a little of the conflicted emotions he did whenever they were together.

He didn't need the distraction of Laurel as anything more than a friend, helping him to help Tommy. He had more than enough to deal with putting his life back together again. He'd promised himself a long time ago he'd never commit to a woman unless he could give her everything and right now, he had a lot less than everything to offer. Besides, he'd only known Laurel a short time. Putting her and commitment in the same thought was ridiculous.

Unfortunately, he couldn't seem to keep her in that just-casual-friends category in his head. She kept straying into other places she had no business being and then sticking there, despite his best efforts to push her out.

Which was why he was on his way over to Sawyer's house before seven on a Saturday morning. He told himself it was because he wanted to talk to his brother and sister-in-law about Tommy, maybe get some ideas for reaching the boy.

It was partly true but the larger part was he'd woken up with a sudden, strong need to do something. Laurel was the cause of that, too. Her struggles to start over sharply reminded him of how he'd been standing in one place for too long, uncertain of which way to go, hanging on to things he couldn't have any more because to let them go meant giving up a part of himself.

For the first time in nearly a year, he wanted finally to be done with the past and move on. Only he wasn't sure exactly how he was going to do that. So he found himself on Sawyer's doorstep, at an obnoxious hour and risking his brother's pre-caffeine grouchiness, with a vague but persistent idea that he wasn't sure whether he wanted Sawyer to support or talk him out of something.

Sawyer opened the door to him after only a few moments, although Cort suspected from his brother's unshaven, rumpled appearance he hadn't been long out of bed. He shrugged off Cort's apology for the hour, didn't even ask why he had shown up so early, only waved Cort into the kitchen and began to make coffee.

"Joey and Nico are always up by now, anyway," Sawyer told him. He shrugged as he was interrupted by a loud squeal and a shriek of laughter from the opposite end of the house. "As you can hear. We'll be invaded in a few minutes so be prepared." He leaned back against the counter after starting the coffee maker and eyed Cort. "Long night?"

"I haven't had one of those in a while."

"Sorry," Sawyer said with a wince, "I know you miss it."

"Yeah, I guess." At his brother's skeptical look, Cort relented. "I did, for a long time. Sometimes I still do."

"Is that what this coaching basketball and helping the kid is all about?"

"Part of it."

Sawyer stood looking at him for a few moments, saying nothing. Then he said, "And part of it's her."

"Her?" Cort put on his best poker face. "There's no her in this."

"Nice bluff, little brother, but I don't believe that. This has got something to do with Laurel Tanner, doesn't it? I knew it last night. That's the first time I've seen you with an actual date in years."

"It wasn't a date. And it's got nothing to do with her. We both want to help Tommy, that's all."

"She didn't seem your type," Sawyer went on as if Cort hadn't spoken and Cort stopped himself from asking for details on just what Sawyer considered his type. "But she was quick enough to defend you and tell us how great you were with the kids. And Maya and I agreed you guys seemed pretty comfortable with each other."

There didn't seem much he could say without giving Sawyer and Maya something else to talk about and any outright denials would be lies so Cort decided to change the subject. Hesitating, he tried the words out in his head before saying, "I'm thinking about going back to law school."

Sawyer stared. "Helluva way to distract me."

Cort smiled a little. He couldn't blame Sawyer for being surprised. He'd surprised himself by having the thought to begin with. "I know, it's probably crazy."

The coffee ready, Sawyer began pouring them both large mugs. "No, it's not crazy. It's just not what I expected."

"Me, neither." Cort took his coffee, fidgeting with the handle before cautiously taking a sip. He grimaced and reached for the creamer Sawyer offered him. "Damn, do you think you could get this any stronger? Why don't you just inject the caffeine and get it over with?"

"It's either that or Maya's weed tea—take your pick."

"Don't start on my tea this early," Maya said. She came into the kitchen with Nico on her hip and shared a smile with Sawyer as Joey, dragging his stuffed buffalo, ran past her to hurl himself into his father's arms. "Hi, Cort." She stretched up and kissed him on the cheek then handed him Nico. "Here, hold your nephew for a few minutes while I get breakfast going. You're staying, aren't you?"

Finding his hands full of squirming, babbling baby momentarily robbed Cort of a reply and Maya took his silence for a yes before he could say otherwise.

Sawyer snagged his wife around the waist before she'd gone two steps. "Hey, where's my morning kiss?"

"You've already had yours," Maya told him, kissing him anyway, "several times over and then some."

"Buff'lo wants juice!" Joey interrupted loudly.

Laughing, Maya moved away to start breakfast and Sawyer motioned Cort into the small sunny room next to the kitchen that served as a casual dining area. Cort spent the next thirty minutes mostly just watching the organized chaos and marveling at how far his brother had come from the guy who was so sure he'd never make a good husband and father to a man whose wife and sons were his world. He envied Sawyer, especially lately, when he'd had to face up to having most of his own world shot to hell.

It was Sawyer, when the kids were busy eating, who returned to the subject Cort had tentatively tossed out earlier. "Cort's thinking about going back to law school," he told Maya.

Maya shot Cort a startled look. "Really?"

Cort held up a hand. "It's okay. It sounds weird to me, too."

"It's not that." She and Sawyer exchanged a glance.

Sawyer studied Cort for a moment and Cort could sense his brother weighing his words. "After what happened with Sandia and your quitting the first time... I never thought you'd want to go back to it."

"Me, neither," Cort admitted. Having to revisit his past with Sandia was one of the reasons why he'd been doubtful about the idea of going back to school. "I'm still not sure I want to. I think I'm half hoping you two will tell what a bad idea it is."

"Sorry, not happening," Sawyer said. "That's your call, little brother."

"What makes it a bad idea?" Maya asked.

"I don't know. Going back to law school at my age, starting over again."

Getting up to refill Joey's juice cup and his and Cort's mugs, Sawyer said over his shoulder, "You make it sound like you're ready for retirement. Besides, you were top of your class."

"That was a long time ago." Cort paused then said, "Maybe it's more about changing. Becoming someone I'd decided I didn't want to be."

Sawyer, back with the refills, looked at him as if he were searching for something and Cort could read the concern in his brother's expression. But before either Sawyer or Maya could say anything in reply, his cell phone rang. Not sure whether to bless or curse the caller, Cort answered it, surprised to hear Laurel's voice. He'd given her his cell number the other night at the diner, but he'd doubted she'd ever use it.

"Cort? Can you meet me at the diner?" she asked, hurried and low. "I know it's early, but Tommy's here with me."

She didn't elaborate but Cort could hear the urgency in her voice, telling him it was important. "I'm on my way," he told her, keeping it casual even though from the way Sawyer and Maya watched him, Cort knew they'd probably guessed it was Laurel. "Gotta run," he said to them after he'd punched the end button. "Something's up with Tommy. Thanks for breakfast. I'll catch you later."

"You do that," Sawyer said, "and tell Laurel hello."

Cort didn't bother with a snappy comeback. Hurrying out to his Jeep, he made it to town in under twenty minutes. It was early enough that the diner wasn't overcrowded and after a quick glance, he found Laurel and Tommy sitting in a corner booth.

He moved toward them at a casual pace, not wanting to startle Tommy into running away again. From the way Laurel held herself, tensely, poised on the edge of her seat, he sensed it was a definite possibility. He wondered how she'd managed to keep the kid here as long as she had.

Laurel looked up, saw him and her expression relaxed a

fraction. "Thanks for coming," she said as Cort slid in next to her.

"I'm not going back there!" Tommy blurted out before Cort could say anything.

Cort glanced at Laurel. Her expression said she'd already heard it and hadn't succeeded in changing Tommy's mind. "Maybe you should define *there*," he said slowly.

"To Mrs. Barraca's."

"Your foster mother?"

"I hate it there. You can't make me go back." His hands fisted together, Tommy glared defiantly at Cort, challenging him to argue. But Cort had seen enough false bravado to know when defiant was a cover-up for scared.

"What's wrong at Mrs. Barraca's?" he asked. "Did something happen?"

Tommy's mouth tightened and he glanced at Laurel. Cort looked, too, trying to get some useful information from one of them.

"Mrs. Barraca is fostering three younger kids, as well as Tommy," Laurel told him. "Tommy said she spends most of her time with the youngest ones. I guess they need the extra attention."

"They're all messed up," Tommy muttered.

"It doesn't mean Mrs. Barraca doesn't care about you," Laurel said gently.

"She doesn't! You don't know. She just wants someone to help her with the chores and the little kids. She doesn't want me." Tommy swiped hard at his eyes. "No one wants me."

Tommy's expression, part determination to keep up a facade of toughness, part vulnerability that showed itself in his tremulous lower lip and the angry unshed tears, resurrected a memory for Cort. He'd been five and Sawyer seven. Sawyer had looked like that, facing down their father in defense of his younger brother, protecting Cort from Jed's abuse. As a kid, he'd always had Sawyer to look out for him. Tommy didn't have anyone.

"Is that why you ran away?" he asked.

"So what? She won't miss me."

"Even if that's true, where were you planning on going?"

The question threw Tommy. He stared at Cort uncertainly then said, "I dunno. Somewhere."

"Tommy, you just can't wander the streets," Laurel protested. "You need a safe place to stay. You need to go back to Mrs. Barraca's." She looked to Cort, silently urging him to back her up.

Thinking fast, Cort tried to come up with an answer that wouldn't alienate Laurel and wasn't, for Tommy's sake, taking the obvious and easy way out. "Mrs. Tanner's right, you do need to go back there, at least for now." He held up a hand to stop the protest he saw coming from Tommy. "But I've got an idea. I have a friend who lives not too far from town and he's been taking in foster kids for years. I think he's only got one other boy there now and he's a year or two older than you. I could talk to my friend, see if maybe you could stay there for a while."

Tommy didn't say anything but Cort didn't miss the quick dart of the boy's eyes in his direction, the spark of interest. Just as quickly, it was doused, replaced by a deliberate guardedness. The kid was wary of trusting him and anyone else who made promises that sounded too good to be true. Considering Tommy's past, Cort couldn't blame him.

"I'm not telling you this is going to work out, but I'll do everything I can. That means, though, you have to do something in return. Go back to Mrs. Barraca's."

"No—"

"I've got no chance of making this happen unless you work with me."

When Tommy retreated into another brooding silence, Cort decided they all needed a break. "Have you had breakfast?" he asked Laurel. She shook her head and Cort immediately flagged the waitress over and ordered pancakes for her and Tommy. After the waitress left, Cort told Tommy, "Think on it while you eat."

"What if I say no?" Tommy asked him, his tone hard and resigned, as if he'd already decided what Cort's answer would be.

"I don't know," Cort answered honestly.

"Whatever you decide, we'll be here for you," Laurel said. She reached over the table and touched Tommy's hand. "I promise you that."

Tommy threw a frown at Cort. "What about him?"

"*Him* has a name and can speak for himself," Cort said. "It's Cort and you can count on me being there whether you want me or not."

The arrival of breakfast offered a temporary reprieve from the tension. As Tommy and Laurel ate, Cort nursed a cup of coffee that tasted like flavored water after Sawyer's brew. As he drank Cort hoped he was saying the right things instead of making the situation worse. He had only Sawyer's example to go by. Neither of his parents had ever been protective or supportive. So he tried to act like he imagined his brother would, not knowing if he was close to getting it right.

With nothing left on his plate but crumbs, Tommy drew circles in the leftover syrup with the tip of his fork for a few moments. He didn't quite meet Cort's eyes when he said, almost too low to hear, "Okay. I guess I'll go back. But I'm not gonna stay very long."

Cort stopped a satisfied grin before it started. "I hope it won't be much longer. You've got to be patient, though, and give me a chance to talk to the right people and make things better."

Since Laurel had been out running and didn't have her car, Cort drove the three of them to Mrs. Barraca's house. It was obvious to Cort the woman had been worried about Tommy and she seemed genuinely to care about him. But it was equally obvious she was overworked and overwhelmed by the responsibility of four needy children, three of whom were under the age of five.

"I hate leaving him here," Laurel said the moment they were outside.

"I know, but we don't have a lot of options right now. Look," he tried reassuring her as he started the Jeep and began pulling out of the driveway, "I'll give Joseph Charez a call about him possibly fostering Tommy. And I've also got a friend in social services who might be able to help."

Laurel stared down at her hands. "I just don't know what's best. I don't think he's ever had a real home."

"Probably not, at least not for long. I'll do what I can, I promise."

She smiled then, straight into his eyes. "I know you will. You've been terrific."

"Keep that up and I'll promise you anything," Cort said lightly but with an unsettling suspicion that he might not be teasing. He suddenly wished he could do something to make her feel better about the whole thing. Maybe earn himself another smile. "We aren't going to fix this today," he said at last. Then, acting on an impulse he didn't want to examine too closely he added, "Why don't we get out of here and do something that'll get your mind off it for a while?"

Laurel eyed him suspiciously. "Like what?"

"I'm guessing you haven't seen much of the area since you moved here. Do you ride?"

"If you mean horses and not that motorcycle you're so fond of, I used to, back home."

"Great. How'd you like to go this morning? I need to get out and clear my head and I know a great place to do it."

"I don't know." Her expression wavered between wariness and an obvious desire to accept. "This sounds a lot like a date to me."

"And, what? You've decided never to date again or is it just me?" Before she could answer Cort urged, "Come on, Laurel, I'm not asking for a lifetime commitment here. We could both use a break and I'd like the company of a friend. I spend too much time brooding these days and I don't like it. I need to remember how to have a conversation that doesn't have to do with what I'm going to do with the rest of my life. How about you?"

"Cort, I—" She stopped, took a breath. Finally, she smiled, the gesture lightening the shadows in her eyes. "Okay, you're right. I could use a break, too. But I need to go home first to trade my sweats for jeans."

"Just tell me where I'm going." Cort felt absurdly pleased she'd agreed to his impromptu invitation.

It was probably going to complicate things more than they already were, but it felt good and for now, that was more than enough.

Chapter Six

Less than five minutes later, Cort pulled into the driveway of the small adobe *casita* Laurel rented.

"Give me a few minutes to change," she said once they were inside.

"Need any help?"

Laurel flushed and then shook her head. "Find some other way to entertain yourself. I'll be right back."

She left him alone in her living room and Cort took the opportunity to look around. The little house with its red-tiled roof was neat and clean, painted in light earth-colored pastels, with large windows that let in the sun, and a fresh scent of sage and pine. But a sense of emptiness lingered, as if Laurel had deliberately kept herself from bringing too many memories into it.

Several haphazard piles of photographs spread over a coffee table caught Cort's eye and he moved closer to look at them. From the boxes on the floor and the careless way the pictures had been tossed over the table, it appeared Laurel had been sorting through past memories. Most of the photos were of Laurel and, what he decided from the resemblance, must be her family. Only one showed her with a light-haired man, their arms draped around each other's shoulders as they grinned for the camera. They both wore wedding rings so Cort guessed the man must be her ex-husband.

They looked young and happy, but their pose struck him as odd, reminding him more of two best friends rather than lovers. Then again, what would he know about it. He and Sandia had been passionate and adventurous lovers, they'd shared interests and ambitions, but he'd never thought of her as a close friend. For all the intimacy they'd shared in bed, neither of them had been willing to lay open their heart and soul for the other to see.

"That's Scott." Laurel stood a few feet from him. She'd changed into faded jeans and a denim shirt over a white t-shirt, her hair caught back in its usual ponytail. "It was taken right after we were married," she said quietly, "before everything went wrong."

"You look very young," Cort said, not quite sure what else to say.

Laurel took the photo from him and studied it, almost dispassionately, as if the couple pictured were strangers. "Scott was my best friend in high school. I never dated anyone else. We got married when I was still in college. I suppose we were very young. But at the time it seemed right." She tossed the photo, face down, into one of the boxes, staring at it a moment before seemingly shaking off whatever emotions looking at it had resurrected before turning back to him. "What about you?"

"Me?"

"Trina said you were engaged once."

"Trina apparently said a lot of things." Cort definitely didn't want to go there again, but he felt compelled, after her revelations, to give her more than a one-word confirmation of what she already knew. "I was engaged."

This was harder than he expected. He'd sidestepped it this

morning with Sawyer. But he knew if he were serious about trying law school again, this was another part of his past he'd have to settle with. It had been a long time since he'd gotten this close to his feelings about Sandia, though, and the reunion promised to be painful.

He started to take the easy way out and change the subject when Laurel asked, "What happened?"

"Sandia died," he said. Suddenly Cort couldn't look at the sympathy and understanding on her face. It hurt somehow. He turned away, pretended to find the books on her shelves intensely interesting while he said the rest of it, quickly. "We met while we were both in law school in Albuquerque and I moved in with her after a couple of months. We were living in her old neighborhood because she liked it there, but it wasn't very safe. When we decided to get married, I stayed because I figured we wouldn't be there much longer. One weekend I had to go back home. I wanted her to come with me, but she was studying for finals and insisted on staying. I didn't like leaving her, but my mother was sick and she'd taken a turn for the worse. Sandia told me she could take care of herself."

Cort could hear himself, the dead tone of his voice. But he felt it all inside again, painful and very much alive.

"While I was gone, an addict broke into the house, looking for money, and killed her." Laurel's breath caught, but he kept staring, unseeing, at the books. "After that I decided I wasn't cut out to be a lawyer, and eventually I came back here to chase bad guys. You already know how that turned out."

He didn't say anything else. How he still felt guilty for not protecting her, for not insisting Sandia go with him or move out of that area altogether. But mostly for not loving her with everything in him. Maybe if he had she would still be here.

She stepped closer and put a gentle hand on his shoulder and he finally faced her. The compassion and understanding in her face and touch nearly made him spill it all to her. He held back, though, not willing to leave himself more vulnerable to her than he already was.

"It's not your fault," she said softly. "You couldn't have known."

"Yeah, that's what everyone said. Sometimes I believe it." He shook his head. "You want to hear something funny? I'm thinking about going back."

"To law school?"

"I think all those months of sitting around doing nothing have given me delusions," he said with a half laugh, inviting her to smile the suggestion away.

Instead, she frowned a little. "Why would you think that? It seems worth considering."

"Does it? I quit at the beginning of my second year. It'd almost be like starting over since I haven't been in a classroom in over ten years. I'm not even sure I'd be any good at being a lawyer even if I could manage to finish school this time."

"If you're trying to talk yourself out of it then tell me now and I'll just nod and agree with you."

Cort laughed outright then. "I'd rather hear what you really think."

She looked at him dubiously, as if she doubted her opinion would matter to him. "What I really think," she said carefully, "is that you're scared."

It was the last thing he expected to hear from her. He put on his best look of cocky assurance, the one that hadn't been working so well lately, to cover the fact she'd thrown him off balance. "Hey, I was the big, tough cop. I'm not supposed to be scared of anything."

"Maybe. But I think I understand how you feel. I know the whole idea of starting over and becoming someone I'd never thought I'd be scares the heck out of me."

Her words, almost an echo of his own to Sawyer and Maya earlier, unexpectedly touched him. He'd lost his job and part of his physical ability, but she'd lost love and a child. He could go a different direction, regain most of what he'd lost, albeit an altered version. It wouldn't be as easy for her because letting herself believe in the possibility of a new love and family would mean being vulnerable to the same heartache and loss all over again. If he was afraid, she must be terrified.

"If I confess I'm scared, will you promise not to tell anyone?" he asked lightly. "It'll ruin what's left of my reputation."

Laurel hesitated as if she wanted to say something else. She settled for a smile. "Bring back the black leather and the motorcycle and no one will believe me even if I did."

"Ah, it comes out. You like the bad boy in leather look."

"Now you are delusional."

"Probably," Cort said, grinning at her flushed cheeks. "Come on, let's get out of here for a while. You can tell me what you do like on the way."

"Where are we going?" she asked as Cort backed the jeep out.

"I still keep a few horses at my grandparents' estate. It's not far. And there's an easy trail to the mountains from there."

"I thought your father owned a ranch."

Cort blew out a breath. He supposed she didn't do it on purpose, but Laurel had a knack for bringing up awkward subjects. "Yeah, well, he hasn't been my father for a long time."

He felt her watching him and deliberately kept his eyes on the road. "Estate sounds pretty grand," she said lightly, telling him she'd gotten the message he didn't want to explain any more.

"I guess. I did most of my growing up there but I was never that impressed with it."

"You must like Luna Hermosa though. You came back."

Cort glanced at her. "Maybe like you, I just wanted to get away from the memories."

"That doesn't really work though, does it?" Laurel sighed then she caught his eye and smiled. "You just end up dateless with no place to go on a Saturday night."

"Well, it's Saturday day and we've got some place to go. So we can pretend it's a hot date."

He said it flippantly but as soon as he did, there was a subtle shift in the air between them, awareness breathing in the silence of how alone they were and for reasons that had nothing to do with their mutual concern for Tommy.

Pulling onto the road that led to his grandparents' property, he thought it was going to be a lot harder to pretend this was just a friendly outing, like last night, with no strings attached, when it felt like something a lot different.

Cort pressed a series of numbers into a keypad. As the expanse of elegantly wrought iron gate slid open, Laurel reminded herself not to let her jaw drop. This was so far removed from anything she'd grown up with, it might have been another world.

"Well, you did say *estate*, didn't you?" Her eyes darted from side to side along the winding piñon-lined drive that finally led to a massive hacienda. From a distance, it almost looked like part of a Pueblo complex, several adobe structures, varying in height and size, all melded together with round timbers and earth-toned stucco.

She tried to imagine Cort growing up here. It was difficult because he didn't act the way she'd expect someone born to money and privilege would. He obviously had been, though, and it reemphasized to her how completely out of her experience he was.

"It's way too big for the two of them, but they'll never give this place up," Cort said, pulling to a stop on a driveway set off to the side of the main circular drive. He glanced out the window and shrugged. "But it's not as though they have to do anything."

They both got out of the vehicle and Cort gestured toward a bricked path near the driveway. "That leads to the gardens and beyond those are the stables. I need to say hello to the grandparents then we'll go saddle up. I'll try and keep it short, but my grandmother will probably insist on feeding us something first. They put me up for about five months when I was recuperating so I don't feel right any more going out of my way to avoid them."

"Is there a reason you'd want to?" Laurel asked.

Cort walked around to where Laurel stood and took her hand, drawing her eyes to his. Out of her recent habit of keeping everyone back, she almost pulled away. Except she suddenly had the impression the gesture was more reassurance than a ploy to touch her. "Several. I'd better warn you now. They're not what you'd call warm and fuzzy."

Laurel laughed. "I think I can manage. I've dealt with my share of cool and prickly."

"Okay, but if they start talking about anything even vaguely resembling restaurants do me a favor and immediately interrupt before I do something I'll seriously regret."

"Restaurants? Why would they?"

"Trust me," Cort muttered, as he led her toward the front patio entrance, "they will."

"I don't think it's a good idea for you to be exerting yourself like this." Consuela Morente looked at her grandson over the rim of her china teacup with an expression both worried and disapproving.

As Cort had predicted, his grandmother insisted they stay for tea and coffee. They were sitting in a room that looked like a designer's dream and spoke of old money and impeccable taste. Laurel felt out of place in her jeans and boots, sipping tea from a delicate gilt-edged cup, while, posed beside his wife of sixty years like a patriarch in a nineteenth-century painting, Santiano Morente watched her as if he were judging her worth.

But Cort disconcerted her more. He'd introduced her to his grandparents without any explanation of where she fit into his life then sat down next to her on the small loveseat as if him by her side was only natural. His grandparents, from their speculative glances, seemed to be drawing their own conclusions and Laurel had the uncomfortable feeling it was that she and Cort were a couple.

Either it didn't bother him or he was deliberately ignoring it because Cort kept a smile and an easy flow of comebacks up to the point his grandmother questioned his decision to go riding.

"I'm fine," he said shortly, and Laurel got the impression he'd repeated that phrase so many times recently it had become automatic and meaningless.

"We've heard that enough from you not to believe it," Santiano said with a frown. "But perhaps some good has come out of this. It has forced you to reconsider your choice of job. A job, I might add, that was a mistake from the beginning and a waste of your talents. Now maybe you'll give serious consideration to finally assuming responsibility for your mother's share of the business. Heaven knows your brother never will. We'd like to be open here in the next month, but we can't do that without a manager."

"We've had this conversation before." *Too many times,* Laurel thought, if the barely controlled irritation in his voice were any indication.

"What else are you going to do?" Santiano pressed him. "It's been almost a year and you haven't shown any ambition to do anything else. This is an opportunity for you to avoid following your brother's example. He could have done anything he chose. Instead, look where he is now."

Cort's expression hardened. "If you mean Sawyer, yeah, he's happily married with two great kids and a job he loves. I'd say of the two of us, he's the lucky one."

"Of course he means Sawyer," Consuela said. "I will never understand why you insist on claiming those two Garrett boys as your brothers."

"Probably because they are."

They stared at each other and then Consuela smiled as if their mutual test of wills had never happened. "You would be doing us a favor." She glanced at her husband before adding, "Perhaps just for a few months, until we're established. Your grandfather has been taking on too much these past months and with your uncle managing the expansions in Arizona, there's no one we can count on here to help."

Rubbing at a spot just above his right brow, Cort sighed. "What makes you think I could help? I can bus tables with the best of them, and I can mix a pretty decent margarita. Other than that, I don't know a damned thing about managing a restaurant."

"I don't think you'd have the time, if you're planning on going back to law school," Laurel spoke up.

Consuela and Santiano looked startled. Cort turned to her with a raised brow and Laurel hoped she hadn't put her foot in it.

"I must say this is a surprise," Consuela said finally. "Isn't it a bit late for you to become a student again?"

Laurel began to get an idea of why Cort had reason to regularly avoid his grandparents. "I'm sure Cort would make a success of it, if that's what he decides to do," she said firmly, "especially if he has his family's support."

Taking Laurel's hand, Cort got to his feet. "Look, I'm not making any promises, but I'll think about it, okay? Thanks for the tea but we need to get started. I want to show Laurel some of the mountains. I'll call you in a day or two and let you know about the job."

"I appreciate the show of confidence," Cort told her as soon as they'd escaped outside and had started walking toward the stables.

"It wasn't a show," Laurel said. "I meant it. You don't seem like someone who gives up easily. If you want to go back and finish law school, you will."

He grinned, his good temper suddenly restored. "I think I'll keep you around for whenever I need some ego stroking. You can see how deprived I was in the months I stayed here."

"Your grandparents do seem a little, um, severe."

"Very tactful of you, but I grew up with them and *severe* is one of the nicer things I can say about them."

"It sounds like you don't have a lot of happy memories of this place."

"It was better than living with my father," Cort said shortly.

Laurel was curious, particularly after the exchange between him and his grandparents. She'd never directly asked him about his family though. It would be too much like prying and she'd had enough of that in her own life to know how uncomfortable it was.

But when they'd reached the stables he stopped, facing her. "Look, if you haven't already you're going to hear a lot of talk about my family. My father is a nasty SOB who drank too much and then took it out on Sawyer. My parents split when I was six and after that, Jed Garrett decided Sawyer and I didn't exist. My parents had adopted my brother Rafe, and Garrett kept him, remarried and had Josh. What we didn't know until recently was that Garrett had an affair with Rafe's mother and Rafe really is his son. And the big secret that everyone's sure to find out soon is that Garrett had a son before any of the rest of us so we've got a brother we've never met. He's a captain in the Army reserves and got called up and we haven't been able to connect yet."

Laurel felt a little dazed. "You've given me a new appreciation for my everyday, two-parent, three kids and two dogs and a cat family. Although compared to you, I feel kind of boring," she added with a lightly teasing smile.

With a grin that made her blush, Cort led her into the stables. "Let's see what I can do to convince you you're anything but."

Chapter Seven

It felt great to be in a saddle again, Laurel thought, checking her stirrups for length. She hadn't ridden much since college, but as a girl, she'd spent every free moment riding at her best friend's ranch. Today, with the bright autumn sun streaking down through flames of orange, yellow and copper leaves, a brisk autumn bite in the air, for the first time since she'd been in New Mexico, she began truly to relax.

Beside her, Cort had mounted a large chestnut stallion. She stroked the neck of the smaller dappled gray mare he'd chosen for her and turned to him. "Thank you."

Cort looked up from adjusting the reins in his hand, the wind ruffling his dark hair. "For what?"

"For this." Laurel shifted her reins to one hand and gestured with the other at the vista of mountains, trees and turquoise sky. "For reminding me how fresh the earth and pines smell. For getting me out and away from my routine and letting me forget everything else for a while."

The corner of Cort's mouth lifted in a satisfied smile. "Oh, yeah. That was a feat, wasn't it?" He pulled his horse close to hers and leaned out of the saddle toward her. "So, what's my reward?"

Less than a breath away, his scent, leather, earth and sage, wafted through her senses, teasing her. Trembling on the edge between wanting to move closer and thinking it was a bad idea, she felt momentarily paralyzed. The slightest encouragement from her, he would kiss her.

The slightest encouragement. The barest shift forward.

She never knew if she actually made that move or whether Cort made it for her but in the next moment he slid his hand around her nape to draw her closer and kissed her. His mouth gently explored hers at first, as if he were unsure of his reception.

Laurel softened, his hesitation making her bolder, and without thinking, she kissed him back. He responded instantly, deepening their kiss from a light caress to something more sensual, more suggestive. A sharp pleasure spiked inside her, knocking her off balance and leaving her teetering toward abandoning any reserve and wallowing in the feeling. She might have fallen completely except at that moment, Cort's horse let out an unwelcome snort and with a jerk, broke them apart.

Laurel caught her breath, bemused by the sudden jolt out of the sensual haze fogging her brain.

They stared at each other and she saw the same questioning confusion in his eyes. *What just happened?*

Then Cort, with a rueful laugh, seemed to shake it off. "Guess Atrevido can't stand the mushy stuff," he said. As if on cue, his horse surged forward and Cort let the stallion have his head, taking off at a gallop up a sagebrush-dotted path that led into the foothills. Glancing at her over his shoulder, he called back, "C'mon, I'll take you on a little adventure."

Never one to shrink from a physical challenge, Laurel nudged her mount and chased after him. They rode at a hard gallop until the path grew too steep for more than a brisk walk. Ponderosa pines flourished, along with oak, juniper, spruce and Douglas fir, braced for the promise of snow, rustling all around them in the breeze. They climbed up the path through huge, sienna shaded boulders, towering pines and scrub evergreens to a level spot at the top of the smallest of several peaks.

Cort reined in his horse and motioned Laurel to dismount under a lumbering old piñon tree. "I'm impressed you kept up," he said, breathing hard as he threw one long leg over his saddle. "That was no easy climb."

Laurel followed suit, finding him waiting for her as she lowered herself down. "I told you I could ride."

Cort rubbed his shoulder. It ached some, but not enough to keep him from riding. "So you did. Now that I know how good you are, we should get out like this more often."

"Should we?" Standing close to him, without the distraction of the challenging ride, she tried to match his casually friendly tone and forget that he'd kissed her. And not a casually friendly kiss but one that made promises and stirred desires. She shouldn't have let that happen. Because now she wanted to kiss him again. If she did that, then they wouldn't be able to continue to pretend they were only friends, working together to help Tommy and it was a pretense she couldn't afford to let go.

Hurriedly, she stepped back. "Is your shoulder okay?"

He smiled. "Better every day."

"That's great," she said, strolling a few paces away to look out over the mountains. "It's beautiful here."

Cort came up behind her. "Yes, it is." Laurel turned to find him looking at her. That provoking half smile slipped up the side of his face. "You know, you weren't so eager to get away from me when you kissed me."

"I didn't kiss you. You started it."

"Does that mean you don't want to do it again?"

"I thought we'd agreed to just be friends," she threw back at him. "You said you didn't want to get involved with anyone, especially me."

"Yeah, and I'm pretty sure I meant it." He stopped, then said quickly, "I still mean it," though more to himself than to her as if he were trying to convince himself it was true. With a sigh, he pushed a hand through his hair. "Maybe I don't anymore. I don't know about you, but now I'm having a hard time sticking to it."

"Cort, I… It's not that I don't want—" Laurel stopped, struggling to put words to her conflicted feelings. "I like you, I like spending time with you. But we don't know each other that well yet. You told me I don't trust anyone and after what happened with Scott and Karen, maybe that's true. I can't. Not now."

Cort reached out and brushed the back of his knuckles gently over her cheek, smiling softly. "Okay, I can live with that. Especially the *yet* and *not now* part." When she looked confused, he added, "I figure that means there's hope for both of us for a *one day* and *later.* Besides, it gives me new incentive to come up with ways we can get to know each other better."

"I'm not sure if I should be happy or worried about that," she said, eyeing him dubiously and making him laugh.

Inside, though, she was smiling.

It was early, but not too early for dinner by the time Cort pulled up in front of Laurel's place. They'd spent an hour hiking before the return ride and their conversation during the trip back had been light and easy.

Underneath it though, Laurel wrestled with an unsettling restlessness. She wanted to blame Cort for kissing her but to be honest, she'd known from the moment she'd agreed to spend time with him for Tommy's sake that she was endangering the defenses she'd built up to protect herself from being made vulnerable. She'd let what happened with Scott and losing her baby isolate her because she was afraid to face that kind of heartbreak again. She was afraid getting close to someone would revive old cherished dreams and hopes and that could only lead to pain because those dreams and hopes had died with her marriage and child. And that was something she couldn't tell Cort; something she'd never told anyone.

Still, Cort had given her the best day she'd had since coming to New Mexico. Being with him, she didn't feel alone. His show of understanding and caring prompted her to offer, "Why don't you let me thank you for today by fixing you dinner?"

Cort turned off the ignition and cocked his head at her. "Are you offering me home cooking? I vaguely remember that concept."

"I am, but I don't do Mexican food. Yet."

"As a matter of fact, that's the one kind of home cooking I do get. The woman who was Sawyer's and my nanny, Regina, still brings me care packages. She used to do the same for Sawyer, but I don't think she's cooking as much for him since he got married. Although Maya is a vegetarian, so I'm sure mother hen Reggie makes certain Sawyer gets his regular meat allotment."

"Well, I'm not a vegetarian and not likely to become one. And I'd be happy to whip up a mean fried chicken, biscuits and gravy dinner."

Cort seemed to consider. "You must be tired after riding and hiking today."

"Please, I teach eleven- and twelve-year-olds. Today was a cakewalk."

"In that case," he said with a grin, "fried chicken sounds great."

Laurel breezed through dinner. It was a meal she could practically make with her eyes closed and a good thing since she had the distraction of Cort leaning in the kitchen door, watching her work after she refused his offer to help.

"You're right, you are a pretty good busboy," Laurel teased when, a leisurely hour later, they'd finished eating and Cort was helping her with the cleaning up.

"It's the least I can do. Dinner was fantastic. I don't think I've eaten that much in months."

Laurel smiled, pleased. "Me, neither. Maybe it's because—" She stopped herself and busied herself wiping at a nonexistent spot on the counter.

Cort put a hand on her wrist, stopping her. "Because why?"

She let out a little sigh. "Because I usually eat alone." Before he could comment, she moved away. "I think I'll start some coffee. Do you want dessert? I've got a cherry pie in the fridge."

"Are you trying to kill me?"

They finished the last of the cleanup and Laurel brought a tray with coffee and a few thin ginger snaps into her tiny living room. Cort had already settled into her well-weathered couch. He looked relaxed, content and impossibly sexy. His dark brown hair was tousled from the day's activities and a shadow of a beard darkened his angular chin and jaw. He stretched his long legs out in front of him beside the coffee table, jeans taut against his muscular thighs.

Stopping herself from staring, Laurel took a seat beside him and busied herself pouring coffee. "Cream?"

Cort sat up and leaned forward, his thigh and forearm brushing hers. Her body warmed instantly to his touch. "Not unless your coffee is like Sawyer's and threatens to eat through the cup," he said, thanking her with his knee-melting smile.

As she handed him his mug, their fingers touched. Her pulse quickened and she hoped he didn't notice how his every move prompted a purely adolescent response in her. She felt ridiculous. After all, she'd been married. She'd been used to the close company of a man for years. But the fact she'd had no close male company for years made her wonder if it wasn't like riding a bike. Could you forget how to behave and stay cool with a hot guy so he couldn't read you like an open book? Of course since she'd only dated Scott, her experience with hot men was seriously limited. And no man but Cort had ever made her feel like this—jumpy, edgy, excited, quivering with anticipation—all those things she shouldn't be feeling for a friend.

"So is your lack of aspiration to join the family business one of the reasons for considering law school again?" she asked, needing to push her thoughts in a different direction.

He leaned back, nursing his coffee mug. "One of them, I guess. It's more about getting on with my life. Although it feels strange to be thinking about going back to something I thought I was done with."

"It's not really going back, though, is it? I mean, you probably don't want the same things now that you did when you were twenty."

"No, a lot of things have changed since then."

"Then it's more like building something new." Laurel put down her coffee cup and pulled off her boots before curling her legs up under her. "Where would you like to be in five years?"

Cort looked amused at her question. "Is this a test?" He smiled away her embarrassment that she may have strayed too far into his personal territory. "It's okay. I haven't given it much thought but maybe it's time I did." Laying his head back against the couch, he shifted to look at her. "You know, when I look back, this is the first time I've ever thought this much about any major decision. Law school, joining the sheriff's department, even asking Sandia to marry me. I never considered the consequences. I did it because I knew at the time it was right and I didn't see any reason to debate all the reasons why or why not."

He fell silent, staring into space a moment, then turned back to her. "But to answer your question, in five years I'd like what my brothers Sawyer and Rafe have—a job and a beautiful woman I love, and maybe even a couple of kids. The whole happily-ever-after package."

Without warning, his lightly spoken words unleashed a painful wash of emotion in Laurel. He had unwittingly echoed the dreams she'd once had, of marriage, satisfying work and a family. All that was left to her was the work and that didn't begin to satisfy the ache for things lost to her forever. Her marriage was over and with the loss of her baby she'd also lost her ability ever to have children of her own.

It hurt, more than it had in months, and Laurel abruptly made to get up, not wanting Cort to see, sure he'd be able to read her secrets in her eyes.

"Hey," he said. He grasped her hand, stopping her and then very gently slid his hand against her jaw, lifting her face to him. Laurel tried to force back the tears but they came anyway, spilling onto his fingers. "What's wrong? I didn't…oh, damn. I'm sorry, I should have thought—" Ignoring her attempt to evade him, Cort pulled her into his arms, cradling her against his chest like a child. "I'm sorry," he repeated. "With everything you've lost, that was about the worst thing I could have said."

Everything I've lost. You don't know everything. I can't tell you everything. Because then you'll know how broken I am. Because you could never want what's left of me.

For long minutes, Cort held her close, stroking her hair, letting her cry and saying nothing. She appreciated his silence the most because he didn't offer any meaningless words of comfort or tell her everything would be okay. He just offered himself to lean on and let her grieve, even though he didn't know all the reasons.

Finally, when the worst of it had ebbed, leaving her drained, Laurel eased herself out of his arms and sat up, swiping her fingers under her eyes. "I'm sorry," she said.

"Don't be," Cort said. "I think you needed that."

"I don't think you needed it, though," she said. Feeling awkward for breaking down in front of him, she started to think of some way she could end the evening and salvage some of her dignity without making him feel unwelcome. Then she looked at him more closely and frowned. "Are you okay?"

Cort pinched the bridge of his nose, closing his eyes. "Fine."

"*Fine* as in okay, or you're saying *fine* when it's really not because you're tired of answering that question?"

"Fine as in I'm getting another one of those damned headaches and I am tired of answering that question," he said without opening his eyes.

"I'm sorry, this is—"

"Not your fault." He looked at her then, though Laurel could see even the muted lamp light in the living room was painful for him. "I've been having these off and on for the last year. The doctors call them trauma induced migraines or something like that. Another thing they can't fix." Slowly, he got to his feet, offering her a hand up. Not letting go of her hand, he brushed his fingertips over her cheek. "Are you okay?"

"I'm fine."

"*Fine* as in okay, or you're saying *fine* when it's really not because you're tired of answering that question?" he quoted back to her.

"*Fine* as in I'll be okay. It's you I'm worried about. Should you be driving alone?"

"It won't be the first time," he said lightly.

Though she couldn't stop worrying, she didn't want to annoy him by making any more of a fuss. Instead, she walked him to the door, waited as he shouldered into his jacket and wished she could do something to help.

"I'll give you a call later. We can talk about Tommy," he said, with a shadow of his usual teasing smile. He bent and kissed her cheek. "Or something."

"Be careful," Laurel murmured as she watched him go, the cool night air unable to penetrate the warmth he left behind.

Chapter Eight

The following Saturday afternoon, Joseph Charez led Cort and Laurel into his living room. Sounds of boys' laughter and the clatter of dishes and silverware echoed from the kitchen. The house smelled of macaroni and cheese and freshly baked peanut-butter cookies.

Joseph had welcomed Cort as a friend and immediately put Laurel at ease. He smiled often, listened well and she guessed there weren't too many kids, or adults for that matter, who didn't respond to his warm, sympathetic manner. It made Laurel even happier that Cort had been able to arrange for Tommy to come here.

"Tommy's just finishing lunch with his new pal, David," Joseph said, leading them into a room that looked well used. A half-finished puzzle decorated the coffee table, the couch pillows were in disarray and Joseph bent and picked up a boy's dirt-stained running shoe wedged between the couch and a side table. He held up the lone shoe. "You can see that Tommy's feeling at home here."

Laurel smiled, relaxing even more. Maybe the Charez home would feel comfortable enough for Tommy to stay all the way through high school. She hated the idea of him moving again and again. Still, despite Joseph's warmth, Carlos and Inez, the live-in couple who helped Joseph and David in the house, making it seem more like a family, Tommy wouldn't even consider the idea of the Charez home being any more permanent than his last foster homes. He continued to stubbornly insist he wanted to be in a *real* family with a mother and father and *real* brothers and sisters like the other kids at school had.

"How is he doing?" Cort asked, taking a seat next to Laurel on the couch.

"Better, I think," Joseph said. "David has helped. He's been here about a year. He's a little older than Tommy and is good about treating him like a younger brother."

"Does he seem happy?" Laurel wondered aloud. "I mean, he rarely smiles or plays. He's so withdrawn compared to the other kids at school. He seems to pour all of his emotions out in his writing rather than letting them show."

Cort squeezed Laurel's hand. "At least he has that outlet, thanks to you."

She smiled, a little embarrassed. "I can't take credit for that. Tommy's a born writer."

Joseph nodded. "You're right about that. He's always curled up in one corner or another, scribbling in his journal. He said you gave it to him, Laurel, and you're the only one who he'll let read it."

"He's shown me some of his entries. They all seem to come back to wanting so desperately to be adopted into what he calls a *real* family. Please don't take that to mean you haven't done everything to make him feel wanted, Joseph. Even though Tommy's only been here a short time, I know he thinks a lot of you."

"I understand. It's only natural for a boy like him to want parents and siblings and a traditional home. I wish I could find that for him. But even if I could, the legal system is so convoluted, placing a child in an adoptive family can be a frustrating and often painful process that often doesn't work out for one reason or another."

Laurel turned to Cort. "What the system needs is more good children's-advocacy lawyers."

"You're the only person I know who would say the system needs more lawyers, period." Cort shifted in his seat. "It doesn't sound to me like there's much chance of Tommy ever getting the home he wants."

"I keep my eyes open, of course," Joseph shrugged, "but, no, not really. Boys his age aren't in high demand when it comes to adoptions."

Though he seemed to be avoiding looking at her, Laurel knew Cort was listening intently. She didn't want to be pushy but she couldn't help but imagine how effective he could be in defending and assisting children in need. "Cort's thinking about going back to law school," she blurted out, hoping Joseph wouldn't make her regret it, but instead would dangle bait in front of Cort that would help sway his decision.

Cort flicked a warning glance at her. "Joseph isn't interested in my career plans."

"On the contrary, that would be marvelous, Cort. You don't have a lawyer in your family, do you? I always say every family needs a lawyer!"

A tall, elegantly dressed woman carrying a large portfolio briefcase strode into the room. "Am I missing out on a joke?" she asked. "I could use some humor today, please tell it again."

Joseph stood and walked over to kiss the young woman on her cheek. "Aria, this is Laurel Tanner, the woman who brought Tommy to us. Laurel, this is my daughter Aria. And you know Cort, of course."

"Sure," Aria said, "haven't seen you in months." The two exchanged a hug, then Aria turned to shake Laurel's hand. "Cort and I are old high-school buddies. I used to do his French homework for him in exchange for rides on his motorcycle. It drove Dad crazy," she said with a wink at Cort. "I've been wanting to meet you."

"You have?" Laurel couldn't help but wonder why such an impressive looking woman would be interested in her. She was already feeling intensely unsexy and plain around all of the curvaceous, dark, olive-skinned women in town. But Aria, though she had all those traits, also had a way of taking the local style, a feminine and seductive look, one step further. She translated it all into what Laurel would have called sultry, understated elegance.

"Oh, absolutely," Aria was saying, her tone gracious.

"That's nice...but why?"

"Because I hear you are doing amazing things with children who need a little extra something at school. I mean, extra care, attention, tutoring."

"Giving something extra is Laurel's expertise," Cort said, smiling.

"Oh, really?" Aria's voice had a distinct teasing note.

Cort laughed. "Shame on you, Aria. You've made Laurel blush."

"I'm sorry." Aria laid a hand on Laurel's arm. "Cort's just too easy a target. I can't help giving him trouble." She turned to Cort. "That is your middle name, isn't it?"

"Not anymore."

Though only a slight hint of bitterness tainted his tone, Laurel knew Aria's comment had unwittingly hit a nerve.

"Oh, I'm sorry, Cort. You know how terrible I am about taking a joke to far. How are you doing?"

"Better. A lot better, thanks. And, no offense taken, by the way." He leaned a little forward. "Besides, you know I'll get even with you."

"So what are you up to these days?"

Laurel tensed. She knew how he hated that question, but it seemed Cort and Aria had known each other a long time and that if anyone could get away with asking it, it was this woman.

"Trying to pull things back together, figure out where I'm

going." Glancing to Laurel he added, "I'm thinking about going back to law school. Laurel's decided I need to specialize in children's advocacy."

Laurel could hardly believe her ears and Aria smiled warmly at her. "She's a smart woman. It would suit you perfectly, you know."

Cort raised a brow. "That so?"

"Of course. When you were a detective, you were always getting the bad guys. If you became an attorney for children's rights you could get the bad guys who hurt them."

Joseph put an arm around his daughter. "Aria's on a crusade to staff her new children's ranch."

"I was beginning to get the impression there was a hidden motive here."

"What ranch is this?" Laurel asked.

"For a long time I've been hoping to build a place for children with special needs," Aria explained. "We don't have anything like it in town."

"My daughter grew up with a houseful of foster children, you see, and a lot of the kids my wife and I fostered had special needs. It was difficult at best trying to find resources to help them. So ever since she finished her degree in architecture, Aria's had a dream of opening a ranch for children who need a little extra attention."

"That's a wonderful idea," Laurel said, her respect for Aria deepening. Not only was she a classy dresser, she was a successful professional woman with a big heart. "Are you building it here on your property?"

"Oh, no, we still call this place a ranch but Dad had to sell off a lot of land years ago when I was still a girl." She glanced at Cort, her eyes teasing. "Competition's pretty tough around here thanks to the Garretts."

"Sorry about that. Jed and Rafe are tough businessmen."

"We got a good price for the land," Joseph said, "enough to allow the wife and I to concentrate on the kids we took in."

Aria nodded. "And then after Mom passed on and I got so

busy with school, we even sold the horses," she said, kicking off her high heels. "It'd be nice to have the land we sold back now, but we needed the money more at the time and we'll find another location for our ranch. We're closer to town than I'd like to be, anyhow."

Laurel understood her meaning at once. "You want the kids to feel like they're sort of on vacation, right?"

Aria brightened. "Exactly."

"Can you move ahead without the land?" Cort asked.

"Not really. We're still mostly at the dreaming stage right now. But we are gathering a core group of people interested in making it happen. Speaking of which, Laurel, you're a teacher, and a darned good one, too, from what Alex Trejos is saying. We could use someone like you."

"Aria, don't scare the poor girl away," Joseph reprimanded. "She's barely been in town long enough to settle in much less to join in your cause." He shook his head. "I apologize for my daughter's overzealousness."

Ignoring her father, Aria turned to Cort. "We could also use a good children's lawyer."

Laurel, Aria and Joseph all looked at Cort.

"Is it getting warm in here or is it just me?" Everyone laughed a little and he added, "Like I said, I'm thinking seriously about it. I'll let you know when I make up my mind, I promise. But for now we'd better take Tommy out for that ice cream we promised him before I run out of time. I have to go take some measurements for my grandparents at the new restaurant they're opening in town. I told them I'd help them get the thing up and running."

That was news to Laurel. He hadn't mentioned anything about getting involved in the restaurant business since their visit to his grandparents last weekend.

"Really? That's exciting," Aria said. "It's always been well worth the drive to Taos or Albuquerque for the Morentes' famous steak diablo and flan, but how great will it be to drive around the corner instead?"

Laurel could read Cort's mind, knew *exciting* was hardly the word for it and the only reason he'd agreed to help was because he felt he owed his grandparents. But she said nothing. She hardly wanted to open that can of worms right then.

"Thanks. I hope it all works out," was all Cort revealed.

Joseph motioned with a wide smile. "How can it fail?"

Cort was sorry they didn't have more time to spend with Tommy, but he'd made an appointment with the tile man to look at replacing some damaged spots on the floor of the building his grandparents were renovating for the new restaurant site. The replacement tiles had to be ordered from Mexico, so time was of the essence to get them to Luna Hermosa in time for opening night.

"Let's plan to take a horseback ride soon, would you like that?" he asked Tommy as they pulled into the drive at the Charez ranch.

Tommy eyed him warily. "I only know how to ride my bike."

"We can teach you to ride a horse," Laurel assured him, as she climbed out of the Jeep and pulled the seat forward for Tommy to get out. "You'll catch on in no time."

"Yeah, maybe," Tommy said, avoiding her eyes.

Cort came around to the other side of the jeep to walk Tommy back to the house. "Horses can look pretty big if you're not used them, but I think you'd enjoy it once you get used to them. A horse can be a great friend, you know?"

He shrugged. "I got friends. I don't have a mom and a dad."

Cort and Laurel exchanged glances over the boy's head. Cort struggled for something to say and saw the lost look in Laurel's eyes mirrored his own. His first instinct was to tell the boy parents weren't necessarily all they were cracked up to be. He wouldn't wish Jed Garrett on anyone. And although his mother, in her own way, had loved him and Sawyer, she'd never been the warm and nurturing type.

"People who care for you can be as good as real parents,

sometimes better." Cort appealed to Laurel for help. He was drowning here.

"Cort's right," she said. "Mr. Charez, Aria and the people who help them care very much for you. I think you know that by now."

Cort opened the gate to the small front patio and let Tommy walk in ahead of them. "They're okay. Mr. Charez is kinda like a grandpa and I like David. Aria is nice but she's not around much 'cause she's always working." Finally the boy looked up at Cort, then Laurel. "But they're not like having *real* parents."

With that he rushed inside the house, slamming the door behind himself and leaving Cort and Laurel staring awkwardly after him.

Cort blew out a frustrated breath. "I was hoping this would make things better for him. But I'm starting to think this wasn't such a good idea."

"It was." Laurel put her hand on his arm, drawing his eyes to hers. "It's just neither of us can give him what he really wants."

"I wish I could. No kid should have to grow up the way he has."

"Maybe that's another good reason why you should give the idea of law school some serious consideration."

"Persistent, aren't you?" he said, grinning at her embarrassed flush.

"I just think you'd be a lot better at that than you would working in a restaurant."

She was probably right, but Cort had promised his grandparents he'd give the manager's job a try for a couple of months, until they could find a permanent replacement. He didn't particularly want the job, but it was something new and didn't involve sitting behind a desk all day, and he could repay the obligation he felt to his grandparents at the same time.

"Speaking of the restaurant, it's getting late," he said, avoiding answering her unspoken question. "Do you mind joining me there for an hour or so? I'm not sure I have time to drive you home before the tile guy comes. And at this point, I can't afford to miss him. Besides, I do make a mean margarita."

Laurel accepted the change of topic without comment. "Sure, no problem. I'd like to see it."

"Well, to me, it doesn't look like much yet, but the grandparents seem to think it has potential. I'm just not sure if I know how to help it get there."

Laurel climbed into the Jeep beside him. "That's what tile guys are for."

"And electricians, and decorators and plumbers and roofers and carpenters—and I have to stop thinking about it or my head's going to start pounding again."

Laurel reached over to lightly massage the side of his face. "Don't get stressed about it. It'll all come together."

Cort leaned his head back against the seat, already feeling the tension ebb at her gentle touch. "That feels way too good. Maybe we should skip the restaurant and go back to your place so you can finish this massage."

"No can do," she answered softly. "Apparently, you've got a restaurant to tend to."

"Okay, so after I tend to the restaurant, maybe you can tend to me?"

Laurel stopped her massage and pushed him playfully on the shoulder. "One thing at a time."

"Fine. Then the one thing I want to do right now is this."

Before she could tell him no, Cort leaned over and pulled her to him, his fingers seeking the petal soft skin beneath the silk of her hair covering her nape. Gently entwining his fingers there, he bent and brushed her mouth with his.

Laurel let out a little sigh and the longing in it sparked a flame in him and he deepened the kiss. She yielded to his touch, melting against him, encouraging his exploration. He continued to savor her sweet taste and fresh windswept scent, allowing his fingers to return the favor of a massage to her shoulders and back as he shifted to bring her even closer.

He couldn't remember the moment when massage became caress and slow and easy became a shade hungrier, more urgent, only that his body decided to take charge and his body wanted more from her than this teasing promise of passion.

But it was probably the same moment Laurel eased away from him. She didn't completely break contact, but her palms flat against his chest between them sent the clear message she didn't want this to go any further than it already had.

Avoiding looking at him, she said, "That was nice."

"*Nice?*" Cort didn't know whether to laugh or seriously wonder if he'd lost his touch. "If that's the best you can say, I need some work on my technique."

"Um, no, I don't think so." She blushed. "I mean—"

"It's okay." He brushed a light touch of his lips to her temples then down one cheek to settle in a supple spot behind her ear. "We could still skip the restaurant," he murmured against her skin. "You could help me practice."

"You said you have to meet the tile guy and you were already running late," she reminded him softly.

Reality, slithering through the haze of desire, had him pulling back. "Oh, hell. I hate this job already."

Laurel straightened, vainly attempted to smooth her mussed hair and checked her face in his visor mirror. She laughed a little. "I can't remember when I actually made out in a car last. Probably in high school."

Cort tried to remember when he'd done the same. He started the engine, thinking. Then he'd remembered too well. That was the night Nova had showed him her tattoo. *Best to keep that to myself,* he thought, saying only, "Yeah, me, too."

"With whom?"

Damn, leave it to a woman not to let it go. But if he lied to her, she might sense it and even though it didn't mean anything to him, the way she was about trust it could be enough to destroy what little he'd built up in her. "You first," he said, stalling.

"Scott, of course. Who else? My lack of dating experience is pathetic."

Cort messed with the radio, the windshield wipers, anything to distract her.

"It's not raining."

"Better to be prepared in case it does."

"It was Nova, wasn't it? The last woman you made out with in high school."

"I'm damned if I do and I'm damned if I don't admit it, so, yes, it was Nova. But it didn't mean anything. We were just kids. It was just a way to kill a boring evening in a small town."

"That's all sex meant to you?"

"We didn't have sex. We just made out."

"Why did you stop?"

He stopped at a light then turned onto the road that was the fastest route to get to the other side of town where the new restaurant was located. "I don't remember." That was the truth at least. "Probably because we were both sixteen and afraid of getting caught or into something we weren't ready for. Making out is a lot different than having sex."

"Not where I grew up."

"And I thought Luna Hermosa was small." As soon as he'd said it, he regretted it. His sarcasm came across way too loud and clear.

"Excuse me?" Laurel said, crossing her arms and facing him directly. "What exactly is that supposed to mean?"

He didn't like the turn of this conversation one bit but he was already in so deep it would take a miracle to get out unscathed. "Only that I know you must have been sheltered, growing up. And, you've already made it clear your ex-husband was your only boyfriend. Which I respect, don't get me wrong."

"But?"

Cort felt the heat of Laurel's rising temper. "But, you can't expect me to have the same background. First, I'm a guy. Second, I've traveled a lot. Third, it's just more typical to have had some experience by the time you're done with college and have been around." He knew she didn't relate and that was kind of sweet to him, but he wasn't exactly getting that message across too well.

"Well, apparently, from what I hear, you've been around with Nova quite a bit."

"And? I never tried to hide we were lovers. When I moved back after Sandia died, Nova and I were together for a while, but it was never serious, on either side."

"Just a way to kill a few boring evenings?" she flung back at him.

"Why can't you get past this? It was long before you. It has nothing to do with us now." He took a breath, fighting his growing irritation. "Look, it's good that you haven't been around. I like that about you, your innocence."

"Innocence! I've been married. I'm not innocent. Maybe I'm innocent compared to Nova Vargas and women like her, but I don't want to have had *her* experiences." In what seemed to be a sudden surge of nervous self-consciousness about her appearance, she pulled her simple jacket tight around herself and crossed her cargo pant clad legs. "And that goes for her experience with you, too!" she finished with a snap and then turned abruptly away from him to stare out the window toward the setting sun.

"Is that right?" Now his temper was beginning to flare. Unknowingly, he stepped harder on the gas. Glancing over at her, he struggled to keep his tone even. "Correct me if I'm wrong, but didn't you say that part of the reason you left your small town in Montana was to challenge yourself, to prove you could take a chance? I interpreted that to mean you wanted to have new experiences."

"I wanted—no, needed—a new life."

"I know that feeling. But you said you came here to run away from the pain. As it turns out, you didn't come here to expand your horizons and *grow*—as women are always so fond of saying."

"If by that you mean, did I come here so that someone like

you, someone apparently so worldly and experienced, could seduce a poor sheltered girl from Montana, then you're absolutely right."

Cort's head was beginning to pulse with pain, this time brought on by frustration and mounting anger. "That was uncalled for and you know it. If all I'd wanted to do was seduce you, I'd have done it by now."

Laurel glared at him. "You're so arrogant, you know that? How dare you treat me like a dumb schoolgirl? If *I'd* have wanted to seduce *you,* I'd have done it by now. "

Cort heard her falter a little. She was out of her league here, and they both knew it. But she wasn't finished yet. He didn't say anything, wondering where she was heading. In the next moment, though, he wished he'd stopped her.

"Why would I want to bother getting any more involved with you when you don't even know what you want to do with yourself?" she threw at him. "You're like a Ping-Pong ball bouncing out of control from sitting around sulking and feeling sorry for yourself for a bad twist of fate, to trying your hand coaching children, to running a restaurant to making noises about going back to law school. Apparently you were so used to being in constant motion when you were a detective, now you're worse than some of my kids. You couldn't sit still through classes and endless hours of studying. If I ever decided to get involved with anyone, I'd want a man with stability, someone I can rely on. I don't need a man who acts like a child. I teach them all day."

That one knocked the wind out of him and even though he was on a main street, he unconsciously slowed down. Her words cut deeply enough to draw emotional blood because she was partly right. He had been lost, bouncing around out of control. He still was. They were on their way to see a restaurant he was supposed to be managing, but he had no idea how to do that or why the hell he'd let himself get into a position of having to do it. And he had wasted too much time ruminating over the incident that had cost him his career.

He knew he'd never be any more satisfied coaching children full-time than he would be running the restaurant. But law school, though it was starting to make more sense, felt uncomfortable. Like Sawyer, he'd gotten hooked on challenging, active work; and in his case, to flirting with danger and the excitement of the chase. Unlike his brother, though, he didn't have an arm and shoulder that could take the stress of a physically demanding job. And despite what he kept telling everyone, he hadn't quite settled with that yet.

Preoccupied with his solo conversation, he drove for several minutes before he realized he'd missed the turn to the restaurant.

"Can you just take me home please?" Laurel asked quietly. "I think it's a bad idea for me to go to the restaurant with you now and we're only a couple of minutes from my place."

"Yeah, sure. I missed the turn anyhow."

"What about the tile guy?"

"Guess I'll have to find another one."

They rode on in silence, Laurel staring out her window, Cort staring straight ahead. Not liking the tension hanging between them, he was momentarily tempted to try to mend fences before dropping her off and make a joke about not getting that massage tonight.

Glancing at her set expression, he thought better of it and instead said, "I am trying, you know, to get that Ping-Pong ball back on the table."

She looked back over at him, her blue eyes sad, her tone still defensive. "And I'm trying to get over what I've lost, too. Maybe it's nothing to you because you've lived other places and seen the world, but coming here was a challenge to me. Maybe I did come from a sheltered life in a small town, but this was a big move for me. New Mexico is a long, long way from home in more ways than I can explain to you." She grabbed her purse and zipped her coat. "In fact, I've been seriously missing my family, especially since I couldn't spend Thanksgiving with them. Maybe it's time I think about going back where I belong."

Cort pulled the Jeep to a stop in front of her *casita* and started to step out to go around and get her door but she laid a hand on his arm, stopping him.

"Laurel—"

"Don't. I'll let myself in," she said. And then she was gone.

Chapter Nine

"Mrs. Tanner, is this how you spell *strength?*" Tommy looked up from his writing journal. "Mrs. Tanner?"

"Mmm? Oh, sorry, yes, that's right." Laurel realized she'd been sitting for the last few minutes with her chin propped on her hand, staring into space, instead of focusing on the four students she was supposed to be helping with their reading comprehension. Luckily, the five of them, Tommy included, were absorbed in answering questions about the book they'd been reading together. Unfortunately, that gave Laurel time to think.

She'd been thinking about Cort. Actually, if she were honest with herself, he was all she'd been thinking about for the past week. Their argument bothered her more than she liked to admit. They'd both said hurtful things and she hated that they'd left it unresolved. Several times she'd considered calling him and trying to set things right. But she'd stopped herself, trying to convince herself it was for the best.

Except she couldn't believe it and she couldn't keep him out of her thoughts, waking or dreaming.

Glancing at the clock, she realized she'd nearly kept her kids too long. "That's all for today. You guys did a great job. Finish your journal work this afternoon and we'll talk more about it tomorrow."

The rest of the students grabbed up their things and hurried out but Tommy lingered, taking more time than needed to stuff his notebook in his backpack.

"How are things going with Mr. Charez?" Laurel asked.

"Okay, I guess." He fingered the edge of his book a moment before shoving it in the backpack and slinging the pack over his shoulder, heading for the door. Laurel thought he was going to leave without telling her anything else but at the last minute, he turned around. "I'm coming to basketball practice today."

"Really?" She tried to hide her surprise but not her pleasure. "That's great."

Tommy shrugged. "Cort kept bugging me about it so I told him I would try it."

"I didn't know he'd been to see you."

"He's there a lot. He's been showin' me some stuff. I gotta go," he said when the first buzzer signaling the end of the period sounded.

"I'll see you this afternoon," Laurel called as he darted out the door.

She sat back in her chair, trying to decide whether to be pleased that Cort was being true to his word and taking time to develop a relationship with Tommy or pleased but a little hurt he didn't seem to have the same interest in pursuing their relationship any further.

Though if he didn't, she could hardly blame him after the accusations she'd hurled at him about not being able to move forward. Remembering the things she'd said about him and Nova made her cringe. She couldn't have sounded more naive and unworldly if she'd tried.

The worst of it was, she suspected her motivations were less about not trusting him and more because she was jealous of Nova. Not so much that Nova had been Cort's lover, although she didn't like to think about that, but because Nova reminded her of everything she wasn't. Whenever Nova was around she could hear Scott's voice in her head, loud and clear. *You're not very good at being a woman.* She wondered what ever possessed her to think she could compete on the same playing field with someone like Nova Vargas. And why she even wanted to play the game to begin with.

"You're not eating alone again, are you?" Laurel looked up, startled out of her thoughts, to see Alex standing in the doorway, smiling. He tapped his watch. "Lunchtime. Want to grab a sandwich with me? I was on my way to the faculty room."

Laurel hesitated, not wanting to encourage his interest in her, then decided she could use the distraction. "Okay, thanks, company would be nice."

"You know, you're starting to remind me of Cort these days," Alex said as they walked up the hall to the faculty room and he opened the door for her, "sitting around brooding about things. Is everything okay?"

So much for a distraction. "Everything's fine." She wasn't about to tell him about her and Cort's fight.

"Doesn't look that way to me," Alex commented. They both retrieved their lunches from the refrigerator and sat down at one of the tables. "Is something wrong with you and Cort?"

"Not really," Laurel hedged. Inwardly she winced, not at the small mistruth, but because she was more or less confirming Cort's fiction that they were a couple. She added, settling for a version of the truth, "Cort just seems a little short tempered these days."

She expected Alex to agree and use her admission as leverage to gain some points with her. Instead, he frowned a little. "I know. I'm worried about him." He smiled at the lift of her eyebrow she couldn't stop. "It might not seem like it sometimes, but Cort's one of my best friends and I really am worried about him. Cort's the most easygoing guy I know, or at least he used to be, when he wasn't on the job. But he's been through a lot in the last year. I guess you can't come that close to dying and not have it change you."

Dying? The word slapped her. "I didn't know. I didn't realize it had been that bad."

"We weren't sure for a while if he was going to make it. Then it took three surgeries to put his shoulder and arm back together and all those months of therapy. But the worst of it was him losing his job. He says otherwise but I don't think he's gotten over being angry about it. He spent so many years living on the edge with all the undercover work he did and he was good at it. Maybe too good. It's got to be hell trying to find something to replace it."

Hell, indeed, Laurel thought as they finished up lunch and she got ready to return to her classroom. Considering everything he'd gone through, it was surprising he wasn't more bitter and angry, that he was at least trying to move forward instead of focusing on what he'd lost. Remembering the times he'd comforted and supported her, Laurel regretted even more the accusations she'd flung at him.

Maybe they'd both been wrong but knowing what she did now, she had to try once more to make things right.

"Great shot, Tommy. That's three in a row." Cort's praise earned him a flicker of a smile from the boy and it felt like he'd won the grand prize. Making a one-handed grab at the basketball, he flipped it back to one of the other kids. "Let's get in a little more work on those free shots and then we'll call it a day."

He didn't get as much grumbling as he'd had at the beginning when he insisted on the practice drills, and as the boys trotted off toward the free-throw line, Cort noticed one or two make a comment to Tommy about his shooting. Tommy's first practice was going even better than he'd hoped. He hadn't been too confident the boy would even show up today and even less sure Tommy would join the other kids if he did.

That something he'd said managed to convince the kid to do both was more satisfying than he'd expected.

A lot more satisfying than being in the same gym with Laurel and not knowing what to say to her, even if he'd had the opportunity. From the way she kept glancing over at him during her practice, he got the idea she felt the same way.

At the end of the hour, when the rest of the team had left, Tommy lingered behind, waiting for his ride, and Cort played some one-on-one with him for a few minutes while Laurel finished up with her girls. She came over to watch once she was done, clapping as Tommy ducked behind Cort to make a quick basket. "Great shot," she called.

"Lucky shot," Cort pretended to grumble, then grinned and cuffed Tommy on the shoulder. "You're a lot faster than me."

"Yeah, well," Tommy said, returning Cort's grin, "you're a lot taller than me. So it's fair." The smile transformed the boy's face and for a few moments, he was a typical eleven-year-old kid, enjoying being able to best an adult.

"Looks like you two have been practicing," Laurel said, coming up to them.

Tommy glanced at Cort. "Some."

"Keeps us out of trouble," Cort said, and started to suggest Laurel join them next time when a loud, "Hey, Tommy!" interrupted him.

David hung in the doorway, gesturing to Tommy. "Time to go. We're gonna be late for dinner."

"I'll see you Saturday, okay?" Cort told Tommy, who nodded, and with a hurried, "see you," ran after David, leaving Cort alone with Laurel.

An awkward silence filled the space where Tommy had been. Cort wasn't sure what to do about it. Since their argument, he'd been questioning whether it was worth his time and effort to pursue things with her any further than he already had. He didn't need the additional frustration and she seemed to be going out of her way to make it as difficult as possible.

Seeing her again changed his mind.

"About the other day, I'm sorry," he heard himself saying before his brain had time to protest. "I shouldn't have."

"No, I shouldn't have. I'm sorry, too. I said awful things."

"A lot of them were things I needed to hear."

They looked at each other. Voicing it made things better, but it didn't make them easier. He still felt like he was walking in a minefield, afraid his next move would detonate another bomb that would blow their tentative beginnings all to hell again.

"I think I understand now why you're reluctant to go back to school," she finally offered.

"Is that because you've decided I'd make a lousy student?" He smiled to make it into a joke.

"No, but I wanted you to know, that if you do decide to go back, I'd be happy to help you get your bearings again. I mean, that is my job."

"Helping me? Or taking on other people's problems in general?" he asked, a little amused she'd seemed to be adding him to her list of caretaker projects that included Tommy and Aria's ranch idea.

She blushed but didn't look away. "Teaching."

"I knew that. But thanks. It's nice to know I've got a tutor if I do decide to give the student life a shot again." He thought for a moment, wondering if he should act on impulse or leave now before he got himself into trouble. *The worst she can do is tell me to get lost. And I've done a pretty good job of that all on my own.* "Look, I've got a few things to check on at the restaurant. I'd still like for you to see it. You want to come back with me and have a drink? I wasn't kidding about being able to make a wicked margarita."

She hesitated to the point where Cort was sure she was going for get lost. Then she nodded. "This is your last chance though," she said lightly. "You promised me one last time and never delivered."

"Then it's a good thing you're letting me redeem myself." He took a few minutes to change back into his jeans and sweater. "You're welcome to ride with me," he offered with a sly grin as he pulled on his gloves and helmet and started for his bike. "There's room for two."

"Give it up. You're not getting me on that thing, ever."

"That sounds like a dare to me."

"It's a promise," Laurel said firmly, though he could hear the laughter in her voice.

"Two weeks?" Laurel glanced around at the mess of plastic sheeting, sawdust and tables, chairs and equipment waiting to be installed stacked in various piles, and turned a doubtful glance on Cort.

"Yeah, I know. But the grandparents are determined to be open by the first of the month so we can benefit from holiday traffic." He'd cleared her a seat at the bar and, unable to find a blender to make the planned margarita, had substituted a glass of white wine. He leaned backward against the bar beside her, nursing a beer and trying to sound confident that he'd be able to pull everything together before opening day. "I'm sure it'll all come together sooner or later. Probably later," he added as she took a sip of wine to hide the twitch of a smile.

"Later as in a few extra weeks?"

Cort pretended to think it over. "I'm thinking July sounds pretty good."

Laurel laughed. "It can't be that bad."

"Other than I have no idea what I'm doing and everyone knows it, it's great," he said, and gestured with his bottle and grinned. "I figure if I stay away from the kitchen, I can at least avoid burning the place down or poisoning anyone. After that, what's the worst that could happen?"

"Do you want me to answer that?"

"No, I'd rather live in blissful ignorance for a while longer. Besides, I have a backup plan. If things start going too wrong, I'll put somebody else in charge and take over bussing tables and mixing drinks. Those I can do."

"I'm sure your talents stretch a little farther than that," she said, smiling at him.

"Think so?" He set his own drink down and shifted to face her. She dropped her eyes, running a fingertip around the rim of her glass. Cort watched her and the slow motion of her hand. A thick lock of hair had slid out of her ponytail and lay against her cheek, pale gold against ivory. Knowing he was pushing his luck, but unable to resist, he reached out and brushed it back, just grazing her skin. His touch drew her eyes to his.

"Are we okay?" he asked softly.

"Better, I think."

"You think?" He took a step closer to her. "Is there anything I could do to make you sure?"

"Maybe, I mean, I don't know—" She broke off, blushing.

"I do." Leaning in, he slid his fingers into the hair at her nape and decided to go for broke.

"Cort, I need to ask you about—oops, sorry. I didn't know you had company." The moment broke instead. Nova stood there, a knowing little smile causing Laurel's blush to deepen and Cort to groan inwardly in frustration. "I didn't expect to see you here, Laurel."

"The feeling's mutual," Laurel said with a smile of her own, except hers looked like she'd pulled it out of a box and pasted it on.

The awful fight they'd had the other day and Nova's silent part in it grated on his mind. She glanced at Cort then at Nova, in her figure-hugging denim skirt and long-sleeved black T-shirt, and Cort knew he was in trouble. Why couldn't Nova have worn something that didn't scream seduction just this once? Laurel was undoubtedly thinking about his past with Nova, doubting him all over again. "I didn't know you were working here," she said coolly.

"I haven't had the chance to tell you," Cort said quickly. "I talked Nova into leaving the diner and giving me a hand here. She knows more about this business than I ever will."

"He's working me harder than I ever did waiting tables," Nova said, coming to stand by Cort. She put an idle hand on his forearm. "But the benefits are much better," she added with a wink in Laurel's direction.

Cort threw a scowl at Nova. He doubted Nova was going out

of her way to mess with Laurel. Nova flirted as easily as she breathed. But she wasn't making his life any easier right now.

"I hate to interrupt," Nova said, "but I need to run this by you. I promise, in a few minutes, he's all yours," she told Laurel.

As he listened to Nova, only half processing what she said, Cort was very aware Laurel watched them and did his best to make it clear, whatever was between Nova and him now was strictly business.

"Get him to make you a margarita next time," Nova said, as she made to return to the back-room office. "He's pretty good at it, when he can find the blender."

"I should go, too," Laurel said, standing up. "I have a test to write up."

She tried, failing miserably, to sound cool and uncaring, unaffected by it all. The facade didn't fool Cort for a moment.

"Laurel, look, about Nova—"

"You don't owe me an explanation," she said stiffly. "In fact, I'd rather not hear any more details than you gave me the other night."

"That's good, because the only details I've got are about hiring waitresses and keeping the chef happy and something about a stove that doesn't get hot enough. And maybe I don't owe you an explanation but I don't want you thinking what you're obviously thinking. I'm not your ex. I'm not going to lie to you."

She wouldn't look at him. "It doesn't matter."

"It matters." Very gently, he slid his fingers under her chin and lifted her face to his. "I know you think this is the wrong way for me to go and maybe it is. But I'm trying to pull things together because of you. You threatened to go back home when we were fighting. I plan on helping you forget that threat."

"No, you can't," she said.

"Yes, I can. What I can't do is pretend anymore that this is about being friends." He reached over and slid the confining band from her hair, letting the heavy mass slip over his fingers in a sensual caress. "I don't think you can, either."

Panic flashed in her eyes and Cort cut off the denial he saw coming by pulling her into his arms and kissing her.

At first—her palms pressed flat against his chest—she didn't respond. Cursing himself for pushing her too far, too fast, Cort started to pull back. At the same moment Laurel yielded, leaning into him and kissing him back.

And then he stopped thinking.

She was still unsure of him, unsure of herself, but Laurel wanted this, wanted Cort, like a craving she couldn't satisfy, and she wrapped her arms around his neck, drawing him closer. Cort took full advantage of her response, pulling her closer still, parting her lips under his, the intimate caress heating her blood, heightening her senses and crumbling to dust any rational thoughts.

He wanted this, too, she knew from his low needy groan that found its echo in her, the hot urgency of his mouth on hers. Some tiny part of her brain protested her surrender when only moments before she'd been ready to walk away from him. But it didn't stand a chance against the sinful dark pleasure that Cort created with his hands and mouth. She'd never been daring when it came to lovemaking but being with him emboldened her, pushed her to forget all the reasons why she shouldn't be doing this.

At the same time, she didn't know how to deal with it. All her experience had been with Scott and his lovemaking had been unimaginative and undemanding, never overwhelming. Nothing had prepared her for Cort.

Despite all her doubts about him, against his sensual attraction, she was weak. He made her feel like a woman she didn't recognize, needy and demanding, her senses sharpened, her skin sensitized so that every touch made sparks.

His hand tangled in her hair, tipping her head back as he dragged his mouth from hers to kiss and taste her throat. "This is what I want back," he murmured hotly against her skin. "I want to go forward and not look back."

A touch of ice cut into the fire he'd started. "Some things you can't have back." She pressed her hand to his shoulder, as if she could feel the scars there, a reminder that the future for both of them would always be tainted by the past. "Isn't that why you're still angry about what happened?"

"Isn't that why you won't trust me?" His hold on her loosened and he moved back enough to look her in the eyes. "You're right, I was angry. Part of me still is. But it's not going to change anything. Any more than you can change what your ex did."

It was so much more than Scott and Laurel almost told him, wanted to tell him, to tell someone, so the burden of knowing wouldn't be hers alone any longer. Except she couldn't make herself say the words. Tears burned her eyes and she pulled out of his arms. "You're right, I can't change what happened. I'll never get my baby back."

Cort gently brushed away the tears on her face. "No, you won't, but that doesn't mean you have to push everyone out of your life. I can't make every bad thing that ever happened to you in the past go away. But if you give me a chance, maybe we can start something new."

The tears threatened to choke her now. "Cort, I want to." He didn't know how much she wanted to forget, forgive, believe, refind her faith in the future. "I don't know if I can."

A loud thud from the vicinity of the kitchen followed by an agitated scrabbling sound and a string of cursing interrupted whatever reply Cort might have made. Without even a flicker of interest in that direction he said, "Ignore it."

"Maybe we should finish this somewhere else," Laurel said, glancing uneasily at the kitchen. She could hear several voices now chorusing in increasingly loud debate.

"Great, good. Let's get out of here." Taking her hand, he began looking around for her coat.

Laurel put a hand on his chest to stop him. "Not now. You need to take care of things here."

"You're more important." Someone in the kitchen started yelling and he blew out an irritated breath. "I'm about two seconds from using one of those fifteen dozen pans we've got in there for something besides cooking."

Despite everything, she smiled. "That doesn't sound very managerlike."

"This might come as a surprise, but I'm not very managerlike. Besides *managerlike* sounds kinda boring." He flashed a wicked grin. "And if it means giving up the bike and leather jacket, you can forget about me ever achieving that particular goal."

"I'll try not to be too disappointed."

A sudden slam of metal against metal punctuated the argument in the kitchen. Cort rolled his eyes. "This is starting to remind me of those biker bars I used to hang out in. I'd better go make sure no one's got my idea for using pans." He hesitated. "Laurel…"

"Go on," she said quietly. "We can talk later."

"Yeah, I guess we could do that, too." Snagging her coat from the chair where he'd draped it, he kissed her quickly as he put it into her hands. "How about I stop by your place when I'm done here? It shouldn't be too late."

She nodded and he kissed her again, drawing out the sensual caress until the noise from the kitchen became too much to ignore. "I'd better go."

He let her leave this time, wondering when what she wanted and what she needed had suddenly become the same thing.

Chapter Ten

Cort shoved a stack of papers into the restaurant safe, twisted the handle and started to stand.

"Damn!" he cursed into silence, grabbing his right shoulder with the opposite hand as a twinge of pain shot down his arm. He glanced at his watch and saw it was going on 1:00 a.m. He'd been working nonstop undertaking every task from pounding nails into cabinets to hanging draperies to sweeping up sawdust for hours. And his body, particularly his shoulder and head, were suffering the effects of what felt like one endless day and night.

He flipped the light switch in the office and headed outside telling himself that a desk job was looking better and better. In spite of his exhaustion and the hour, as he tugged his helmet gingerly over his aching head, he realized the ache to see Laurel was stronger. She'd be getting up for school shortly, but he couldn't help himself from turning his bike toward her place.

What would she look like when she was sleeping, he wondered, suspecting she'd appear nothing short of angelic. He spent his short ride letting his tired mind drift to images of her in bed…what would she wear, anything or nothing? Flannel pajamas, probably, he thought, laughing to himself. But underneath those, oh, yeah, her soft ivory skin, warm from the sheets and blanket, her hair loose and wild like a halo around her face, he couldn't wait to see her, even if it meant suffering her complaints for disturbing her at this hour.

Trying to avoid waking the neighbors along with her, as he entered her driveway, he killed the engine of his bike and coasted to a stop. A single light shone in her front window, giving him hope she'd waited up for him despite the hour.

He started to ring the bell when a muffled sound, halfway between a scream and a moan, followed by a *thump* froze his motion. He instinctively reached to the shoulder holster that wasn't there. *Damn.* The sound came again and he briefly considered kicking open the door. He checked the lock, astonished when he realized she'd left the door open. *Is she crazy?*

Easing it open, he took a quick look inside and immediately exchanged one concern for another.

Laurel lay on the couch, twisting in the throes of a nightmare, tangled up in a blanket, and half crying, half babbling things he couldn't make out. An overturned vase at the foot of the couch told him the source of the thump.

Dropping his helmet onto a chair, he went down on one knee beside her, gently shaking her shoulder. "Laurel, wake up. Laurel!"

She screamed, jolting upright.

Cort caught her upper arms, steadying her. "It's okay. It's me, Cort. You were having a nightmare."

"Cort?" Slowly, Laurel slumped back on the couch, trembling. In her oversized flannel shirt she looked small and fragile, in need of someone to hold her. He put his arm around her and she leaned into his side. Stroking the tangled hair back from her face, he brushed his fingers against her cheek and felt the dampness from where she'd been crying.

"Sorry," she mumbled, pulling away and sitting up a little. She shoved her hair back with an unsteady hand.

"Don't be," Cort told her. "Are you okay?"

"Yes. I'm used to waking up like this. Well, not with you sitting next to me, but like this."

"Does this happen a lot?"

She made a vague shift of her shoulders. "Off and on. I've had versions of the same nightmare since my baby died and Scott left."

Cort didn't press her for an explanation. Whatever it was had obviously upset her and he didn't want to make it any worse.

She glanced at the mantle clock that read one-thirty and her mouth twisted in a grimace. "When did you get here?"

Cort raked his fingers through his hair. "Just now. I finished the last of the cleanup and paperwork at the restaurant around half an hour ago."

"Oh, my gosh, you should have gone home. You must be completely wiped out."

"I promised you I would come by tonight." He attempted a tired smile. "It's morning, though, does it still count as a promise kept?"

Laurel lifted her hand to brush her fingers down his cheek. "It counts a lot."

"By the way, your front door was wide-open. You'd sure as hell better not be making a habit of that or I'll come over here myself every night and lock it for you."

"I left it unlocked for you. I was waiting up when I fell asleep here." She didn't quite look at him and added softly, "I was counting on you keeping that promise."

He felt a little badly for growling at her, but he held his ground. "Thanks, but next time we need a better plan so that front door of yours stays locked."

"I'm sorry for greeting you with the drama. You must have wondered what was going on in here."

"You don't even want to know what crossed my mind. But, hey, don't worry about it. I understand. I had problems with nightmares myself after Sandia died."

"You?"

"Yeah, well, it surprised me, too. There were a lot of nights I didn't sleep at all. Maybe if I'd told someone about it they wouldn't have lasted as long they did."

"Maybe," Laurel said quietly, "but I told a counselor and she said the dreams were just part of the grieving process. She said when I accepted what happened, they would go away. But it's hard."

"Accepting it completely is a tall order."

"Especially when you still feel responsible."

Cort shook his head, not sure these mutual midnight confessions were good for either of them. But he found he couldn't drop it just yet. Something was nagging at him. She'd said her nightmare was about the baby she'd lost and the husband who'd left her. Despite what the jerk had done to her, did she still love him so much he was in her dreams, he wondered, not liking the odd hurtful pang the question brought with it.

"You still dream about him, don't you?" he said.

He half expected her to react angrily, but instead she studied him thoughtfully before she said, "No, he's long gone from my dreams. How about you? Is Sandia still a part of your dreams?"

"Hardly. I don't know that she ever was in my dreams to begin with. I told myself I loved her, and maybe I did, as much as I could then." He gave a short, harsh laugh. "You said you married your best friend, I was ready to marry my best lover. Sandia never wanted more than I was ready to give and I thought at the time it was a good thing. I called it love but we were never what you would call emotionally intimate. I never shared anything with her that mattered. But if I had really loved her enough, I wouldn't have left her alone that day and she wouldn't have died."

"That's not true," Laurel said softly. "You know it isn't. Maybe she wasn't the love of your life, but you obviously cared about her enough to want to make a life together."

"Yeah, well, you've gotten a taste of how good a blueprint I had for a loving family," Cort said, rubbing his throbbing brow. "I should never have asked her to take a chance on forever with me when I knew from the start I couldn't give her everything."

"Maybe not and maybe I shouldn't have married Scott, and maybe we should never try it again. Maybe alone is better. But I'm getting tired of being alone." Her last words came out as a trembling whisper and Cort felt a shudder go through her.

"I know that feeling," he admitted softly.

"Let me try to help your headache," she said, reaching to touch his temples.

Gently, he took her hands in his, kissing the back of each. "The best thing you can do is go to bed. Come on." He got to his feet and pulled her with him, dragging the blanket behind him as she led the way to her bedroom.

When she got into the bed, he stripped off his jacket and sat down next to her, gathering her into his arms. She said nothing, leaning her head on his shoulder in silent communion. They stayed like that for several long moments when words seemed unnecessary.

Finally Cort murmured, "You need to get some sleep. Can I get you anything?"

"No, I just hate these dreams." She glanced at the beside clock. "Six o'clock is going to come pretty quickly," she said with a weak attempt at a smile.

"I don't think I've been helping here with all the confessions." He was starting to feel slightly uncomfortable with the intimacy of the situation, and not just the emotional revelations.

He'd come here with the notion of a quick assurance he hadn't forgotten his promise and maybe stealing a good-night kiss. Sitting next to her in bed, so near he could smell the wild rose scent of her, with her pressed against him and her hand still clasped warmly around his, his body started to get other ideas.

"You don't have the market on confessions tonight," Laurel said. She covered another sudden yawn with the back of her hand.

"I think it's way past your bedtime."

"I know. I just…"

"Have trouble getting back to sleep afterward?"

She nodded. "It's stupid, really. I mean, I'm not five years old."

"No, it's not." Deliberately ignoring the alarms going off in his head, Cort scuffed off his boots and then nudged her over and got into bed beside her, punching up one of her pillows to prop up against.

Laurel's breath hitched in surprise. "Cort, I don't think—"

"Me, neither. So let's just both stop thinking for a while. Between my head and my shoulder, I'm not up for much more than a couple hours' sleep." He gathered her close against his chest, tucked the blanket around her and began slowly stroking her back.

At first, she tensed, holding herself stiffly in his embrace. But gradually, the warmth and his rhythmic stroking lulled her into relaxing and after a few minutes, her eyes fluttered closed and her breathing evened and slowed.

"If I didn't know you were telling the truth about your headache, it would almost be a funny irony, wouldn't it?" she asked sleepily.

"Almost."

When she'd fallen asleep, Cort started to ease out of the bed. But Laurel made a little sound of protest and draped her arm over his chest as she snuggled closer, sighing softly.

Cort stifled a groan. This was right up there with the top stupidest ideas he'd ever had, starting with his deciding to come here at this hour in the first place. But he resigned himself to sitting here a while with her until she was sleeping deeply enough for him to extricate himself without him waking her.

He settled back against the pillow and made the mistake of closing his eyes.

Laurel lay wrapped in Cort's arms, watching her alarm clock. Five minutes before it went off, she reached over and stopped it to keep from waking him. She could hardly believe he was still here beside her, in her bed. After her awful nightmare and their disturbing moments of true confessions, she was glad he'd finally fallen into a deep sleep.

She wished she could stay in bed with him, partly to avoid the risk of waking him, mostly because it felt so good to be with him. Sometime in the night, they'd shifted positions, with her lying on her side, his arms around her and the length of his body fitted to hers. She'd awakened in the best way with her senses filled with him. She loved the feel of the even rise and fall of his breath against her neck, the scent of him on her skin and bed, his warm, solid body cradling hers.

They hadn't made love, yet she felt an intimacy with him in a way that went beyond physical. He'd touched her heart when he'd willingly opened up to her and revealed some of his vulnerabilities and regrets about his past. It had been so long since she'd let herself get this close to anyone and it surprised her how easily it had happened with Cort, seemingly from one moment to the next without her being aware of it.

Being with him had replaced the cold loneliness inside her with warmth and peace and despite their argument the other day, after he'd come to her and to her bed, the past hours had been the best she'd slept in years.

Unfortunately, a sharp ray of morning light reminded her it was a school day and it was getting late. Sunshine was already streaking between the slats of the blinds, starting to wash the room in diffused light. Laurel eased Cort's arm from around her waist and slid out of bed. Though he'd collapsed in his jeans and shirt, she pulled a light cover over him. Then she grabbed her clothes and crept out of the room.

She quickly showered and dressed and grabbed a cup of coffee. She left Cort a note with instructions on where to find bread, jam, eggs and bacon, at the same time almost wishing he'd woken with her. She hadn't told him last night, but her car battery had died and she'd been lucky to get her poor excuse for a vehicle as far as her driveway.

Reluctantly, she'd called Alex to ask for a jump. He'd hadn't been able to come by last night but promised her a ride to school this morning and then to help her start her car when they had more time after classes. "I'm glad you called me," he'd said.

She wasn't, particularly, but at the time, her options seemed limited since she hadn't been sure whether or not Cort would be able to keep his promise to stop by and she didn't want to call him at the restaurant when she knew how buried he was in work.

Before heading outside to wait for Alex, she looked in on Cort. He'd rolled over on his back, tossing the sheet aside, and was still sleeping soundly. She fought an urge to sneak back in the room and kiss him good morning, restraining herself lest she wake him—firmly quelling a traitorous thought that whispered she should do just that and enjoy the consequences. Instead, she sent him a silent kiss and quietly closed the bedroom door.

A few minutes later she heard Alex's car and she went out to meet him as he was getting out. He stopped, staring at Cort's motorcycle.

"Cort has a migrane," she said lightly as she walked over to him. "He can't drive."

Alex stepped around to open the car door for her. "So I see."

Laurel had expected an awkward situation with Alex, but she didn't feel any particular obligation to explain in detail what had happened. She climbed into his car and before he shut the door behind her said only, "Cort's under a lot of pressure with his grandparents and their expectations for the restaurant."

She could tell by the expression on Alex's face, he was itching to ask more questions and at the same time struggling to bite his tongue. Thankfully, the latter impulse won out and as they drove to school Laurel chatted about anything and everything except the fact that Cort Morente was still asleep in her bed.

Clang, clang, clang. Clang, clang, clang.
The irritating noise interrupted the dream Cort was having of Laurel in his bed and—

Clang, clang, clang.

Trying to drown out the noise, Cort buried his head under a pillow that smelled like—wild roses and Laurel? Coming to life, he tossed the pillow aside, realizing in the instant when the brain finally accepts night has turned to day, Laurel was not in his bed, he was in hers and his cell phone was about to find its way through her front window. Grabbing the cursed thing from her nightstand he flipped it open and growled, "What?"

"This a bad time?"

Cort recognized Rafe's graveled voice at once. "No, sorry. I was, um—I mean, I had a late night at the restaurant."

He could almost hear his brother smirking. "That the reason you're not answering your phone at home? You're sleeping at the restaurant?"

Cort groaned. "Not yet." Eager to change the subject he asked, "What's up? Did something happen with the old man?"

"No. He's the same. It's something else. Look, I hate to bother you, but I'm desperate."

Cort sat up and shoved a hand through his hair. "What's wrong?" he asked, suddenly worried. Rafe rarely called, and never for help.

"One of my hands quit recently and another busted himself up trying to corral a bad-tempered bull. Josh is off in Texas and I've just inherited three-dozen bison from my relatives up the mountain. It's a bad time of year, but they have to get rid of them right away. There's more snow than there's been in fifty years up the mountain this year. They'll starve if I don't move them down to the ranch. And I could use the head after losing so many last winter."

The phone went silent and Cort knew his brother was working himself up to ask for help. That was something Rafe Garrett didn't do without a fight. Rafe's stubbornness and his independent pride had always been his strength and his downfall. In fact, Cort suspected Rafe wouldn't be calling now if Jule hadn't prodded him into it.

"You want some help getting them down to the ranch?" he offered, trying to make it easier on Rafe.

"Yeah," came the short reply.

Neither Rafe nor Jule had any idea how swamped he was with the restaurant or he knew Rafe would have called Sawyer instead. After years of bitterness and resentment over circumstances their parents had created, Sawyer and Rafe had finally mended long-broken fences and were on much better terms than ever before. Of course, it had taken him nearly getting himself killed to bring his brothers to the point of reconciliation, but Cort figured at least something good had come out of the whole mess.

"No problem," he said.

"You sure?" Cort could hear the relief in Rafe's voice. "It's gonna be a few days' work."

"Hey, what are brothers for?"

Rafe laughed and Cort smiled at the sound he'd started to hear more often from his brother since Jule came back into his life. "I'm starting to figure that out."

"Give me a couple of hours to get some things squared away then I'm all yours."

"Thanks, Cort. I mean it."

"No problem. And I mean that."

The first part was about as far from reality as could be, but it was the truth because he did mean it.

A longer morning, Laurel couldn't remember. She'd yawned her way through her classes, practically nodding off during a quiet reading period. Her spirits lifted seeing Tommy, especially when he said he'd be at basketball practice today even though it wasn't Cort's day to coach, but it didn't help with the drowsiness that had her considering spending her lunch period napping in her car.

A little after eleven, when the lunch periods started, she straightened her desk a bit and found herself wondering, a little wistfully, how long Cort had slept. Had he made himself breakfast? Did he take a shower at her place? All morning questions—silly questions, she reminded herself—had been distracting her, reminding her how much she liked the idea of Cort being in her home.

But right now, she had to focus on the rest of her day and finishing out her classes and then coaching basketball. She was going to need a ride again but if she hustled this afternoon, she could avoid having to ask Alex, and could catch the school bus and ride over with the kids at least as far as the community center.

"You keep frowning like that, and I'm gonna think you aren't glad to see me."

Laurel spun around to Cort's easy smile. He leaned in her doorway, his faded jeans and leather jacket, tousled hair and the days' old beard giving him a slightly disreputable look she found irresistible.

The sight of him gave her heart a little jolt and for the first time all day she felt alive. Straightening, he sauntered over to her and surprised her by pulling her close and kissing her soundly, right there in the middle of her classroom. In plain sight, where anyone walking by and glancing inside could see them.

"Cort," she gasped after catching her breath.

He grinned and her heart flipped. "What's the matter? Ashamed to be seen with me?"

"Not hardly. It's just, here—you're going to make me the hot topic for gossip in the staff room."

"I think I did that already this morning when Alex picked you up and my bike was in your driveway."

"How did you know?"

"Your car was in the driveway and Alex seemed the most likely person you'd call for a ride. Although I'd have been happy to do the honors."

"I didn't want to wake you," she said. "You aren't getting much sleep lately."

"Ah, the caretaker thing again. Well, just to show you two

can play that game, I found your extra key hanging in the kitchen so I checked your car out. For future reference, when the battery is coated in nasty green stuff, it's time to buy a new one. It's all taken care of, except I couldn't get it here because I'm going to be tied up this afternoon."

"It's okay, I can take the bus to practice and I'll find way home from there."

"Nope, I've got that covered, at least the after part. I asked Maya if she'd pick you up after practice today on her way home from the clinic. She has to pass right by there at almost the same time you're done. Here's her cell-phone number in case anything changes," he said, fishing a slip of paper out of his jacket pocket and handing it to her.

"Wow, thanks," she said, paused, then added, "by the way, I wasn't going to ask Alex for a ride again."

He rewarded her with a smile. "He'll be disappointed, but I'm glad to hear it."

"Jealous?" she asked, only half joking.

"Every time." And he sounded serious.

To cover the fact he'd flustered her, Laurel asked, "How did you sleep? I tried not to wake you. I felt badly about my nightmare keeping you up half the night."

"Keep me up all night if it means I get to sleep with you," Cort said. The wicked glint in his eyes suggested activities other than sleeping and the room suddenly seemed warm and much smaller. "And you didn't wake me up. Rafe did. He needs some help at the ranch, that's why I can't be your chauffeur today."

"The ranch?"

"Rancho Piñtada, my father's ranch. Rafe's foreman there and he's in a bind moving some bison down the mountain. It's not far, but it's a few days' work and he's short on help."

"But you're buried in work with the restaurant, doesn't he realize that?"

"No, and I didn't tell him. You don't know Rafe. It cost him big-time to even call me and ask. We've been trying to mend fences in this family and I'm not about to refuse my brother the one and only time he's ever asked me for help."

Laurel stared at him then shook her head. "You're something else, you know that? Last night at the restaurant and with me, and all of this going on and you still managed to jump my car and arrange a ride for me. No wonder sitting behind a stack of papers sounds like a jail sentence to you."

"You're the one who said I couldn't sit still," he reminded her. "Honestly, though, some days it's looking a lot more like freedom."

"Maybe there's hope for you yet," she teased.

"Think so?" Sliding his hand over the nape of her neck, he tugged her close and kissed her, lingering, until the second lunch-period buzzer reminded them that the outside world was about to intrude and they both needed to be somewhere else.

"Yeah," he said, before he left her to pull her scrambled senses together, "I think so, too."

Chapter Eleven

Maya pulled into the community-center drive and waved Laurel over to her car. It was a hybrid, of course, Laurel thought with a smile. What else would she be driving?

"Hop in," Maya invited. "It's warm in here, but it won't be a quiet ride, I warn you."

Laurel glanced to the back where Maya's little boys sat strapped into their car seats, Joey chattering a mile a minute, his words punctuated with car and animal noises. His stuffed bison was strapped in with him and his little hands were busy zooming cars through the air. Beside him, Nico rocked back and forth singing a song that made sense only to him, his miniature hiking-boot clad feet kicking to his beat.

Laurel tried not to let her own emptiness overshadow the joy watching the boys gave her. "Thanks for picking me up," she said, climbing in beside Maya.

"I hope it wasn't too much out of your way."

"No problem, I pass right by here from the boys' day-care center and the clinic. I'm glad I could help." She glanced back over her shoulder. "Boys, you remember Mrs. Tanner. Say hello."

"Buff'lo says hi." Joey helped his stuffed friend's hoof to wave.

Nico also curled his fingers in a babyish wave at Laurel without interrupting his singing.

"You can take that as a greeting," Maya said, pulling the car around to the main street.

"They're so cute. But I'll bet you have your hands full, what with work, two kids, a big house and a husband."

Maya laughed. "That's the understatement of the century, but I enjoy all of it. There's nothing I'd give up or change, except maybe to have more time alone with Sawyer and a few more hours' sleep."

"I hear mothers say the same thing all the time. Especially single parents. I don't know how they manage."

"I don't, either. They have my absolute admiration. I mean, Sawyer is terrific, so helpful, and I have Regina part of the time, too, but even so, I'm always behind on things. Sawyer says he wants another baby or two, but I might have to learn how to clone myself first."

"If you figure it out, let me know. I'm always behind, too, and I have no excuse."

"You certainly do. Your work doesn't end when school lets out, and I understand that you also coach basketball and give extra help to kids like Tommy after school hours."

"Yes, but none of that is like being a mother." With the commotion in the backseat, Laurel hoped Maya hadn't heard the wistful note in her voice.

But Maya looked over at her, her eyes questioning. "Well, you'll have your chance to do that, too, one day, I'm sure. Then you can experience another level of exhaustion." She looked at her sons in the rearview. "And joy."

Laurel's heart twisted. She wished she could confide in Maya that she'd never know that kind of happiness. Of any woman she'd met here except Aria, perhaps, who was also very warm and open, Maya was the easiest to talk to so far. But she didn't dare tell her about her infertility because it was a certainty it would get back to Cort.

"You still there?" Maya was asking, a frown on her pretty face. "I think I lost you. Though it is hard to concentrate with the backseat ankle biters in full swing."

"Sorry, I was just thinking about something. What were you saying?"

Maya looked across at her again, this time for the length of a stoplight. "I was just asking you if you'd seen Cort lately. He was in such a rush when he called this morning I didn't want to bother him with questions."

"Yes, he came over to my place last night—well, actually, very early this morning. He'd spent almost all night at the restaurant working to get it ready for the opening."

"Poor Cort. I can't believe he let his grandparents talk him into doing that. Although knowing Cort, he felt obligated because they're family." A screech called her attention to the backseat and she glanced over her shoulder. "Nico, do not put your shoe in your mouth. It's dirty. Joey take that shoe away from your brother." Laurel reached back to help and when Joey had secured the shoe and threw it out of reach, Maya turned again to Laurel. "I'm sorry, it's impossible to have an uninterrupted conversation."

Laurel smiled. "Goes with the territory."

"You seem to understand. Do you have friends or brothers and sisters with children back home?"

"Yes. My brothers do. I used to help babysit before I moved here."

"Sounds like you'd like to have one for yourself."

Laurel's voice caught in her throat, stifling an answer.

"Laurel, are you all right? Did I say something wrong?"

"No, no, it's just…" She swallowed back the lump in her throat. "I lost a baby a few years ago. It's one of the reasons my ex-husband and I split up."

"Oh, I'm so sorry. What a klutz I am. I didn't know."

"You couldn't have. Don't worry, I'm coping with it. It just takes time."

Maya reached over and put a hand on Laurel's lap. "A long time. But someday, you'll be ready to try again, right?"

Once more words failed her and Laurel turned to stare out the window.

"Laurel, this is the second time I've seen you go pale like that. The same thing happened the night of the festival in the town square. I know this is a really personal question and I don't mean to pry, but are you worried about having another baby because you miscarried?"

Refusing to face Maya's perceptive eyes, Laurel continued to look unseeingly at the passing town. "Something like that."

Thankfully, Joey interrupted with an impatient, "Are we there yet? Buff'lo's hungry."

"Almost, sweetie. We're just going to drop Mrs. Tanner off at her house first. Her car is broken today."

Laurel turned around. "I have some cheese sticks at my house. Do you want one to take with you for the rest of the ride home?"

Joey nodded, clutching his stuffed animal a little tighter. "Buff'lo have one, too?"

"Of course, he can."

"I usually have snacks in the car, but I got such a late start this morning, I forgot to bring them. A cheese stick would be a lifesaver, thanks."

"I live on those things. Quick protein."

"Meatless, too."

They sat in silence for a few minutes, but Maya, as if she couldn't stand it any longer, turned to Laurel, caring and concern in her eyes. "I'll just say this much and then I'll quit. Promise. If you're worried about conceiving again, I'm sure you've been checked by your doctor, but there are a number of holistic and integrated medicine treatments, too, including acupuncture, believe it or not, that have helped many of our patients at the clinic with getting pregnant again after a loss like you've had."

Laurel wanted so badly to tell Maya it would take more than modern medicine, natural or otherwise, to help her get pregnant. It would take a miracle. "Thanks. I'll keep that in mind." She knew she sounded a bit off-putting but it was the best she could do. She didn't want to encourage Maya into thinking she harbored any hopes of having a family of her own. "Over there, on the left where the old hitching post is," she said, pointing out the front window. "That's my street. Just pull back behind the big house. I live in the *casita.*"

Maya pulled into Laurel's drive. "Looks like a very nice place—oh, and you have a little patio." She reached out and squeezed Laurel's hand. "Listen, you can come by the clinic anytime, please. We're very relaxed and very private there. No pressure, I promise."

"Thanks for the offer. I'll keep it in mind," Laurel repeated. "Wait here a second and I'll run in and get some snacks." When she came back out, she handed them to Maya, and then said a rushed goodbye to her and the boys.

Backing out, Maya paused and rolled down her window. "We didn't get to talk about Cort, but please tell him Sawyer and I will are available if there's anything we can do to help get this restaurant launched."

"I'll do that, thanks again." As they left, Joey's buffalo, pasted up against the car window, waved goodbye. Laurel waved back, her heart constricting so painfully it felt broken.

"I owe you several," Rafe told Cort when they'd unloaded their backpacks and saddlebags from their three-day trip to Rafe's tribe's ranch and back.

"No, you don't. I'm glad I could help." Cort followed Rafe to the barn at Rancho Piñtada. "At least the weather cooperated."

His saddle slung over his shoulder, Rafe unlocked the heavy barn door. "Yeah, it's been an interesting season. I'll need to fatten these head back up before spring."

"After all the trouble you had last year, it's good to hear you think this experiment of yours is going to pay off."

Rafe nodded. "It will. Though you'd never hear the old man admit that."

"Hardly. But your relatives seem pretty proud of you," Cort said. He'd only met Rafe's relations from his mother's side once before this trip, at Rafe and Jule's wedding, and both times they'd been warm and welcoming and supportive of Rafe. "You and Jule spend much time with them?"

"We drive up about once a month. They've been good to us. I wish I'd gotten to know them when I was a kid. But Jule and I are going to see to it we don't make the same mistake with our kids. They're going to know my tribe, the other half of who they come from."

"The better half, I'd say." Cort hung his saddle and folded the saddle blanket. He thought for a minute about Laurel, her family in Montana and wondered what her people were like. What kind of grandparents would they make? Probably great, if Laurel's love and devotion to them were any indication of the type of parents they must be. Good thing, because with his mother long passed away and Jed for a father, Cort, like Sawyer, didn't have much to offer a kid in the way of grandparents.

"Damn," Rafe muttered. "Speak of the devil."

Cort followed his brother's glance to where a golf cart was slowing as it neared the barn door. "What's he doing out of bed in this cold?"

"What do you think? He's a control freak. Wants to know about *my* new bison."

Jed turned the cart and drove down the wide path between the stalls. "You get 'em all here in one piece, boys?" he called out stopping the cart but not getting out of it.

Rafe nodded. "Thirty-six head. Skinny, but healthy. Jule'll check them out in the next day or two."

"You be sure she does." Jed coughed then turned to Cort, eyeing him up and down with a look that said he wasn't sure he liked what he saw. "'Bout time you took some interest in this place, seeing as it's gonna be part yours."

Cort saw Rafe's jaw tighten and silently cursed the old man

for bringing up the one subject sure to get his brother's back up. When Jed found out he had cancer, he'd got the idea in his head he wanted to divide ownership of the ranch among his five sons, despite the fact that Rafe, of all of them, deserved to be the one who inherited it. Jed and the man Rafe had believed to be his father had partnered to start Rancho Piñtada, and until recently, Rafe had thought he'd had a claim to at least half the ranch. Discovering he was Jed's son changed all that.

He couldn't speak for Cruz, having never met the guy, but neither Cort nor Sawyer wanted any part of the ranch. Josh, continually chasing the next rodeo title, spent as little time here as possible. Only Rafe had put his heart and soul into the land and as far as Cort was concerned, the sooner he, Sawyer and Josh found a way around Jed's determination to split the ranch up, the better.

"My only interest is helping Rafe," he told Jed.

"I'd of thought you'd be too busy with your new job to do that. The wife says the ladies at her tea party told her your grandparents finally wore you down. Guess they're glad one of you took up the family cross after all these years." He let out a dry snicker. "Better you than me, boy. You wouldn't catch me wearin' no apron, dead or alive."

Rafe looked confused. "What's he talking about? I thought you were just helping out with some construction."

"That, too." He'd been vague in talking to his brothers about exactly what he'd agreed to do, knowing all three of them would call him *loco* for taking on the manager's job. "I agreed to manage the place, at least until they get it open and running."

"You sure those doctors got your head back on straight? Because that seems about the last thing you'd do," Rafe said, not disappointing him. "When does it open?"

"Less than two weeks," Cort admitted. "I was planning to invite you and Jule. I'm running a little behind."

"And you took off three days to help me."

"Like I said, what are brothers for? Besides, getting out in the fresh air on a horse and busting my ass was the best thing I could have done. I'm suffocating in the damned place."

"This brotherly bonding has got me all choked up," Jed interrupted, shoving his cart into Reverse. "I gotta get back to bed before the wife catches me out here and gives me more misery than I'm already in. Oh, I almost forgot my news. Speaking of brotherly bonding, since none of you has been doin' anything lately to reach Cruz, I did it myself."

Rafe and Cort exchanged a suspicious glance. "What have you done?" Rafe asked.

"Sent him a letter. I'm tired of waiting on the four of you to help me find your brother and bring him back here. I want this inheritance business settled while I'm still standing."

"He's over in Iraq fighting for his life and you're telling him in a letter you're his father?" Cort asked. "Nice."

"If someone doesn't tell him, the way it's going over there, he might never know. I want this done and not later." With that he gunned the golf cart and left Cort and Rafe staring after him.

When he'd left Cort shook his head. "Figures, doesn't it? Just like him to drop this on Cruz while he's over there and can't do anything about it."

"Like you said, it figures. Maybe we'll get lucky and that letter'll get sidetracked for a couple of years." Looking bothered, Rafe paced the barn aisle, putting up the tack, stopping to check a stall or two before turning to face Cort, his expression dead serious. "You know I wouldn't have called you with this if I'd known about the restaurant."

"I know." Cort stopped him with a hand to his shoulder. "That's why I didn't mention it. I did this because I wanted to. Okay?"

Reluctantly, Rafe nodded. He fell awkwardly silent a long moment, busying himself with unpacking his saddlebags. "You hungry?" he asked at last, glancing over his shoulder to Cort, who was tossing trash out of his backpack. "Jule called earlier and said she had a big pot roast in the oven. Why don't you call that teacher friend of yours and bring her to dinner?"

Cort thought about the offer, stress over the restaurant weighing heavily on him now that he was back in Luna Hermosa. But his stomach rivaled it, growling over his missed lunch, and besides, he reasoned, his arm and shoulder were too sore to take much more abuse tonight. "Sure, that sounds great. But we'll have to make it an early night because I need to go by the place later and at least pretend to care what new disasters happened while I was gone."

"Like I said, that seems all wrong," Rafe said. "You want work that badly, I've got plenty of it here."

"Thanks, but I don't think I'd make a very good rancher."

"Don't think you'll make a very good restaurant manager, either."

Following Rafe back to his and Jule's house, Cort wanted to tell his brother he was probably right.

Relief and more than a little excitement washed over Laurel when she got Cort's call. She took down directions to Rancho Piñtada, changed into a simple sweater and jeans and got into her car to drive over. Cort's cell phone hadn't worked up in the mountains and for the last three days, she'd been worried about everything from weather to him reinjuring his shoulder or arm, and other less likely disasters such as a stampede or a riding accident.

The dinner invitation pleased her because she hadn't felt comfortable calling Jule to ask about Cort while the men were away. If Cort decided in the future to go on another bison-herding adventure with Rafe, it would be nice to know his sister-in-law well enough to keep in touch with her.

In the next instant she thought how silly she was to be thinking about a future with Cort in it. Their relationship was uncertain at best and to think of getting to know his family better seemed presumptuous. Yet, after talking with Maya again, she found she wanted to know Jule, too. She needed girlfriends, missed the ones back home almost as much as she missed her family.

And somehow, getting to know the women connected to Cort through his brothers was a comfort. They weren't like Nova or Trina, not competitive or women who'd been or wanted to be involved with Cort. Like Aria Charez, they both seemed to be genuine and caring.

Laurel turned on her car light and bent over her steering wheel to read the directions she'd scribbled down. She was almost there; one more turn and the sign for Rancho Piñtada showed up in her headlights. The massive iron gates had been left open and she drove past the main ranch house to where Cort said Rafe and Jule lived in a small adobe house. As soon as she parked and killed the lights, Cort appeared in the doorway. He strode out to her, closing the door behind him, smiling as if he'd been waiting for her all his life.

She's barely made it out of the car before he wrapped her in his arms, lifted her and swung her all the way around. "I missed you," he said, bending to kiss her soundly before she could get a word in.

Dizzied by an unexpected rush of emotion at seeing him again, she retuned the kiss with equal enthusiasm. "Feeling's mutual," she managed when at last they both came up for air. "I was worried about you."

Cort cupped her face in his palms and, concerned, looked deeply into her eyes. "Worried, why?"

"Oh, it's probably silly, mostly. But I was afraid of a bad snow or a stampede or something."

"A stampede," Cort said, then laughed, the sound rich, deep and sexy. "You've seen too many old Westerns."

"Probably," she admitted. "My mind was playing tricks on me the whole time you were gone."

"The whole time, meaning a few days? Wow, what did I do to earn that much of your attention?"

She smiled, teasing him. "Oh, this and that. It surprised me, too."

Pulling her close he nuzzled her neck. "It did, did it? Well, it didn't surprise me that I couldn't get you off my mind. I kept seeing your face, hearing your voice, imagining what you were doing without me. Maybe what you wanted to do with me—" He paused to brush her mouth with his. "Nights were the worst," he admitted, the husky rasp of his voice against her ear making her shiver. "That frozen ground was a heck of a reminder of how warm your bed was just before I left."

Laurel nearly told him her bed had felt colder than ever after the one short night he'd spent next to her there, but something stopped her and instead she said only, "I can't believe you camped out in the dead of winter."

"It was beautiful. I'd forgotten how much I love it. We should go together some time, take Tommy. I know you'd like it. Maybe it'll convince you to start a new family tradition."

No. Traditions implied years together, permanency, faith in a future that included love and children. None of which she had. Pulling her coat more closely around her, she tried to muster a little warmth against a chill that came from inside.

"You're shivering," Cort said, putting his arm around her shoulders and ushering her toward the door. "Let's go inside. Jule's made a dinner that smells like heaven in a roasting pan, especially after three days of Rafe's idea of camp cooking."

"Sounds great," she lied. Suddenly, she wished she could leave, return to her lonely house, retreat back into her shell.

But when they walked inside the cozy house, Laurel had to admit the smell and the warmth of the little house were irresistible. Pot roast and fresh bread from the kitchen and piñon and sage from the fireplace. Candles lined the mantle and dotted sconces on the wall. The house was simple, but filled with warmth and quiet elegance.

"Come in, please, let me take your coat," Jule said. "Cort, did you go out there without yours? Rafe said you kicked your way out of your sleeping bag, too."

"Sorry, I've outgrown that particular lecture. Besides, old habits die hard," Cort replied lightly. "I used to spend a lot of time out in the cold. I got used to it, I guess."

"Who gets used to that?" Jule asked as she led Cort and

Laurel to the dining table. "I can't imagine you miss it, that part of it anyway."

Laurel glanced at Cort, expecting to see his expression tighten in irritation. Instead, he shrugged it off, smiling easily.

"Not that, no," he agreed. "And I'm pretty sure I can learn to live without having to dodge bullets, knives or pickup trucks. Although I'm not convinced the restaurant's a lot safer. I've already broken up three shouting matches, and that chef we've got has a bad habit of waving a meat cleaver around when things don't go his way."

"I hope that's not what you're going back to tonight," Jule said with a laugh as they sat down to dinner.

"You need a hand?" Rafe asked.

"Thanks, but you've got your hands full here."

"During the day, yeah. At night I can put in a couple of hours for whatever you need."

"You can bring me," Jule said smiling at her husband.

"I wouldn't turn down free help if I were you," Laurel prodded Cort. She knew how stressed he was over the impending restaurant opening. Having his family's help might let him cut back on the hours he was spending there, pushing himself to meet his grandparents' deadlines and expectations.

Rafe and Jule's willingness to help reminded Laurel of her own family, and how caring and supportive they were of one another. She decided she liked them both. Though Rafe was far more gruff and serious than his brothers, he had a sincerity to him that was infectious. And Jule, all manners and breeding, obviously knew how to handle her husband's rough edges.

"I appreciate the offer," Cort said.

"Surely there's something I could do, too," Laurel added. She had to admit to herself that after finding Nova there, she'd had a bad taste in her mouth, so to speak, about the place. But hearing how willing Rafe and Jule were to help out, she realized how selfish she was being. And having them there would be a buffer against Nova.

"At this point, I have to admit there's probably a job for

everyone," Cort said. "Even an hour here or there would be a huge help."

"Then count us in," Jule promised.

Rafe gave his wife a stern look. "No heavy lifting for you, though."

"Oh, Rafe, don't be a worrywart."

"Are you hurt?" Laurel asked.

"No," she paused, stealing a glance at Rafe. "We're trying." Rafe smiled and Jule blushed. "We're hoping to get pregnant."

For the first time since they'd sat down, Cort put down his knife and fork, a wide grin on his face. "No kidding? That's the best news I've heard since Maya and Sawyer announced Nico was on the way." He reached over and planted a friendly slap on Rafe's back. "Way to go, my man. Who'd have thought you'd be a family man this soon."

"You forget I've loved this woman since she was only a few years older than Joey. We're making up for lost time."

"That long?" Laurel asked, burying the rise of emotion in her chest over news of the couple's plans for a child, and glad for the change of subject. Between Maya and now Jule and Rafe, she'd been constantly reminded today of her own losses.

Jule passed a basket of buttery rolls to her. "We were childhood sweethearts." She paused to gaze lovingly at her husband. "But it got complicated for a while."

Rafe nodded gravely. "Too long."

"But look at you now, married and about to start a family. Makes a person believe in second chances." Cort looked deliberately at Laurel. "Doesn't it?"

All eyes on her, she felt cornered. She wanted to say simply, yes, but for her it wasn't simple at all. "It certainly can," was all she could muster, knowing her upturned lips were a poor imitation of a smile. "This roast is amazing," she rushed to add, turning her attention to cutting a bite.

"One of the few things I can do without a guaranteed mess," Jule said, seeming to sense Laurel's discomfort. "Lucky for me Rafe's a decent cook."

"I take it you've never eaten his camp food," Cort said.

"This from the guy whose cats eat better than he does," Rafe muttered, but he quirked a smile as he said it and Laurel relaxed a little as the conversation turned to a bantering exchange over each other's various kitchen disasters.

When Jule finally got up to start cleaning off the table, Laurel followed. "Let me help."

"Thanks," Jule said glancing back over her shoulder. "Normally I wouldn't but it's getting late and I know Cort needs to get over to the restaurant."

In the kitchen Laurel thanked Jule for offering to help Cort. "He's really stressed about this whole thing."

"I can imagine." Jule started the coffeemaker and then began stacking dishes. "It's not at all what he's used to doing. Rafe, tactful as he is, more or less told Cort he was crazy for agreeing to do it to begin with. But in this case I have to agree."

"I think he's just looking for something to replace what he lost," Laurel said, feeling compelled to defend Cort, even though she knew with his family, it wasn't necessary. "It's hard, starting over."

Wiping her hands on a dishtowel, Jule stopped to look at Laurel appraisingly. "I'm sure that's true. We're all just worried he's looking in the wrong direction." She hesitated. "What happened really changed him. But I guess you know that."

"Only what I've heard. We haven't known each other that long. He used to be a lighthearted tease, from what I understand."

"He was always fun, and tonight, to tell you the truth, he seemed more like the old Cort than I've seen him in a long time."

"He seems happier to me, too. Being outdoors with Rafe must have been therapeutic."

"For both of them, believe me. But, you know, Cort's always been a positive force in this family, dysfunctional as it is. He was always the one trying to pull everyone back together. Of all of them, he's by nature the most family oriented."

"You all seem so close," Laurel said. "It's hard to imagine you as dysfunctional."

"That's because you haven't met Jed. Believe me, things haven't always been this good, and Jed's at the center of it. But Cort never stopped trying to make peace. And tonight, the way he lit up about the prospect of a new niece or nephew, I think the wheels are turning in his mind about his own future family." She smiled warmly, her dark, delicate features radiant. "Given the fact that he's never been seriously involved with anyone since Sandia died, I'm sure that has something to do with you."

Wishing she had something to do with her hands as a distraction, Laurel avoided Jule's eyes. "I'm not so sure about that. Maybe it was being with Rafe, out riding, sleeping under the stars. It must have brought back memories of when they were kids."

"Not likely. They didn't do anything like that. At least not the two of them. Maybe Sawyer and Cort did. Rafe was always the outsider. That's why what Cort did for him this week means so very much to all of us."

"I know he was glad Rafe called him."

Jule nodded enthusiastically as she poured four steaming mugs of coffee. "Just wait until he has a family of his own. He's going to be a great husband and father."

Murmuring something she hoped sounded like agreement, Laurel focused on the mugs Jule handed her. *Yes, he will. But not with me. Because with me, that wait would be forever.*

Chapter Twelve

"Okay, somebody should've warned me these kids don't have an off button."

The male voice, amused and slightly breathless, at her side had Laurel looking up from snagging a loose basketball. Too quickly, because Alex's rueful smile told her he knew his wasn't the male voice she'd been missing, hoping to hear for the last four days. "Sorry, just me."

"Not just you," she said lightly. "And don't mind me, I'm a little distracted today."

"Or disappointed. You and Tommy both." He inclined his head toward Tommy who was half-heartedly bouncing a basketball off the wall. "I think I've fallen short as a substitute for Cort."

Laurel didn't want to admit it to him but she had been disappointed when she'd come to basketball practice, expecting Cort and finding he'd asked Alex to stand in for him today because he was tied up at the restaurant. Part of her understood; he'd been working long hours to get ready for the opening this weekend. Part of her vacillated between being irritated and let down because he'd made no attempt to contact her in four days. And apparently he hadn't seen Tommy, either, from the way the boy had sloughed through practice, responding to Alex with sullen silence or shrugs.

"He's gotten attached to Cort," she mused, half to herself.

"I think you have, too."

Laurel flushed. "We're just friends."

"Not according to Cort," Alex said. He paused, expecting her to either deny or confirm it, and when Laurel did neither, glanced over at Tommy. "I'll go check on the bus. Maybe you can do something to console Tommy."

Doubtful she'd be an acceptable substitute for Cort, either, Laurel walked over to where Tommy was smacking the ball against the wall with short, hard jabs. "So what did the poor basketball do to you?"

Tommy practically threw the ball at the wall. "Nothin'."

"I know you're disappointed but Cort would have been here, if he could. He's just really busy right now."

"Whatever."

"It's not that he doesn't care about you."

"Then why's he been gone so long?"

Laurel sympathized with Tommy's thinking four days was *so long*. It had felt that way to her, too, more than she cared to admit. Jogging a few steps forward, she grabbed the basketball before it slammed the wall again to get Tommy's attention on her. "He's trying a new job and he's not very good at it yet, so he's having to take a lot of time to learn it. I haven't seen him, either, but I know it's not because he doesn't want to spend time with us, it's that he can't right now."

Tommy looked at her and Laurel could see he was trying to make up his mind whether to believe her or the voices from his past that said Cort had given up on him. "Do you like him?"

The question caught Laurel off guard. "Who? Cort? Of course, yes, he's a good friend."

"Oh." The boy scuffed at the floor with the toe of his shoe.

Studying a streak of dirt, he said, "I think he likes you more than just a friend."

Laurel's heart jumped despite herself. She forced her voice to express only a casual curiosity. "Why would you think that?"

Tommy shrugged. "I dunno. Just stuff he says. You know, about how pretty you are, and how good you are at helping people. How he likes doing stuff with you."

"He likes doing things with you, too," Laurel said, wanting to divert him away from the subject of Cort's feelings about her. She had a suspicion that Tommy, for his own reasons, had decided to play matchmaker and she didn't want him to be disappointed if and when things didn't work out the way he wanted them to.

But Tommy refused to be sidetracked. "Maybe he doesn't want to tell you 'cause he thinks you'll laugh at him or something." He frowned. "Girls are hard to talk to."

"I've seen you talking to Anna Tamar sometimes."

"Yeah, but I don't tell her stuff like, you know, stuff like that." He heaved a sigh and kicked at the floor again. "Cort says girls are confusing and you shouldn't try to figure 'em out 'cause it'll make you crazy."

Laurel couldn't help laughing at that. "Oh, he does, does he? Well, I'll be sure and tell him the next time I see him that you boys make us girls crazy, too." She looked at Tommy, still staring glumly at the floor, and impulsively said, "Let's go see him now."

Tommy's head came up. "Cort?"

"Yes. I'll call Mr. Charez and tell him where we're going and that I'll bring you home later. I'm sure he won't mind," she said as she started for her gym bag to dig out her cell phone. "Maybe we can talk Cort into having dinner with us, if you want."

"Yeah, sure." Tommy tried to sound uncaring one way or the other but his eyes brightened.

Laurel made a quick call to Joseph, who enthusiastically approved her plan, and then bundled Tommy off to her car.

Maybe it wasn't the right thing to do in her case since she wasn't quite sure where she and Cort stood, but it was worth the effort to see Tommy smile again.

As soon as they stepped inside the restaurant, they were greeted by Cort's voice, tight with aggravation. They found him pacing in front of the bar, gripping his cell phone as if he'd like to give it the same treatment as Tommy had the basketball. "I have no clue what that is or why I should care, but you promised me delivery yesterday. If it's not here first thing tomorrow, I'll find someone else to do the job." He jabbed the off button and turning slightly, noticed Laurel and Tommy for the first time.

His frustrated glower immediately changed to a pleased grin. "Hey, this is a surprise. You two are the best things I've seen all week."

Before Laurel could get her bearings, he strode up and quickly kissed her then turned to Tommy. Tommy immediately looked away. "You're not gonna kick me in the shin again, are you?"

Tommy's mouth twitched slightly, but he only shrugged in response.

Cort got down on one knee in front of him and put a hand on his shoulder. "Look, I know you're mad at me and maybe I deserve that kick. I've been thinking about you a lot and if I could have gotten away from here, believe me, I would have. But I promise, from now on, no matter how crazy things get, I'll make time for you." He glanced up at Laurel. "Both of you. No job is worth having the two of you thinking I don't care." He gently knuckled Tommy under the chin so the boy looked at him. "Because I do care. Okay?"

Tommy nodded and Cort smiled, ruffling his hair before he got to his feet.

"So I guess things aren't going too well?" Laurel asked, glancing around. The place didn't look much more organized than the last time she'd been here.

"That's an understatement. I'd have bailed weeks ago

except I promised the grandparents I'd at least stay long enough to get it up and running." He ran a hand over his hair, following Laurel's look around. "Although if one more thing goes wrong, I may not keep that promise."

"You should just tell them you hate it," Tommy said, jumping up on one of the bar seats. "Then you could quit and do somethin' better."

Laurel bit her lip to keep from laughing. "Good advice, I'd say."

"No fair ganging up on the overworked temporary manager," Cort said, trying and failing miserably to look affronted.

"We were hoping the overworked temporary manager had an hour or so to spare to have dinner with us."

"Not here," Tommy added.

"Definitely not here," Cort seconded. "Tell you what, how about we go back to my place and order pizza? It'll give me time to catch up on a few things there and spend some time with you guys without someone here interrupting."

Laurel hesitated but Tommy was already up and halfway to the door and Cort was smiling at her in that way that made it impossible for her to tell him no. And she didn't want to tell him no, not when they were all happy at the same time. "I guess you've got yourself some dinner guests."

"Watch out for my roommates," he said to them fifteen minutes later as he unlocked the door to his second floor apartment. "They're a little territorial."

"Your roommates?" Laurel started to ask.

But Cort didn't have to explain as two plump cats, their fur motley patches of gray, marmalade and white, greeted him with loud purrs and meowing the moment he stepped inside.

Laurel shook her head in disbelief as he bent to give each one a scratch behind the ears. "I've imagined a lot of things about you…"

"Yeah? Like what? Or can I guess?"

"No," she said, flushing. "Just lots of things. But not cats."

"I found them locked in a birdcage during a raid on a meth lab a couple of years ago. They'd been abused and no one else wanted them, so they sort of adopted me. I kept meaning to find a home for them but never got around to it."

"They look pretty at home to me."

"Yeah, well, I've kind of gotten used to them."

Tommy stretched out his fingers to one of the cats, who sniffed it tentatively and then allowed him to pet it. "What're their names?"

"Cat."

"Both of them?" Cort nodded and Tommy eyed him doubtfully. "That's kinda weird."

"They don't seem to mind. Sorry about the mess." Cort sidestepped the cats and tossed his cell phone, helmet, gloves and keys in a heap on the low bar dividing the living room from the kitchen before stripping off his jacket. "I haven't had much time lately for housekeeping."

Glancing around at the books, newspapers, various free weights, weekend dishes, cat toys and clothes scattered around the small space, Laurel bit her lip to hold back a smile. "I could have guessed that."

"There's a couch around here somewhere," Cort said, gesturing in the general direction as he took their coats and tossed them on top of his. "So what's your preference in pizza?"

"Pineapple and extra cheese?" Laurel suggested.

"I was thinking more like jalapenos and chorizo."

Tommy, sitting on the floor, dangling a string for one of the cats to bat about, made a disgusted, strangled sound. "You're both gross. Nobody eats that stuff on pizza."

"You better make it three," Laurel told Cort, going over to the couch and pushing aside a jacket to sit at one end. "Tommy's obviously a traditionalist and you know I'm not very adventurous."

"Guess we'll have to keep working on that," Cort said, flashing her a wicked smile before he went to order dinner.

They lingered over the pizza, talking and laughing and

lightheartedly debating the merits of the various names Tommy came up with for the cats, after the boy insisted Cort's pets needed real names. Laurel couldn't remember feeling so happy and relaxed in years.

Afterward, Tommy sat on the floor and used Cort's coffee table for a desk to do his homework while Laurel and Cort sat on the couch near him. Cort slouched into one corner, pulling her with him and put his arm around her and she curled up against his side, her head on his shoulder, as naturally as if they did this every night. Closing his eyes, he leaned his head back, toying with her hair, and Laurel let herself believe for a moment that this—this feeling of belonging together—was real and lasting.

"I almost forgot," Cort said lazily, not opening his eyes. "The opening's at five on Saturday. I wanted to ask you both if you'd come."

"You want me to come?" Tommy asked, sounding uncertain.

Cort raised his head to look at him and grinned. "Definitely. I have to warn you, though, they wouldn't let me put cheeseburgers on the menu so I may have to smuggle in a few for you and me. So will you come?"

"Yeah, sure," Tommy said, grinning back.

"How about you?" Cort asked, shifting to look at Laurel. "The rest of the family's said they'll be there, but it won't be the same without you and Tommy."

The rest of the family... When had she and Tommy slipped into that category of *family* for Cort, even on the periphery? That could never be real, at least for her. Yet it sounded so good, so right, she couldn't disagree. "I'll be there," she promised.

The contented warmth of their evening together stayed with Laurel the whole drive back to Joseph's house. She said good-night to Tommy shortly after they arrived so he could hurry off to get cleaned up and ready for bed, happier still when Tommy allowed her a quick hug before darting off.

"Are you sure that's the same boy?" Joseph asked, smiling

in wonder after Tommy. "Because it sure doesn't look like the same one who was moping around here all week."

"He missed spending time with Cort," Laurel said.

"If he had his choice, he'd be spending all his time with Cort and you." Joseph rubbed a hand over his bristle of gray hair, eyeing her as if trying to gauge her reaction to the idea. "I think he's got it in his head you'd make a pretty good family."

Tears pricked her eyes, the struggle between liking the idea and knowing how impossible it probably was robbing her of a ready reply. She nearly kissed Aria when the other woman came into the living room, giving her time and space to regroup.

"Hi, Laurel, I thought I heard you," Aria said.

"I'll leave you two to talk," Joseph said. "I need to check on the boys."

"Dad said you and Tommy were out with Cort," Aria said when they were alone. Dropping into an easy chair across from Laurel, she smiled. "I'll bet that cheered Tommy up. He's been one unhappy guy all week with Cort not around."

"I know. But Cort's been so busy at the restaurant he hasn't been around for anyone lately."

Laurel wanted to take back the words as soon as they came out of her mouth. From Aria's knowing expression, she saw Aria had substituted *me* for *anyone*. "Okay, that sounded whiny, even to me," she said.

"No, just a little frustrated." Aria paused then said, "Cort's been through some rough times lately and I would guess it's changed him in some ways. But I've known him a long time and one thing I am certain of. You can always count on him to be up front with you and to be there when you need him."

But would he be there if he knew the truth? "I know how busy he's been. It's just that I wish he were spending his time doing something more satisfying and challenging to him, because managing a restaurant isn't it."

"Tommy thinks he'd make a pretty good dad," Aria said. "And I'd have to agree. He's great with Tommy."

Cold, hard and gray, squeezed Laurel's heart. She'd have to agree, too. Except that even if it became her most cherished desire, she could never give him that—a real family, children of his own. Pushing away the pain, she said quickly, "He's invited Tommy and me to the restaurant opening Saturday."

"We'll see you there then. Cort called right before you got here and invited Dad and David and me, too. We're looking forward to it." Aria cocked her head and looked Laurel up and down. "You don't seem to be, though."

"I want to be there for Cort but to be honest, I would rather not."

"Why? Good food, a great looking guy at your service and a chance to ditch the jeans for a killer black dress. What's not to like?"

"The part about the black dress. I don't own one and even if I did, I doubt I could compete."

"Compete? With whom?"

"Just about every woman in town." Laurel flushed, a little embarrassed at blurting out her insecurities to Aria, who'd probably never felt insecure in her life. "I'm sorry, there's that whiny sound again."

Aria waved the notion of whiny away. "You're too hard on yourself. Cort seems to like what he sees so why worry?"

"Maybe because when I see the kind of woman he's been with in the past and then I look at myself, I don't understand why he'd be attracted to me. To be honest…" She hesitated and couldn't help thinking of the last time she'd shared her feelings with a friend. But Aria wasn't Karen; if she'd harbored any secret desire for Cort, she would have acted on it long before now. Laurel couldn't believe that Aria would use anything she said to undermine her relationship with Cort. "I grew up in a small town and I've only dated one person in my life, my ex-husband. I don't have any experience with a man like Cort. I'm not sure I'd be able to hold his interest, even if I wanted to."

"*Even* if you wanted to?" Laurel blushed and she laughed.

"Sorry, but I thought it was pretty well established you *did* want to. What are you doing Saturday morning?"

"I—nothing, that I know of. Why?"

Aria grinned. "Because I've got an idea."

Chapter Thirteen

If there were a way to do a hundred things at once without bringing on chaos, disaster or insanity, Cort hadn't figured it out.

Fifteen minutes until opening and the only thing he felt confident about was that something would go wrong. Probably several somethings. His grandparents weren't helping. They'd shown up an hour earlier with high expectations he hadn't met and had insisted on two-dozen last-minute changes that had left Nova having to charm the chef out of a temper tantrum and Cort on the phone trying to find fresh salmon at four-thirty on a Saturday in the middle of nowhere New Mexico.

"Stop," Nova said, putting a palm flat against his chest when he came up front to ask her why half the table linens were a different color. "Whatever it is, the answer's no."

"It wasn't a yes-or-no question."

"I don't care. It's still no. It's almost five. Nothing else is getting fixed unless it involves death or my paycheck." Her eyes narrowing, she looked him up and down, assessing the black-on-black jacket, shirt and pants. "Except this." Before Cort could stop her, she pulled off his tie and dropped it into a nearby wastepaper basket, unbuttoned the top two buttons of his shirt and rifled her fingers through his hair. "There. You look more like you again."

"Should I ask who I looked like before," Cort asked, "or do I want to know?"

"The guy who's forgotten how to enjoy life. Definitely not the Cort I used to know."

"That guy doesn't work here."

"I know. And you shouldn't, either." Shaking her head, she glanced back at the seating chart and reservation list stacked on the front podium. "By the way, I know we're pretty well booked, but I invited Alex."

"Alex?" He could have sworn he saw Nova blush. "Did I miss something?"

Nova laughed at what Cort was sure was the clueless look on his face. "Probably. You're good, honey, but that doesn't mean I've given up on every other man. Besides," she smiled teasingly, "maybe seeing me with Alex will convince your jealous girlfriend I'm not still after your body."

Cort nearly laughed at the idea of Laurel in that role. She didn't fully trust him, especially where Nova was concerned, but he doubted it had anything to do with jealousy and everything to do with her ex-husband.

He was beginning to wonder if he could even put her into the *potential-girlfriend* category when, an hour and dozens of people later, she still hadn't made an appearance.

Sawyer and Maya and Rafe and Jule had come together, and had insisted on pushing a couple of tables together to include Tommy, Joseph, Aria and David in their group. His grandparents didn't like it, but all Cort cared about was the smile on Tommy's face when Cort's family accepted him as if he was one of their own and his happiness at being treated as somebody important to Cort.

It was about the only thing that went right.

The chef loudly complained about the missing salmon and having to improvise with mountain trout; Cort had underestimated the demand for tequila and had to clear the shelves at two grocery and a liquor store to restock; and his grandparents had invited a party of ten without bothering to tell either him or Nova and then fussed about the humiliation of their friends' forty-minute wait.

Nearing seven o'clock and the latest minicrisis resolved, Cort made his way back to the front, glancing outside.

"That's the fifth time in the last half hour," Nova commented without looking up from the seating chart she was readjusting.

"I'm—"

"Waiting for Laurel. I know." She glanced over her shoulder as the outside door opened in a whoosh of air. "Finally."

Cort nearly told Nova she'd made a mistake because the woman walking inside couldn't be Laurel. Then the woman slid off her coat to leave it in the cloakroom and he just stared.

Gone were the baggy sweats and in their place was a long-sleeved dress in a deep ruby color that clung to every curve. She'd done something with her hair, too; it was lighter, shorter and had a sexy tousled look to it.

Nova nudged his arm, murmuring, "Stop drooling and say something. You're leaving tongue marks on the tile."

All he could think of was, "Wow," which sounded pretty lame but seemed to please Laurel. Smiling, she walked up to him, slid a hand against his chest and, as if she'd made up her mind to thoroughly mess with his head, kissed him. She even smelled different. Instead of the roses he remembered, her perfume was a subtle, sultry blend of some exotic flowers and spice. "I'm sorry I'm late. Aria and I went into Taos today and it took longer than I expected."

"Um, yeah. That's fine. No problem." He wondered if he was finally starting to crack because for the first time in his life, he felt completely off balance and disconcerted by a beautiful woman. *Who are you and what have you done with Laurel?* "You look amazing."

"Thank you. I thought I'd try something new. I was hoping you'd like it."

"Like doesn't begin to cover it."

It was true in more ways than one. Part of him, the primal, possessive part that didn't take orders from his brain, liked it a lot. But his more rational, questioning side worried their argument the other day had made her feel like she had to remake herself into someone she wasn't because this was what she thought he wanted.

He couldn't ask her now; instead he promised himself later and keeping his hand at her waist, escorted her to sit with his family and Tommy.

Cort didn't feel quite as self-conscious about his earlier gaping since everyone else pretty much reacted the same way. Except for Aria, who just smiled and looked insufferably smug when Cort glanced her way.

"Wow, Laurel, I hardly recognized you," Jule said.

"*Wow* is right," Sawyer seconded. He looked from Cort to her. "You've certainly made an impression," he said to her while looking at Cort.

Tommy stared at her almost in awe. "You look really different," he said.

Laurel laughed lightly, and even that sounded different to Cort. "Is that different bad or different good?"

"Good, I guess," Tommy said doubtfully.

"Very good. If I'd known about the beautiful company, Cort, I'd've been on time." Cort turned to face his youngest brother, who ignored him to give Laurel a thorough once over. "I'm Josh Garrett and you'll make my year, darlin', if you tell me you've been waitin' for me."

Laurel smiled and Cort shifted closer to her, put his hand on her waist again. "Laurel Tanner. And sorry, no, I'm—"

"With me," Cort finished, looking hard at Josh.

Josh grinned, a glint of mischief in his eyes. "Right now, maybe."

"Give it a rest," Rafe spoke up, shoving out a chair for Josh as Laurel sat down next to Tommy. "Cort's got enough to worry about tonight."

"If I had a woman who looked like that, I'd be worried," Josh said, taking the seat and leaning back to smile at Laurel, "about someone like me makin' her a better offer."

Maya gave him an exasperated look. "Josh, there are at least a dozen women here who'd be more than happy to be the center of your attention tonight. Pick one."

"Pick all twelve," Cort added. "Just don't start working your charm on any of the staff until after closing."

Cort half expected Laurel to be uncomfortable left on her own to fend off his baby brother's advances. But then again, maybe her new persona could deal with incurable flirts. Reluctant to leave her until he had more time to either figure this out or just enjoy the hell out of it, Cort didn't have the luxury as one of the waiters came up, murmuring about another kitchen problem. Stopping short of telling the man he didn't care, he said, "Be there in a minute," and running a light caress over Laurel's shoulder told her, "I'll be back."

He spent the next hour hustling around putting out fires, sure he'd mishandled half of them because he couldn't keep his eyes off her. His grandparents were judging his every move; his family and friends drawing their own conclusions about his and Laurel's relationship. All he could think was he wanted to get her alone.

It began to seem less likely all the time until a strange buzzing noise coming from overhead overrode the background music.

Cort looked up at the same moment the sprinkler system activated.

"Here's to Cort—" Sawyer held up his beer bottle "—for managing to get fired on opening night without even trying. And about time, too."

"Best thing that could've happened," Rafe said. His mouth twitched into a smile. "Except you might've picked a drier way to do it."

The malfunctioning sprinkler system had doused everyone with a cold spray for a full five minutes before Cort was finally able to shut it off, emptying the restaurant and leaving everything a soggy mess. Only Cort's brothers, and Maya and Jule stayed behind with Laurel to celebrate Cort's grandparents firing him and giving the manager's job to Nova. They'd mopped up enough chairs and raided the bar and had turned the opening night disaster into an impromptu family party.

Laurel, wearing Cort's leather jacket over her damp and clinging dress, had let herself stop worrying about whether or not she was getting her new role as seductress right and was just enjoying his arm around her and the luxury of being close to him. But what made her happiest was seeing him so relaxed and smiling, as if losing the manager's job had relieved him of a huge burden. Jacket discarded, still wet from his impromptu shower, hair disheveled, he looked happier than she could ever recall him being in the time she'd known him.

His boots propped up on the edge of the table, Josh tipped his shot glass in Cort's direction in answer to Sawyer's toast. "The only problem is you cost me twenty bucks. I bet you weren't gonna last a week."

"That long, huh?" Cort said with a smile.

"Hey, at least I gave you seven days. Sawyer said you wouldn't last three."

"Sawyer!" Maya lightly pushed his arm. Sawyer only shrugged in response.

"You know," Cort told Maya, "that would have been a lot more meaningful if you weren't laughing so hard."

"You guys are terrible," Jule said, but she was laughing, too. "So who won?"

Josh pointed to her husband. "Rafe. He figured Cort's guilty conscience wouldn't let him leave before tonight."

"I said he was too responsible."

"Same thing." Josh downed his tequila shot and then looked at Cort. "Well, if nobody else's gonna ask the big question, I will. What are you gonna do now?"

Both Sawyer and Rafe started to protest and Laurel glanced hurriedly at Cort, knowing how much the question had irritated him in the past. But instead of brushing Josh off with a short-tempered reply, he smiled as if he'd been waiting all night to give an answer.

"Go back to law school," he said. He looked down at Laurel and she could see promises in his eyes. "And maybe start a few other new things along the way."

She scarcely heard the enthusiastic approvals and round of "Cheers!" from his family and Cort's good-natured banter in reply to his brothers' teasing about him at last getting back to being himself again. Though he hadn't said the words, Cort had made it clear to everyone there that he wanted her to be a part of his future. Laurel just couldn't see how they could ever have a future when she couldn't be free of the past.

The party finally broke up around midnight. Laurel stayed behind with Cort, waiting in the dining room while he made the rounds of the back rooms, turning off the lights and locking doors. When he strode back in, she stood up, expecting him to head for the front. Instead, he put himself in front of her, looking at her before brushing his fingertips over her hair, her cheek, the curve of her neckline.

"This is nice. Very nice," he amended. "But you don't need all this to impress me. I think the old Laurel is pretty amazing, too."

"I left the old Laurel in Montana. I need to find out who I am now." Distracted by the slow heat in his eyes and touch that threatened to become a flame, she tried to form words that made sense. "Besides, the old Laurel doesn't know what to do with you."

"What about the new Laurel?"

"She's working on it."

"Need some suggestions?" he asked in a husky, soft voice that caressed her like a touch and made her tremble. As if he had the rest of the night, he slid the jacket off her shoulders and down her arms, letting it drop to the floor. "I have a few."

"I'm sure you do." Something seemed to have gone wrong with her breathing as she waited, poised on the edge of falling completely while he stood just within reach. She thought he might be teasing her, dangling temptation in front of her like sweet bait. But the way he looked at her, she suspected he was doing it to inflame the anticipation in himself, stretching the moment between wanting and having until it broke.

Then, without warning, he pulled her up hard against him and kissed her, an intimate, openmouthed kiss that caught her off guard. All the times before, there'd been a subtle restraint in the way he kissed and touched her, as if he were holding part of himself back, afraid to push her too close to anything more intimate.

He held nothing back now, spinning her senses and her thoughts into chaos. She had no defense against this seduction, no will to resist. He made her feel as if it were inevitable—maybe from the first—they would be lovers. Her body and her heart had chosen Cort, even when her reason argued against letting him too close.

She moved restlessly against him, wanting him closer, wanting him to touch her without the frustrating barrier of clothing between them.

She could tell Cort wanted it, too, felt in the hot urgency of his kiss. Without taking his mouth from hers, he walked her backward until her back pressed against the wall. One hand tangled in her hair, tipping her head back as his mouth dragged from hers to kiss and taste her throat, while the other slid behind her thigh, guiding her leg over his and bringing them even closer together.

Laurel moaned softly as he cupped her breast with a hand that was not quite steady, stroking the taut center, making her whole body burn and tremble.

"You're taking me apart here," Cort whispered hotly against her ear. He pulled back enough to look at her, watching her face as he continued his slow, arousing caresses.

If he asked her to do anything now, anything, she would.

She'd never felt like this, never wanted anyone in the hungry, demanding way she wanted him. No one else had ever made her want to give everything, everything she had, anything he would take. Tangling her fingers in his hair, she kissed him, reveling in the low satisfied sound he made.

She fumbled with the buttons of his shirt, her only thought to touch him.

"Laurel…" Her name came out more of a pleasured groan as she leaned to kiss the pulse jumping in his throat. "You shouldn't," he said.

"You started it," she teased back, made bold by the fantasies she'd spun around his reaction to her new look, the ones he'd brought to vivid life. Finishing unbuttoning his shirt, she pushed it half off his shoulders and watched that slow, sexy smile curve his mouth as she spread her hands over his chest.

It was seeing the white lines of scarring across his shoulder, collarbone and abdomen that tempered desire with tenderness. She wished, suddenly and fiercely, she could take away all the pain and bitterness of his past so he'd never be haunted by them again.

Very gently, she traced the lines on his shoulder until Cort, as if sensing her shift in emotion, covered her hand with his. "You can't change every bad thing that happened to me in the past," he echoed his past words back at her, changed to reflect her thoughts for him.

"But maybe we can start something new?" she whispered. Bowing her head against his shoulder, she closed her eyes. "I want to believe that. I want to." She slowly raised her gaze to his. "I want you."

"Are you sure? Here? Now? Stop," he murmured a trifle desperately as her hands roamed again as she leaned into him, softly kissing his mouth, liking her newly discovered power over him. "I can't think when you're doing that."

"I don't want to think." She wanted to feel. For once, to be like the woman she'd pretended to be and act on her desires with her eyes closed to everything but the feeling.

"That's what I'm afraid of."

Taking both her hands in his, he pressed them against his chest as he leaned his forehead against hers, struggling to bring his breathing under control. After a few moments, he looked at her and let go of her hand to rub his thumb over her mouth. "I want you, too. But I don't want this to be something you're going to regret later, when you are thinking about it."

"Why would I regret it? Because I'm not experienced? Because the only lover I've had was my husband and I don't know what this means?" Laurel felt herself getting angry but mostly with herself, because those were her insecurities, not his. He was right but she didn't want to admit it. She said firmly to convince herself as much as Cort, "I know what I want."

"I know what I want, too, and I want it to be right." Glancing around them he said, "Making love for the first time together in a wet restaurant doesn't seem too right to me." He pretended to think it over for a moment then with a hint of a smile, added, "Memorable, maybe. But not right."

Leaning in, he kissed her, soft and slow, with only a flicker of the previous fire, but with a tenderness and depth of emotion that brought tears to her eyes.

"I'm not going anywhere," he promised. "I'll be right here, waiting for you."

Laurel nodded, not trusting herself to say anything, unsure of which felt stronger, the crippling uncertainty that she couldn't be what he wanted, or the growing conviction he was everything she wanted.

All the way home, with Cort following her in his Jeep, she wrestled with conflicting feelings. She wanted to prove to herself he meant it when he said he wanted her, that him saying he would wait for her wasn't just his way of letting her down easy. Except that made her sound as inexperienced and naive as she claimed not to be.

By the time they pulled in her driveway, she was so deep in debate with herself Cort's tap on the window made her realize she'd been sitting for several moments with the engine running, staring at the steering wheel.

He didn't comment about her lapse as he walked her to her door, waiting until she'd unlocked it and stepped inside with her. Shedding her coat as she went, she flicked on one of the living-room lamps, only then realizing he hadn't moved.

"It's late. I should probably get going," he said, not sounding too convinced of it.

Laurel wished she could be fearless and bold; instead, she felt uncertain about everything except knowing that she didn't want him to leave. She walked back to where he stood and traced her fingertips over his mouth. "You could stay."

Cort captured her hand and kissed her palm. "I could. But then I wouldn't be leaving for at least a week."

"Is that supposed to be a threat or a promise?" She made herself smile but she didn't believe him. If he wanted her as much as he claimed, she doubted it would take any effort on her part to seduce him into her bed. Maybe it was adolescent of her, but she had enough ego to want him to be as overwhelmed by need for her as she was for him.

"You're wrong."

"What? I didn't say anything."

"You didn't have to. I can see it all here," he said, and touched her face. "You aren't very good at hiding your feelings."

"Apparently there are a lot of things I'm not very good at," she said churlishly, then winced at how she sounded. "I'm sorry. You're right, it's late and I'm tired." She started to take a step back, wanting to end this as gracefully as she could, without making more of a fool of herself.

He countered with a step forward, bringing them close again. "You want what I gave the rest of them? Is that all you want? Because if it is, believe me, sweetheart, I'm more than happy to oblige."

Not waiting for her answer, he kissed her hard and deep, one hand around her nape, holding her captive, the other low on her back, pressing her hips to his. He didn't give her time to breathe, let alone think, relentlessly pushing her toward the edge of complete surrender.

Just as abruptly, he released her. Keeping his hands on her shoulders, he stared at her, breathing hard. "You think I don't want you, but you're wrong," he repeated. "I'm about thirty seconds from saying to hell with what's right and showing you just how wrong you are. But I want to give you more than this. I want to make love to you. Not just sleep with you because we've both got something to prove."

"You don't have to prove anything to me." Her words came out in a trembling rush; that they came at all surprised her.

"Yeah, I do. I have to prove you can trust me because I don't think you do, not completely. You don't believe that what we have is going to turn out any differently than it did with Scott."

She started to lie, to tell him he was wrong. She couldn't. Because it was the truth, even though he didn't know the real reasons why.

Cort gathered her close, softly stroking her back. "It's okay. I promise you, it'll be okay. We'll figure it out."

There was nothing she could say, so she held on to him, her head against his heart, for as long as she could.

Chapter Fourteen

Alone in her now empty classroom at the end of a long Thursday, Laurel finished stacking the papers on her desk and stood up to shelve a few books left lying out. The quiet encouraged her thoughts to wander and they did, in the same direction they'd been straying for days now, back to the night at the restaurant, lost in passion with Cort. She couldn't stop herself from wondering how far it might have gone if she'd been more assertive, pushed him a little harder, tempted him to…

The sound of footsteps just outside her door broke into her fantasy. Before she could let go of the books and turn to see who it was, a pair of strong hands caught her shoulders and spun her around. In the next instant she was in Cort's arms, her surprised gasp stifled by his mouth covering hers in a no-holds-barred kiss.

"Wow," she managed, when lack of air finally forced them apart. "What's the occasion?"

"Do I need one?"

He grinned at her and Laurel leaned back to get a good look

at him. He was wearing his biker leather but there wasn't anything cool and dangerous about him today. She'd never seen him like this, practically bouncing with a barely suppressed excitement, an exultant gleam lighting his eyes. He was obviously on some kind of high and although it was a nice thought, she didn't think it was seeing her that caused it.

"No," she answered him, "but I get the idea there is one. Are you going to share?"

"I did it," he said triumphantly. "I finished the application for law school and with any luck I'll be able to start next fall."

"Really? Cort, that's wonderful!"

"I can't say the idea of being a student again sounds too wonderful, and I'm not quite sold on the desk job yet, but when I look at Tommy and think about all the kids like him, it's enough to make all the rest of it worth it. And just so you don't think I've resigned myself to a totally tame life, I let Sawyer talk me into joining the volunteer equestrian search-and-rescue team he heads up. They cover a pretty big region, so they get called out a fair amount of times in a month."

Laurel looked at him doubtfully. "That sounds like it could be dangerous."

"Yeah," he said with a wicked grin, "I'm looking forward to it."

Sweeping her close, he kissed her again with unrestrained enthusiasm that quickly threatened to take the mood between them from celebratory to dangerous of a different sort.

Laurel found Cort hard to resist under most circumstances but with him this wound up, almost reckless with the adrenaline high of his success in getting his life back on track, she found it hard not to let herself get caught up in his mood and damn the consequences of getting caught making out in her classroom.

He started kissing her neck and Laurel clutched at his shoulders, bending back her head to give him access while at the same time wondering how she could keep this from getting completely out of hand.

"This is…a bad idea," she stammered. "Right now, anyway."

"Only if you're expecting another jealous boyfriend who's bigger than I am," Cort murmured, returning his attention to her mouth again.

Another jealous boyfriend? She didn't know for certain that she had one to begin with in him. She tried to think about the implications of that but she couldn't think at all with him kissing her like this. As she teetered on the edge between pulling back and completely abandoning all sense of propriety, Cort made the decision for her, easing his mouth from hers with a last, lingering kiss.

"I'd like to finish this somewhere more private," he said, flashing a tempting smile as he traced the pink flush on her cheeks with his fingertips. "But I've got about a thousand things to catch up on. I just stopped by so I could give you the good news in person."

"I like your delivery system."

"Yeah? I'll remember that next time I have something to tell you. Want to walk me back to my bike?"

Laurel put on an expression of concentration, as if she were giving the matter serious consideration. "What's in it for me?"

"We get to finish this later in private." Cort let her go with a satisfied smirk, following her to lean against her desk as she gathered up her things to go home, then helping her into her coat. Shouldering the case she used to haul papers back and forth, he took her hand and let her lead the way out of the room, in the direction of the front doors.

They passed a few other teachers leaving at the same time and from the avid curiosity she saw in the expressions of the women in particular, Laurel knew she'd again be the topic of faculty-room gossip. She was surprised to find it didn't bother her as much as she'd expected.

Cort's high spirits and the relief that he'd finally made a decision about what to do with the direction of his life made her feel a little giddy. She felt like throwing her arms around him and kissing him passionately so everyone watching would really have something to talk about.

He walked her to her car, lingering for a few minutes to steal a few kisses before reluctantly letting her go. "We still on for Saturday?"

Laurel nodded, anticipating their planned trip to Santa Fe to see the Christmas decorations even more than before. "I'm counting on it. And so is Tommy. He's only asked me about six dozen times if I'm sure we're all going."

"Good. Because I'm looking forward to a real celebration."

The evening was cold and crisp, a perfect winter evening, Laurel thought. Soft flakes of snow fell silently on her nose and cheeks. One touched her lip and she licked it off with a quick dart of her tongue.

Cort caught the gesture and gave her a smile warm enough to melt the snow around them, filled with promise. Leaning close, he murmured for her ears only, "Every time you do that, it reminds me of one of my favorite fantasies." Against her ear, he whispered a suggestion involving warm honey that made Laurel blush.

He laughed and lightly kissed her temple. "Later," he said. "I did promise you luminarias."

She and Cort and Tommy had done some Christmas shopping in Santa Fe earlier that day. Then they'd shared dinner, with lots of teasing and laughter, in a cozy little hacienda restaurant at a table next to a dancing fire in a corner fireplace. Now she gazed slowly around the Santa Fe plaza, aglow from candles in thousands of luminarias.

"It's even more beautiful than I'd imagined," she murmured, curling her hand farther into the crook of Cort's arm as they strolled the plaza, gazing at the winter fairyland of soft candlelight. Tommy, walking beside Laurel, seemed as entranced by the display as Laurel.

"I told you it was magical." Cort bent and touched a kiss to her hair.

"But what keeps the little paper bags from burning? I mean, what if a wind comes up?"

"The candles are sitting in bricks or sand," Tommy answered. "The wind's not gonna make any difference."

"One or two bags might catch fire, but the fire wouldn't spread and the bags are so small that even if they do catch fire they turn to ashes immediately and no harm done," Cort added. "This time of year, there's never much wind up here anyway. You sound like an expert, Tommy. Did you ever put luminarias out at your house?"

"Yeah, my grandpa and I did it once when I was really little. And once he brought me here to see them."

Cort and Laurel exchanged a glance. "I didn't know you had a grandfather, Tommy. Where is he now?" she asked.

"He died."

"Oh, I'm sorry," she said, laying a hand on the boy's shoulder. He felt small and thin inside the oversized winter coat Joseph had given him.

Tommy shrugged. "It's okay. It was a long time ago. I don't remember much about him." He looked around them. "I don't remember much about this place, either, except for that church up the street my grandpa brought me to a few times." He pointed to a beautiful old adobe mission church a few blocks away.

"St. Francis Cathedral," Cort said for Laurel's benefit. He looked at Tommy. "Want to see it again?"

"Yeah, sure." Tommy said it casually, as if it didn't matter, but Laurel could see the anticipation in his face.

As they walked up the snow-dotted sidewalk toward the church, Laurel settled into the moment. Arm in arm with Cort, Tommy running and sliding ahead, glancing back occasionally to make sure they were there, it felt like they were a family. It was a feeling she didn't want to end.

"Listen," Tommy called back to them, "there's singing."

Laurel and Cort paused and the strains of a choir singing a holiday song reached her ears. "'Ave Maria,' one of my favorites."

Cort smiled down at her. "Mine, too."

"Can we look inside?" Tommy asked as he ran back up to them.

"You go on ahead. We'll meet you at the door," Cort said.

As Tommy darted off, Laurel smiled up at Cort. "Can you believe how well he's doing? He's going to be all right, thanks to you."

"And to you. You've been like a mother to him."

Laurel's voiced caught. "No, just a friend and a teacher." *Though he feels almost like a son to me.*

"Tommy would disagree if he weren't too shy to say so. I'm not and I do say so."

"If I were his mother, I could do so much more for him." She couldn't let herself even think about that or she'd break down and turn a wonderful evening into a night marred by sad memories and tears.

At the foot of the steps that led to the picturesque old church entrance Cort stopped and turned Laurel to face him. "You know, you have a bad habit of disagreeing with me at the wrong times." He pulled her to him and kissed her long, deep and slow, stopping her protest and leaving her breathless. "Still want to argue with me?"

"Maybe," she teased. "But not right now."

They climbed the steps to stand with Tommy in the foyer of the church. There they listened in silence to a soloist finishing the last chorus of "Ave Maria" in Spanish. Enchanted, Laurel closed her eyes and leaned back against Cort's chest. He wrapped his arms around her waist pulling her against him, and together they stood close, listening to the divinely lilting notes.

Laurel knew then that Christmas would not be complete unless she spent it with Cort and with Tommy.

When the song ended they walked back outside and Tommy immediately sprinted out ahead of them to take advantage of the thin layer of snow on the sidewalk.

"I've been thinking," Laurel began.

"This sounds dangerous."

"I'm serious," she said, nudging his side. "I want to spend Christmas with Tommy, but I really do need to go home and see my family. It seems like forever since I've been back and I miss them."

She hesitated and Cort looked at her inquiringly. "And?"

"And, I was wondering," she said taking her courage in her hands, "would you like to come with me?"

"To Joseph's?"

"And Montana."

His silence and the dark intensity in his eyes made her knees go weak. She'd risked putting her heart out there, was he about to step on it?

Finally, a slow, easy smile slipped up his mouth. "I think I'd like that a lot."

Laurel couldn't remember being so content or so happy.

She and Cort had spent the first half of Christmas day with Tommy and the boisterous group at the Charez ranch that included Joseph, Aria and her sister, Risa, David and several of Joseph's previous foster kids, Inez and Carlos and two of their grown children and their families. It was noisy, crowded, chaotic and some of the best hours Laurel had spent since coming to New Mexico.

Tommy seemed especially delighted with the celebrations, maybe because it was the first holiday in years he'd shared with people who cared about him. For the first hour, he'd kept glancing at Cort and Laurel when he thought they weren't looking, as if he couldn't quite believe they'd shown up just for him, with an armful of gifts and promises they'd stay for the better part of the day.

Late in the afternoon, as they watched Tommy battle David on the new gaming system they'd brought him, Cort, his arm draped casually over Laurel's shoulders, leaned in close and murmured in her ear, "If we leave soon, I'll have time to take you for a ride before we meet up with the rest of the family. "

Laurel smiled at the suggestive note in his voice, though

she knew what kind of ride he meant. He'd surprised her with his gift to her, a motorcycle helmet and brown leather jacket which at first had her shaking her head at his persistence. But, secretly, the more she'd thought about riding with him, nestled against him, hugging his strong back, fresh air kissing her face, sun or stars leading the way, the more intriguing the idea became. She didn't plan on surrendering too easily though. "I told you a long time ago you'd never get me on that thing. I hope you saved the receipts."

"Five minutes." He smiled, the very picture of temptation. "On a quiet dead-end street."

Her cheeks flushed and he laughed, and she pushed him lightly in the ribs, half embarrassed that everyone in the room knew he could fluster her even if they didn't know why. "Five minutes and I'm wearing a watch. *And,* I'm only doing this because it's Christmastime. You're still going to have to take everything back."

"Deal." He took her hand, helping her to her feet. "But you're going to change your mind."

An hour later, straddling the seat of his bike behind Cort, her arms wrapped around his waist, Laurel had long since eaten her five-minute decree. Maybe it was him, and her heightened awareness of him, but she found the ride sexy and exciting. She hugged against his powerful back, the air against her exposed cheek cold and sharp, a contrast to the warmth of him pressed against her chest and thighs, the smell of wind and leather reminding her of his scent. She snuggled in closer to him, encouraging him to go faster, push harder, the brilliant white of the snow against the clear turquoise sky passing in a blur, dazzling her eyes.

Laurel could not believe she actually felt a pang of regret when Cort finally pulled to a stop in front of his apartment. "Oh, my gosh! That was so great. I want to go again! I had no idea it would be like that. I think you've got me hooked."

Cort stepped back over the bike so that he faced her. His hands on her hips, he slid her closer to him and then bent and kissed her, taking his time until Laurel no longer felt the cold or cared they were in plain sight of anyone around them.

"You've got me hooked, too. On you. Only you." He held her closer still, nuzzling her neck, then pulled back, a boyish grin on his face. "Hey, want to take the bike over to Maya's parents for the party? They're old hippies. They'd get a kick out of it. Come on," he coaxed, when she hesitated, "you know you love it. It'll be fun."

It's not the bike, it's you. The thought startled her. She couldn't. When had her heart ignored her head and decided to fall in love with him? *No, I don't, I can't, I—* "I do." Cort looked confused and she hastily amended, "I mean, okay, sure, yes."

As if he'd read her thoughts, he asked, "Yes, you do?" and the low husky timbre of his voice matched the warmth in his eyes. "Me or the bike?"

She dared to answer with a question of her own. "Can't I have both?"

"Oh, yeah." Leaning in again, he kissed her, with more tenderness than passion, more longing than hunger and then murmured against her mouth, "Maybe both at the same time."

Laurel laughed and suddenly she felt free, simply happy with living and being with him, as if she'd suddenly stepped out of the shadows into a place of promise and light. Maybe it was the motorcycle ride that blew her worries away with the wind, or maybe she'd finally lost the battle with reason and was giving in to love.

Either way, everything seemed possible at this moment and she was going to enjoy it while it lasted.

"So this is your lady." Azure Rainbow, in her colorful embroidered jeans and peasant blouse, a sprig of holly in each of her braids, met Cort and Laurel at the door with a hug and a smile. "I can tell you've been making her happy."

Laurel felt herself blushing. Was it that obvious she and Cort were falling in love? Here she was meeting Maya's parents for the first time and in less than five minutes Azure had figured out their friendship had taken a turn toward something much deeper and lasting.

Cort, though, seemed unfazed. He just smiled and returned Azure's hug. "What, does she have a contented aura or something?"

"Oh, I don't need to read her aura to know that," Azure said. She cocked her head to one side looking closely at Laurel then suddenly beamed at Cort. "Maybe you'll have some news to share with us soon. Your aura is very pink," she told Laurel in a confidential tone. "I can tell you're happy together."

Laurel didn't know about her aura but she figured her face had to be flaming by now.

"There you are. We were starting to think you'd forgotten your way here." Shem Rainbow came up and threw an arm around Cort's shoulders, smiling broadly at Laurel. "You must be Cort's woman. Good to finally meet you." He waved in the direction of the eclectic group of people milling around the house. "Go get yourselves a brew. The party's just getting started."

"Can I find a place to hide?" Laurel muttered to Cort as they made their way farther into the living room.

Cort laughed at her expression. "You'll have to get used to them if you're going to hang with me. They've kind of adopted me since Sawyer and Maya got together. They've even gotten Rafe over here a couple of times and believe me, that's no small accomplishment. To Shem and Azure everyone's family."

That became clearer to Laurel the longer they were there. Although the Rainbows and most of their guests still seemed to be living in the sixties, Laurel found she liked them and the way they immediately accepted everyone as old friends, no matter who they were or how long they'd known them.

Relaxed and enjoying herself as she and Cort mixed with the Rainbows' guests and talked with Sawyer and Maya the only thing that marred her complete contentment right now was a nagging uneasiness about leaving for Montana tomorrow with Cort.

At the time, the impulse to invite him along had seemed like a great idea and it still did, as far as the him coming with her part. But she couldn't help but wonder how her family would respond to him. She'd told her parents she was bringing a friend and while they would never tell her no, their insistence that she and Cort stay at their house had held a note of reservation and questions Laurel put off answering until she was there.

Laurel also wondered how she was going to answer those inevitable questions about the exact nature of her and Cort's relationship. Her family wouldn't be satisfied with any *just a friend* definition. And they'd hardly believe it since being physically demonstrative with her seemed to come naturally to Cort, like breathing. She wouldn't have brought just a friend home to meet her family in the first place, either, and they knew it.

But she couldn't tell them what she wasn't sure about herself. This was going to be awkward, in more ways than one.

"Why the frown?" Cort came up to her after getting her a drink and put his arm around her shoulders. "Are you okay?"

"Better than okay," Laurel said, and she meant it. Still, something must have shown in her face because he eyed her skeptically and she sighed. "It's true. I'm just a little nervous about going back home tomorrow. How about you, have you had any second thoughts about coming with me?"

"Sure, and third and fourth ones, too—but not about going with you. About you having to face your family with me in tow and—" Cort paused, seeming to weigh his next words "—and having to face the memories."

Laurel shook her head. "You can't protect me from the memories or from whatever my family may say. Besides, it's because of you I'm going back at all."

"Yeah, sure it is," Cort said, his mouth twisted in an expression of out-and-out disbelief.

"It is." She touched her fingers to his face, willing him to believe her. "If I hadn't met you, no matter how much I've missed my family, I wouldn't have gone back there. But now, that part of my life that included Scott is over. I can go back now and deal with whatever happens." She meant what she was saying, but the shakiness in her stomach as she spoke underscored her reservations.

Cort didn't say anything in reply but there was something warm and intimate in his eyes as he gently kissed her before hugging her close to him.

A sweet, heady emotion flooded her heart and Laurel refused to let her doubts and fears ruin what her heart had discovered. They hadn't disappeared but tomorrow would be soon enough to wrestle them again. Only after tonight, with Cort on her side, she'd have a whole lot more ammunition.

Chapter Fifteen

"Hand me that ornament, Laurel, honey. No, not the blue one, the one Scott gave us your first Christmas together. You were still in high school, remember? It's always been one of my favorites."

Laurel inwardly winced. Her mother seemed determined not to make this easy. "Mom, please not that one." Even though her family had waited until after Christmas so they could all share the traditional evening of decorating together with Laurel, little of that indulgent spirit seemed present tonight.

"Oh, don't be silly," Helen Bachman chided her daughter. "It's only an ornament. You know, since you're home again, you should go and see him and Karen. You were all such friends. I hated to see the way you left things when you decided to leave."

Laurel just stopped herself from grinding her teeth in frustration. "Here— She pushed an ornament, not Scott's, into her mother's palm. "I don't have any reason to see Scott or Karen. That's not why I came back."

"He still asks about you, you know."

"I can't imagine why. And I'm surprised you see so much of him."

The reproachful look her mother turned on her wasn't enough to make Laurel regret her short reply.

"The Tanners are old friends," Helen said. "And you know Scott took over his dad's insurance business and we've been with Mike Tanner since before you were born. Besides, this is a small town. You can't have expected we'd never see him."

Or stop considering Scott a family friend, apparently. Not telling her parents all the reasons she and Scott had broken up had probably been a mistake on her part. It had given her family the idea it was she who'd wanted out of the marriage. Then she'd made things worse by leaving home for a place her mother, at least, considered as far removed from Montana as Laurel could have gotten.

It was probably unreasonable to feel hurt because her family was still friendly with her ex-husband and former friend. Her mom was right, Barker's Creek was small and her family had been friends and neighbors with the Tanners for more than twenty-five years. But a tiny part of her wanted her parents to side with her without question.

That was just one of the reasons Laurel was starting to believe coming back hadn't been a good idea after all. Her mother's comments about Scott weren't the first her family had made since they'd arrived that afternoon, insinuating a general disapproval of the changes in her life, particularly her relationship with Cort. The moment they'd stepped in the door, her mother had taken one look at her hair, and the low-riding jeans and soft brown sweater that lightly hugged her body, and cast an accusing glance at Cort, as if he were personally responsible for turning her daughter into someone unrecognizable.

Not that her parents and her two older brothers and their families hadn't welcomed Cort, but they'd been strangely reserved. As warm and loving a family as they were, they certainly weren't showing that side of themselves to Cort. And it was beginning to bother Laurel more than a little.

She offered him an apologetic look at her mother's latest attempt to underscore the fact he was the outsider here. Leaning against the edge of the mantle as he watched her help decorate her parents' Christmas tree, he smiled, silently shrugging it off.

He'd been doing that all day, shrugging it off, seemingly unaffected by anything her family said or did. The only difference she'd noticed was he acted a shade more possessive, touching her, holding her hand, putting his arm around her—staking his claim, she thought, reluctantly amused by the idea despite it adding to the building tensions in the house.

Laurel's elder brother lifted his two-year-old son and helped him hang an angel on the tree. "So, Cort, how did you and Laurel meet?" Jacob asked.

"Through a mutual friend," Cort said, winking at Laurel.

She smiled at his inside joke and went over to stand by him. "Cort's mentoring one of my students. Tommy's been going through some rough times and we've both been trying to help him."

"You a teacher, too?" her brother Matt asked.

"No, but I'm about to become a student again," Cort said as he bent to scoop up a large silver ball that Matt's three-year-old daughter had dropped. "Lucky for me I've got Laurel to help me remember those study habits I used to have because it's been a while." Slipping an arm around her waist, he lightly kissed her temple.

Matt frowned. "So you're not working now?"

With a glance at Laurel, Matt's wife, Jannie, quickly said, "Going back to school is work." She smiled as Cort handed her daughter the ornament. "I went back a couple of years ago to finish my degree in accounting so I could work at home and it was a lot tougher than I expected."

Jannie smiled reassuringly at Laurel. Of Laurel's two sisters-in-law, she and Jannie had bonded by far the most.

Jannie was always there to back Laurel up when Laurel had to defend herself to her two overprotective older brothers.

Laurel returned a thankful smile to Jannie for her attempt to diffuse the situation, but she could tell from the look in Matt's eye, he wasn't going to let this pass.

"It's hard to feed a family on a student's salary," Matt said.

Jacob nodded and added, "What kind of work do you do?"

Tired of her brothers' interrogation, Laurel started to intervene on Cort's behalf. He'd gone through all this for months at home; he didn't need her family dredging it all up again.

But Cort's hand tightened a fraction against her waist and he smiled a little as he said calmly, "I used to be a cop. But I got busted up on the job and had to give it up. I'm going back to law school next fall, but I'm not too worried about supporting a family. I inherited a share of my family's business and between that and the disability pension, I can pay the bills until I finish school."

"You boys can stop the grilling session any time now," Harold Bachman spoke up from the depths of his easy chair. He cast a rueful smile at Cort. "My boys tend to forget Laurie is grown up and doesn't need them looking out for her anymore."

"I understand, I've got a couple of older brothers myself."

Harold nodded. "Sounds like you've been through a rough time, too. But you've got a plan for moving forward. That should be good enough for anyone." He looked meaningfully at his sons.

Laurel doubted it would be, at least where her brothers were concerned, but she hoped they'd at least appreciate Cort's frankness. It didn't surprise her; his sincerity was one of the things that made him so attractive to her. But she'd never heard him talk so openly about his inheritance, although she'd guessed from things he and his grandparents had said that both Cort and Sawyer had inherited their mother's share of the Morente money, as well as her portion of the restaurant business. He'd never acted like he cared much about it one way or the other. Laurel suspected he'd brought it up now, not to boast about his financial position, but to make it clear to her brothers he was perfectly capable of supporting a family.

Before she could stop herself she thought, *our family?*

When, a few minutes later, the oldest of Jacob's three children started a rowdy game of hide-and-seek with the little ones, Laurel seized the moment to take Cort into the kitchen where they could catch a minute alone. She poured them both a glass of eggnog and began to apologize for the way her family was treating him. "I didn't expect it to be like this. I'm so sorry."

Cort took the glass from her hand and set his on the counter beside it then took her gently by the shoulders. "Why? They're just worried about you."

"I expected them to be more understanding, more accepting. They're good people, but you're not seeing that."

"Of course I am. I can see they love you and don't want you to get hurt again. I don't blame them for that."

"I know," Laurel said. She put her arms around him, resting her head against his heart, and his hands slid down her back, gathering her close. "But I don't want you to get hurt, either."

"I'm a big boy. I can take care of myself."

She didn't argue with him but thought that sometimes, he needed someone to take care of him. He just wasn't very good at admitting it.

He didn't need to, though. She knew. *I'll be there for you,* she silently vowed, *just like you're there for me.*

"I wish you wouldn't go." Laurel ran her hands over the front of Cort's jacket, smoothing the dark leather.

Despite Laurel's parents' invitation, after a long afternoon and evening of questions, veiled comments, disapproving looks and a general sense that he wasn't the most popular guy in the room, Cort had decided to stay at a nearby mountain lodge. Laurel's mother in particular had looked embarrassed when he made the excuse of not wanting to impose on them and Laurel was upset. She'd made every kind of protest she could think of to keep him here but he stuck to his guns. He was doing it for her. He figured if she were going to find any peace during her visit here, it would be easier if he weren't staying in the same house.

Capturing her hands, he kissed her palm. "I'm not going far. If you need me, call."

"I need you to save me from my family," she said with a slight grimace.

Cort laughed. "I don't think you need me for that."

"I know why you're doing this. And it's not necessary."

"Yes, it is."

"Cort—"

"Look, you need some time alone with them. I don't want to come between you and your family any more than I already have."

"I hate this," Laurel said fiercely. "I hate that they've made me feel like I have to choose sides."

"You don't. I'd never ask you to do that."

"I know you wouldn't. But I feel like I do. We've been here less than a day and I'm already ready to go home."

"Home?" Her easy use of the word in referring to Luna Hermosa sent a spike of happiness through him. "I thought this was home."

"It used to be." She sighed. "I'm not so sure anymore. When I first came to New Mexico I didn't think I'd ever feel I belonged. I thought the only place I fit in was here. Now, so much has changed, here's where I feel like a stranger."

He stopped himself from asking about those changes, though part of him hoped at least some of them belonged to him. "Maybe that's good. Well, not the part about feeling like a stranger," he amended when she raised a brow. "But good in that you've found some place where you can have a new beginning and leave behind the bad memories." He wove his fingers into the rumpled silk of her hair, loving the feel and how it tousled even more. "Maybe it's time to make some new memories, better ones."

"Maybe," she agreed softly. Rising up on her tiptoes, she kissed him, a tender caress that spoke of gratitude and understanding more than passion. "Thank you for trying to make things easier for me. For staying and always being on my side. You don't know how much I appreciate it. Especially since I'm pretty sure any other man with sense would have been running as far and fast as possible in the other direction by now."

"Who says I've got any sense?" Cort murmured before gathering her into his arms and covering her mouth with his, leaving no room for doubt that this time had nothing to do with gratitude and understanding and everything to do with wanting her. He resisted the strong urge to invite her back to his room. A secluded mountain lodge, the room lit with only firelight, and a big bed— He ruthlessly cut off the fantasy before his body clued Laurel in on the direction of his thoughts and concentrated on her in his arms, kissing him back with an enthusiasm that threatened to bust him anyway.

"Laurie, I found— Oh, I didn't know you were still here, Cort."

Cort let go of Laurel as she twisted to face her mother, hovering uncertainly behind them, her cheeks stained red.

"I was just leaving." He lightly kissed Laurel then pulled on his gloves and fished in his pocket for the keys to the rented SUV.

"It's still a date for breakfast, right?" Laurel asked.

"I'll be here at seven-thirty," he promised. Leaning in close, he whispered in her ear, "I'll be thinking of ways you can thank me properly for being such a nice guy."

With a quick good-night to her and Helen, he strode out into the chill of the night, smiling at the remembered look in Laurel's eyes that suggested she might take him up on that offer.

After Cort had gone, Laurel resigned herself to her mother taking the opportunity to comment again on Cort, or their relationship.

Instead, Helen said, "I've put you in your old room. Would you like a cup of tea before bed?"

"Sure," Laurel accepted. She followed her mom into the kitchen, sitting down at the small wooden table, watching as Helen went through the small, comforting motions of making tea.

"This—relationship you have with Cort, it seems to have happened very fast," Helen began, once they had steaming cups of gingerbread-scented tea in front of them.

Laurel kept her reply noncommittal. "Not really."

"I only thought, after what happened with Scott and you're leaving the way you did… Are you sure you're ready to get involved with someone else?"

"Mom, I didn't leave Scott. It was the other way around." She twisted her hands in her lap, wishing Cort were here, maybe not in the room, but at least in the house, so she could have the illusion of him being at her side, encouraging and supporting her to say the hardest things she should have said two years ago.

"But I thought—" Helen began.

"I know what you thought. You thought after I lost my baby that I should have tried harder to keep my marriage together and work on starting a family with Scott. But I couldn't." The tears started but Laurel lifted her head and looked directly at her mother. "After my miscarriage, I found out I couldn't have any more children. Scott wanted a family, a *real* family, as he put it. I couldn't give that to him, Karen could. And she made sure he knew it. He left me, Mom. He said I wasn't very good at being a woman. Maybe that's the way he felt from the start or maybe he didn't want a broken wife. I don't know. That's why I left. I couldn't see him and Karen together, especially after she got pregnant. It hurt too much."

"Oh, Laurie…"

Laurel buried her face in her hands, unable to stop the deep sobs welling up inside her. Helen moved close and put her arms around her, holding her close and gently rocking her, murmuring words of comfort that were more sound and feeling than actual meaning.

The outpouring of old grief and pain emptied her, leaving Laurel oddly calm and almost peaceful. There would always be a place in her heart for the child she'd lost; a bittersweet hurt that would never leave her. But instead of living inside the emptiness as she had for so long, she wanted to fill it with hope, and warmth and love.

"Why didn't you tell us?" Helen asked as Laurel rubbed her hands over her face, pushing away the tears.

"I couldn't tell anyone, especially after Scott seemed so— repelled by the idea I couldn't give him children. I didn't know until later, but he told Karen. All the time I thought she was supporting me, being my friend, she was using me to get closer to Scott."

Helen shook her head in disbelief. "I'm so sorry. I wish you had told us. Maybe things would have been different." She hesitated, then asked, "Have you told Cort?"

"That I can't have children? No. I don't know if I can."

"Laurie, if you care about him as much as I think you do, you have to tell him."

Laurel couldn't look at her mother. "I'm afraid," she confessed, so quietly she wasn't sure her mother had heard.

"He loves you." Laurel's head snapped up and Helen smiled. "I could see it almost from the start. I'm just not sure how you feel about him."

"I don't think he—I mean, he's never…" The idea of Cort loving her was like a dream, fragile and wondrous, but something not to be too desired or clutched too tightly because it could easily vanish the moment she allowed herself to believe it. "I care about him." *I love him. It feels like I always have.* "Too much, maybe." She drew a shaky breath. "He wants everything I thought I could have, once. He wants a family and I can't give him that."

"Just because you can't get pregnant, doesn't mean you can't have a family," Helen said gently.

"Tell that to Scott," Laurel said, a touch of the old bitterness resurfacing. "He said he loved me but that all changed when he found out I couldn't give him children. I can't go through that again. I can't love someone and then have him leave me because I'm not enough of a woman. Because I'm broken."

"You're not broken. And Cort isn't Scott. If you want a future with him, you have to give him a chance to understand."

No, Cort wasn't Scott, he was much more, and she wanted to believe that he would understand and accept her as she was. But telling him might destroy everything that had started to grow between them and she wanted to hold on to what they had for as long as she could.

Because although part of her desperately wanted to believe in the impossible, the part of her that was afraid didn't trust in dreams anymore.

Laurel tried the next morning to act as if nothing had changed but she knew Cort immediately sensed the difference in her. Her mother's certainty he loved her had her watching him when she thought he wasn't looking, weighing every word and gesture for evidence it was true. She didn't know if she wanted it to be or not and that unsettled her even more.

Going into town for breakfast didn't help because she kept running into people she knew and behind their small talk she could almost hear the questions they wanted to ask, about her leaving, the changes in her, and most of all, the tall, dark and handsome stranger she'd brought home with her.

They'd nearly finished breakfast when Cort, after studying her for a moment, asked, "Did something happen last night after I left?"

"Why would you say that?" Laurel hedged.

"Because your mother didn't glare at me once this morning, and you keep looking at me like you're not sure you remember who I am but you're too polite to say so."

"Believe me, there's nothing forgettable about you." She reached across the table of the booth they were sitting in and touched his hand. "I'm sorry, I'm just feeling a little weird yet. My mom and I did talk last night. I told her some things

I should have said a long time ago, about Scott and why he left me. She understands a little better now." She lowered her eyes, guilt pricking at her for the omissions she'd made. It wasn't the whole truth but it was the best she could do for now. "I guess she's decided you're not so bad after all," she added, smiling to tease him a little.

"How about you?" Laurel looked up to the warmth in his eyes and his suggestive half smile. He took her hand in his, slowly tracing patterns on her skin with his thumb. "Have you decided I'm not so bad after all?"

"A long time ago," she admitted.

"So what would it take for me to go from not so bad to incredibly good?"

"I don't know." She pretended to think it over. "Any suggestions? Forget I said that," she added hastily when the glint in his eyes told her he had any number of illicit ideas.

"Oh, you aren't getting off that easily," Cort said. Sliding out from his side of the booth, he moved to her side, nudging her over and putting his arm around her as he sat down beside her. He lightly nuzzled her ear. "Did you miss me last night?"

Laurel's breath caught. "You have to ask? Cort—um…" Brushing her hair aside, he'd kissed the side of her neck, his tongue flicking against a particularly sensitive spot. She shivered, very glad they'd chosen a relatively secluded corner and at the same time feeling exposed to every eye in the room. "This isn't exactly the place—"

"How about this one?" he murmured, his mouth slipping a little lower.

"Cort!"

He leaned back a few inches, smiling wickedly. "Sorry," he said, looking anything but. "I missed you, too. Every minute. Right now…" His voice lowered to a sensual drawl. *"En este momento, todo lo qué puedo pensar alvededor le està besando."*

"My Spanish sucks. But I'm guessing whatever you said is something you shouldn't be doing in a crowded restaurant."

She didn't tell him that it didn't matter what he'd said, if he kept looking and touching her like that, she'd soon be ready to agree to anything he suggested, crowded restaurant or not.

"I said I'd like to kiss you senseless. And I'm available for lessons. Spanish lessons," he said when she lightly pushed his ribs. "What'd you think I meant?"

"If you think I'm giving you any more ammunition to torment me, think again."

"Aw, come on. I know you're the teacher, but I'll bet I could teach you some useful Spanish. How about something simple to start with like, *'Yo le quiero, Cort.'*"

Laurel knew enough to translate that one. *I want you, Cort. And I do.*

Cort shifted a fraction closer. "Or, *'Yo le necesito.'*"

I need you. Yes, more than you know.

"And one of my favorites, *'Quiero que usted muestreme un uso más creador para la esposas.'*"

His miserable attempt at an innocent expression had her eyeing him suspiciously. "Whatever you said, I'm pretty sure the answer is no."

"Damn, and I was on a roll. Oh, well, it's probably for the best," he said just as two of the ladies from her mom's quilting group passed by, glancing their way and smiling at Laurel in recognition, "Using handcuffs like that is illegal in some places."

"Cort!" Heat flooded her face and Cort laughed. "You're evil," she muttered. "Great, now they're watching us. I'll be the gossip for a week."

"Only a week?" Pulling her closer, he kissed her. Not a chaste caress but a lover's kiss, long, intimate and hot enough to raise the temperature around them by several degrees. About the time Laurel was at the point of not caring where they were and who was watching, he eased away and leaning back with a satisfied grin, winked at the quilting-group ladies. They blushed furiously and stared fixedly at their menus. "That should be good for at least a month."

Chapter Sixteen

"Okay, next time, we do the lodge together."

"Only if you keep your promise not to bring up handcuffs in public places again."

"We definitely go backpacking."

"And you give me five minutes head start in any future snowball fights."

Cort leaned around to look at her. "No way. It's not my fault you lost and had to pay up."

"No, but it was your fault you insisted on collecting in the middle of a public park at high noon with half the town passing by," Laurel countered. Her attempt at making it a rebuke fell flat when, with a warm flush of pleasure, she recalled that particular penalty for losing to him. The trip back home had been memorable in more ways than one.

They'd gotten back to Luna Hermosa late yesterday evening and since she had to be at school this morning, Cort had dropped her at home with the promise they'd catch up with each other and Tommy today. Cort had been waiting for her when she got home from classes, and now they sat together on her couch, him sprawled in the corner and her curled up against his chest, his arms around her. Unfortunately, neither of them had been able to connect with Tommy yet. She hadn't seen Tommy at school today and Laurel wondered if he'd come down with some bug over the holidays.

"Maybe you should try calling Joseph again," she murmured, tempted to relax and let herself wallow in the feeling of having Cort close, but unable to shake her worry over Tommy.

"I'll give it another shot, but I'm sure if something was wrong he would have called one of us." Cort reached for his cell phone he'd tossed on her end table at the same moment it started buzzing. They exchanged a glance as he flipped it open. "Then again… Hi, Carlos," he said into the phone. Suddenly tense, Cort looked quickly at Laurel, all lightheartedness gone. *"Qué se está encendiendo? Retrasaron y explican."*

To her annoyance, Laurel couldn't follow most of what he was saying, but she caught the name and guessed Cort was talking to Carlos Biega and that it had to do with Tommy, but she had no idea why Carlos, instead of Joseph would be calling him. She started to get a bad feeling that Cort's grim expression did nothing to relieve.

"No, Laurel es conmigo. Yo la diré." Laurel is with me. I'll tell her. Tell me what? Laurel wanted to shout. It had to be about Tommy, she thought, the bad feeling intensifying.

"Da las gracias para permitirme saber," Cort was saying. *"Diga Joseph que estaré en toca tan pronto como sé algo."*

He snapped his cell phone shut and shifted to get to his feet. "We have to go. Tommy ran away today."

"What? When?"

"Joseph dropped him and David off at school, but apparently Tommy ditched his last afternoon class. Alex called Joseph and Joseph went to the police station to get them searching. He asked Carlos to let me know." He was already pulling on his jacket. "Sorry, I wasn't trying to leave you out of the conversation. Carlos was in a hurry."

"It's not you I'm mad at, it's Alex. Why didn't he tell me Tommy had run off? He knew I was in class today."

"No idea. Maybe he couldn't, for some reason."

"He could have called you, at least. Someone should have called you."

"Joseph did the right thing. He went to the police first."

She could see in his eyes that it was times like this that he hated the most not being a part of that life anymore. She understood his frustration that, as an outsider now, he might not be able to do as much to help, to have an impact in situations like these. But there wasn't anything she could do, except stand by him and offer her support and caring.

"I need to get a message to Jorge and ask him to take the girls' team today," she said, diverting her thoughts on what might, what could happen to Tommy to something practical as she dug out her cell phone to call Jorge. She looked at Cort before she punched Send. "I'm going with you to look for Tommy."

Cort looked at her with approval. "Damned right you are."

"Any other ideas where Tommy might have gone?" They were sitting in the parking lot of the city police station, both as clueless about Tommy's whereabouts as the police had been. Since they considered Tommy a runaway, Cort knew the police wouldn't be mounting an active search for him until he'd been gone longer than a few hours, although they'd promised him and Laurel they'd be keeping an eye out for the boy.

That hadn't been good enough for him and he knew it definitely wasn't good enough for Laurel. She sat stiffly in her seat, her eyes fixed on the dashboard as if she were trying to will Tommy to appear.

"I've been thinking about that. But I just don't know. There is a girl in my class, though, that Tommy talks to more than anyone else, Anna Tamar. Maybe she would have an idea where Tommy might hide. I'm not sure where to find Anna, though."

"I am. Her family owns the tack shop a few blocks from here. It's Josh's second home." He started the SUV but before he stuck it in gear, he took Laurel's hand in his. "We'll find him, I promise."

A few minutes later, Cort flagged Eliana Tamar over from where she was bagging a pair of boots for a customer.

"Cort," she said, reaching up to hug him. "It's been forever since you've come by."

Cort noticed Laurel give him a sideways look as he returned Eliana's gesture and despite the situation, he almost smiled. He'd always liked Eliana although he'd never thought of her as more than a friend. Laurel didn't know that, though, and he noticed her greeting to Eliana when he introduced her was a little stiff.

"We need to talk to Anna," Cort told Eliana. He explained briefly the situation with Tommy and Eliana immediately went to the back room to get her younger sister.

Eliana came back almost immediately with Anna hanging behind until the little girl spotted Laurel. "Mrs. Tanner!" Anna cried, hurrying toward Laurel. "This is my store."

"Hi, Anna." Laurel reached down and hugged her. "It's a great tack shop. Looks like you have everything here. I'm going to have to buy some new riding boots next time I come in."

Laurel chatted with Anna a couple of minutes more about the store and then school. Cort stood by, admiring Laurel's gift for making the shy child feel comfortable and helping her to open up.

"Anna," Eliana finally broke in, "Mrs. Tanner and Cort are here because they have some questions to ask you about your friend Tommy."

"Tommy?" Anna's eyes went wide. "Is he okay? What happened?"

"I'm sure he's fine," Cort said, hoping it was true. "But Tommy's run away from Mr. Charez's house and we thought you might be able to help us find him."

Anna stood perfectly still, staring at Cort. "He ran away?" she whispered finally.

Cort went down on one knee, making himself eye level

with the girl. "Anna, we need your help. Do you have any idea where Tommy might be?"

Anna blinked, twisted her thin fingers together. "Tommy's not in trouble," Cort said gently. "We just need to find him."

"Where do you think he might have gone, Anna?" Eliana asked. "You told me you and he talk sometimes. Has he ever told you about a favorite place, somewhere he likes to go to be by himself?"

"Well, um, he might hide way up at the top of that big old cottonwood tree at the park," Anna said. "He can climb higher than anyone else."

"Okay, anyplace else?" Cort urged.

Anna looked away, dark brows furrowed in concentration. "Maybe the plaza downtown. There's a hole in the lattice of the gazebo where we can climb under and hide—" She broke off and glanced up nervously to her sister. "I mean, I heard that you could do that."

"Don't worry, Anna." He leaned a little closer to the girl, confiding in a conspiratorial whisper, "When we were kids, Eliana used to know all the best hiding places at the park. She used to drive us crazy because she'd disappear and we could never find her."

"Eliana did that?" Anna looked doubtfully at her sister then back at Cort. "That must've been a really long time ago."

Cort smiled, lightly squeezing her shoulder before he got to his feet. "Thanks for your help, Anna."

"If we hear anything about Tommy, I'll give you a call," Eliana said as she walked with Cort and Laurel to the door. She frowned as she looked out into the deepening afternoon shadows. "I hope you find him soon."

"We will," Cort said, with more confidence than he felt right now.

Two hours later, Laurel was at her wits' end. "I don't know what else to do, where else to look."

Cort darted his flashlight through the hole in the lattice

under the gazebo one more time. They'd already been here once earlier but had decided to come back again, just in case. "From the looks of the soda cans and candy wrappers under here, kids definitely use this place for a hideout," he said, straightening and brushing at his jeans. "But if Tommy was here, he's gone now."

They'd searched everywhere Anna had suggested, as well as places Laurel and Cort thought of. But Tommy was nowhere to be found. "It's nearly dark." Laurel gazed upward, suddenly hating the blackening sky over the city park. "What if—"

"Don't." Cort pulled her into his arms. "Don't go there."

"I know, but I can't help it," Laurel said. She held to him, leaning on his strength as worry and frustration began to gain the upper hand in her emotions.

"He can't just have disappeared. Where is he?"

"I wish I knew."

He hesitated, and Laurel looked up at him, sensing he was weighing whether to say more.

"What is it?" she asked. "You've thought of something."

"Not really," Cort hedged. A demand he tell her trembled on the tip of Laurel's tongue but she bit it back when he shook his head, letting her go. "No, not really. It's just that it'll be much harder to search for him after dark. I have a couple of good flashlights, but Sawyer has access to much better equipment at the fire station."

"Could Sawyer get some volunteers together to launch a search?"

"I'm sure he would as long as he's not on duty." He pulled out his cell phone and dialed.

Laurel waited, breath held. Sawyer and maybe some off-duty firefighters, too, would make a huge difference in the area they could cover tonight.

"Hey, I need help with something," Cort said when Sawyer answered. "Are you working tonight?" He explained the situation then waited. "Great. Thanks. I'll meet you at the station in half an hour."

"He's going to help? And others, too?"

Cort nodded and slid a finger under her chin, gently tipping her face to his. "There's nothing else you can do right now. Let me take you home. I promise as soon as I know anything I'll call."

"But I want to go, too. I can search." The thought of being stuck at home, feeling useless and worried about both Tommy and Cort would be enough to drive her mad.

"I know that, but Sawyer had a good point. It's dark and cold, and Tommy's going to be scared. He trusts you enough that he might just come looking for you."

"Maybe. But he trusts you, too, and he has no clue where I live. Wouldn't it be more likely he'd go to your apartment?"

Cort shoved his hands through his hair. "I don't know, maybe. You want to wait there instead?"

"I don't want to wait anywhere," Laurel said. "But if you think there's a chance he'll turn up, then one of us should be there."

Reluctantly, she followed him to his vehicle. At his apartment, Cort helped her out of the car and walked her upstairs. They'd reached the top landing and Cort was fishing for his keys, when the door to the apartment opposite his apartment opened and Cort's elderly neighbor stepped out.

"I've got someone here's who's been waiting for you," the man said.

The door eased open a few inches wider and there, looking both defiant and afraid, stood Tommy.

Cort and Laurel both stood there staring at the boy for ten long seconds before Cort moved. Thanking his neighbor for sheltering Tommy for a few hours, Cort waited until the three of them were inside his apartment and he'd called Sawyer to tell him the search was over and Joseph to let him know Tommy was with him before putting himself in front of Tommy, blocking any retreat.

"What are you doing here?" he snapped. He heard the taut,

angry tone of his voice but couldn't stop as all the hours of fear and worry about Tommy came back to haunt him. "And what the hell were you thinking running away from Mr. Charez? You've had the whole town out looking for you."

Laurel put a hand on his arm. "Cort." She looked at Tommy, who was staring wide-eyed at Cort. "We've been so worried about you. We've been looking for you for hours." As if unable to contain herself anymore, Laurel reached out and hugged the boy to her.

Tommy clung to Laurel for a few unguarded moments, Cort's heart went to his throat, seeing how much Tommy needed and cared for her. Laurel was right. They did belong together, even if it was impossible right now. But somehow, he had to make that happen.

"Are you sure you're okay?" Laurel said, easing back to look at the boy. "You had us so worried."

"I'm okay." Tommy glanced at Cort, then quickly dropped his eyes, obviously expecting Cort to start chewing him out again.

Cort took a deep breath, clamping down on his impulse to do just that. "I'm sorry I got angry with you, Tommy," he said, "but you scared me when you disappeared like that. Why did you run away from Mr. Charez?"

"I don't wanna be there," Tommy muttered, scuffing his foot on the rug.

"Mr. Charez is very nice and you seem happy there," Laurel offered tentatively. "Did something happen that made you want to leave?"

Tommy shrugged his thin shoulders. "No, I told you, I just don't wanna be there."

"Tommy, I thought we had a deal that if I got you into Mr. Charez's house, you'd stay put," Cort said.

Biting at his lower lip, Tommy stared hard at Cort and then suddenly blurted out, "You guys left me. You went away. You said you weren't going to do that, ever."

"Tommy…" The boy's accusation, colored with hurt at

what he considered their betrayal of his trust, knocked out Cort's frustration over Tommy's running again. He put his hands on the boy's shoulders, looking steadily at Tommy. "You're right, we did go away. I'm sorry we couldn't take you along this time but we didn't leave you. We were only gone a couple of days and we told you we were coming back. I know it's hard, but you're gonna have to trust us. We're always going to come back, I promise you."

"Why can't I stay here, with you?" Tommy turned to Laurel. "You could stay here, too, and then we'd always be together."

Laurel looked stunned, torn, wanting, Cort knew, to say yes but knowing it wasn't an option right now. Cort quickly rescued her by dropping down on one knee in front of Tommy, making sure he had the boy's attention. "I wish things were different and maybe one day they can be. But this is the way it has to be for now."

"Why? Don't you want me?"

Cort winced at the anguished cry. A memory, vivid and painful, flashed into his head.

"Mama, why are we leaving?"

"I've already told you." His mother didn't look up from *stuffing clothes into the suitcases she had spread all over the bedroom. "We can't live here any longer."*

"But why? Doesn't Daddy want us anymore?"

She had looked at him then, and the hard, fierce light in her eyes frightened him. "No, he doesn't. He doesn't want us at all."

He never, never wanted Tommy to feel that way about him. Just the idea he could do something, even inadvertently, to inflict that same pain on Tommy sickened him. "I want you to stay. I want us to be together always, too. I just can't make that happen right now. But you need to believe that I'm not going to give up until I do."

Tommy's lower lip quivered and Cort pulled him into a hug. Tommy hugged him back, hard. When they let go, Laurel was watching them with tears in her eyes and Cort found his voice wasn't quite steady. "We need to get you warmed up and fed and back to Mr. Charez's house."

Tommy looked like he was about to protest, but then shifted his shoulders in what Cort accepted as the best agreement he was going to get out of the boy right now. He got to his feet. "And I want you to give me your word you'll stay there this time until we can work something else out because I trust you'll keep a promise."

Tommy looked at Laurel and she nodded. "Cort is right. It's best for now. But it won't be forever, I promise."

"So, do I have your word you'll stay with Mr. Charez?" Cort asked again.

Frowning, Tommy kicked at the rug, then muttered, "Yeah, okay. I promise." He raised his head to look at Cort. "Do I have to leave now?"

"Not until you've had some dinner," Laurel answered before Cort could. With a quick swipe of her eyes, she looked at Cort. "Is there anything in the kitchen that doesn't count as cat food?"

"Microwave burritos?" he offered.

Tommy perked up. "I love those things."

"Hey, me, too."

Laurel shook her head at them. "As Tommy would say, you guys are gross."

She was smiling though as they all crowded into Cort's excuse for a kitchen and raided the freezer. When, nearly an hour later, Tommy was tackling a plate of pastries that Regina had left earlier in the week, and Laurel was sipping a cup of her candy bar coffee, Cort found himself watching them, suddenly aware of a feeling he recognized as a deep contentment.

This was where they belonged, together. They might have come from different places and all have their ghosts of the past to deal with, and maybe it wasn't the traditional way to start a family, but it felt right. Cort wanted the feeling to last. It scared him how much he wanted it.

Laurel caught his eye and smiled, a gesture from the heart that told him she felt it, too.

And Cort knew then that very soon, he had to make good on that promise of forever.

The next day, Cort took Laurel out to the Charez ranch to spend time with Tommy. Laurel brought Tommy some of the schoolwork he'd missed, sat and talked to him a while about the story he was working on for her class while Cort, giving them some quiet time together, spent some time talking alone with Joseph and Aria about Tommy's situation.

When Laurel had finished helping Tommy, they joined the others in the Charez's living room.

"Tommy's just written a wonderful story about an orphaned boy who won perfect parents in a lottery," she said, avoiding Cort's eyes.

"I made them like Mrs. Tanner and you, Cort. The dad even has a bad shoulder, but he can shoot baskets with his other arm just like you."

Cort patted a spot next to him on the couch, motioning Tommy to come sit next to him. "I feel special knowing you would make up a character that reminds you of me."

Laurel followed Tommy and sat down on the other side of him. "Tommy's really got a talent for describing his characters."

"Your story is what we were just discussing," Joseph said, smiling at Tommy. "Parents, well, a parent, that is."

Tommy looked confused.

"Have you been talking about a permanent home for Tommy?" Laurel made herself ask, not sure where this was going, but suddenly afraid it would mean Tommy finding a family that didn't include her. She hated the thought even though she knew it was selfish of her. If Tommy had the chance of a real family, she should be ready to do whatever it took to make sure he got it.

But she wasn't ready for what came next.

"A permanent home with me," Cort said. Tommy stared at

him and he smiled. "You've never had a dad and I've never had a son. I thought we might be able to help each other out. I'd like to adopt you."

Tommy's eyes widened, hope warring with caution on his face. "Do you mean it? You'd really be my dad?"

"If you want me to be."

"Yeah, of course I do!"

Laurel felt as if Cort had struck her. "You...but—"

She didn't know how to finish the thought. Part of her was angry Cort had come up with the idea of adopting Tommy without talking to her about it first, especially since he knew how much she loved Tommy. She wanted to insist that Tommy needed a mother, too, but she'd only appear to be angling for a commitment from Cort that he might not want to make and she couldn't accept even if he did.

Aria smiled understandingly at her. "You're concerned a single guy can't give Tommy everything he needs, right?"

"I can't change the fact I'm single right now." Cort looked pointedly at Laurel and she flushed. "But I love Tommy and that's the most important part. I can learn the rest soon enough," he added, a touch defensively.

Laurel put a hand to her face, her head spinning. Cort, she knew, sincerely wanted to be Tommy's father and he'd make a terrific dad. But she felt so left out, as though suddenly, instead of playing a mother's role to Tommy as she'd been doing, at least in her heart, she was about to be demoted to something akin to a distant aunt.

Unless...

"You guys should get married," Tommy spoke up, echoing what had been in her thoughts, but what she could never say. He looked hopefully between Cort and Laurel. "Then we could be a real family."

"Tommy, that's not— I mean, it's not that simple." Floundering, Laurel turned to Cort for help but he just looked back, his expression unreadable. "Cort and I—we're friends. We haven't talked about anything like that."

"So what? You're always hanging around each other. And, I've seen you kiss. That means you must like him."

"That's a big decision and it's up to Cort and Mrs. Tanner, Tommy," Joseph gently interjected. "They might not be ready to get married."

"Dad's right," Aria said. "Getting married is a really big deal. And it's a private thing between two grownups to make that decision."

"It doesn't mean it'll never happen, though," Cort added.

He reached behind Tommy to touch her shoulder but Laurel pulled away. Marriage wasn't something she wanted to talk about, especially not in front of the Charezes. The confused hurt that crossed Cort's face upset her but she couldn't let him close right now.

Aria was watching them closely and Laurel knew she caught her subtle gesture of rejection. She frowned a little then put on deliberate smile. "You know, I think you've had enough adult talk for one night, Tommy. Why don't you get washed up for dinner and then you and David can help me set the table?"

"I'll need to check on how things are going in the kitchen," Joseph added. He turned to where Cort and Laurel sat awkwardly avoiding each other. "You're welcome to stay for dinner."

Laurel practically jumped to her feet. "I can't," she said more abruptly than she'd intended. "I have papers to grade tonight."

"Thanks anyhow Joseph, can we have a rain check?" Cort said without looking at her.

"You both always have a standing invitation."

After saying their goodbyes to the Charezes, Laurel and Cort walked with Tommy to the front door. He wormed his way in between them, putting his arms around them both to bring them all closer together in a rare showing of open affection.

"If you got married, we could be like this all the time," he said. He hugged them both quickly then broke away, looking embarrassed. "I mean, we could, you know, be a family." He thought about it a moment then added, "You just can't do any of that kissing and hugging stuff in front of my friends."

Laurel smiled, her heart full of love for the boy and aching with worry over Cort. "I promise. But do you think I might get a kiss now?"

Tommy scrunched up his nose, considering. "I guess." He glanced over his shoulder to make sure Aria and Joseph had gone. "As long as nobody but Cort sees. And you can't tell anybody, either," he warned Cort.

Cort put his hand over his heart in a show of making a serious vow. "Never. You've got my word as a fellow guy."

Bending to him, Laurel brushed a light kiss over Tommy's cheek. Though the touch was akin to a mother's caress and echoed all her longing to be a mom to Tommy, she had the oddest sensation at the same time that she was losing him.

Chapter Seventeen

On the drive back to Laurel's *casita* Cort wanted to say so much. He'd been glad the door to discussing marriage with Laurel had been opened at the Charezes. It wasn't ideal the way it came up in front of everyone, but he was happy it had. To him, Tommy's point was a good one. Once the prospect of adoption was out in the open, marriage, maybe not right away, but by the time the adoption went through, seemed a natural progression in every way.

Or so he reasoned. Until he saw how unhappy the idea made Laurel. When the subject came up, she'd pulled away from him, refusing to look at him, as though even his touch would burn her. Then and there his hopes sank.

Now, they were almost to her place and he was still struggling to understand her reaction.

She sat in distant thought, right next to him yet miles away, until at last he couldn't stand it any longer. "What's the silent treatment about?" he asked, almost snapping at her. "Is the idea of us getting married that repulsive to you?"

Laurel crossed her arms over her chest and kept gazing straight ahead. "No, it's not repulsive to me," she answered coolly, "it's just that adopting Tommy and getting married so that he can have parents isn't the right reason to get married."

"Is that what you think? Tommy's only one part of the picture. I see a much larger canvas, a family, us together with Tommy and with our own children. Don't you know that by now?"

She still refused to look at him. "I know you want to adopt Tommy and it would be easier if you were married. And Tommy wants a mother and a father, you and me. We get married and you both get what you want."

"But it's not what you want," Cort said flatly.

"It seems like the right thing to do for Tommy and it's the practical thing to do rather than juggling him between two homes," she went on as if he hadn't spoken. "But I married Scott because we were best friends, high-school sweethearts and everyone said we were perfect for each other. Obviously, we weren't. We were just doing what was expected, what seemed reasonable. I'm not going to do that again. Even for Tommy. It wouldn't be best for him in the long run if we ended up separating."

"And adopting Tommy's the only reason you think I'd have for wanting to marry you? I thought we had something more than that. That we were working toward building something permanent. Apparently I was wrong and you've got other ideas."

For the first time since they'd left the Charez house, her expression softened and she looked stricken. "It's not like that."

"No? Then how is it?"

"It's…" She stopped, glanced at him and then sharply turned aside to stare out the window again.

Cort grew more frustrated, and more hurt by her refusal to even talk to him, by the minute and by the time he pulled into her drive, he was almost glad for the evening to come to an end.

Evidently she was, too, because she had her hand on the door handle before the Jeep even came to a full stop. "I'd invite you in but I really have to finish some schoolwork before tomorrow."

"Yeah, sure." He wanted to stop her, try and fix what had broken between them, but his pride stubbornly refused to allow him to reach out, especially when he was pretty sure at this point, she'd slap him back down. "I guess we don't have anything else to talk about tonight."

Laurel looked back at him and for a moment, he thought she would relent, say something. Instead, her mouth tightened as if she were determined to hold the words back and she only shook her head and then left him watching her and wondering how everything had gone wrong.

Too wound up to go home and have a staring contest with his cats, Cort decided to go to his grandparents' restaurant and have a drink. He walked into the bar and was surprised to find Sawyer there alone and nursing a beer.

"It's been a long time since I saw you hanging out at a bar alone," he said, putting a hand on Sawyer's shoulder in greeting. "What's the matter, did you and Maya have a fight because you insulted another one of her vegetarian delights?"

Sawyer motioned Cort to the stool next to him. "No, nothing like that. I don't really even want to be here. But Josh asked me to."

"Josh? What's up with him?" A bartender Cort hadn't met took his drink order. "Is something wrong with the old man?"

"Nothing more than usual. This is so ridiculous I almost don't want to tell you."

"Come on, I could use some entertainment right now."

Looking a bit sheepish, Sawyer confessed, "It's like this. Josh has a thing for one of the waitresses. But she won't give him the time of day because she's heard Josh goes through more women in a month that most guys do in a year. So he asked me to come in and have a drink so he can bring her over here and have his married-with-children brother vouch for him. I'm the boring respectable brother who's supposed to somehow convince this woman that all the talk about Josh is just vicious rumors and he's really a decent, one woman kinda guy."

Cort nearly choked on his beer laughing. "Good luck! So where's he now?"

"Back in the kitchen with her, trying to convince her to come out and listen to me. I told him he's got exactly fifteen minutes. I want to get home in time to read Joey his bedtime story."

Turning back to his beer, Cort tried to ignore an unexpected pang of yearning.

Sawyer noticed the change though. "Hey, what's up?"

"Jealous, I guess," Cort said lightly.

"Jealous? Of me?" Sawyer sat back and eyed Cort as if meeting him for the first time. "That doesn't sound like you. Did Tommy's disappearing act get to you that much?"

Cort finished his beer and ordered another. "I don't know, that's part of it, I guess." He paused trying to find words to come close to explaining how he felt. "Things have changed in ways I never saw coming."

"Almost getting yourself killed has a way of doing that."

"It's not just that. It's Laurel."

"Yeah, I've known that for a while now."

"Nice of you to let me in on it," Cort said with a small smile. He let the smile go, toying with the neck of his beer bottle. "After I lost Sandia, I realized we'd gotten together for all the wrong reasons. I made the mistake of settling for less than everything. But I don't think I honestly believed I'd ever find anyone that would make me want everything, want to give everything. And then Laurel came along. Now, here I am ready to start chasing papers instead of bad guys and thinking it's a good thing."

"Isn't it?" Sawyer asked.

"It should be. You're right that Tommy's a big part of it. Until you had your kids, I never understood what I was missing. But I look at you and I see I'm missing a big something.

I want that with Laurel and Tommy. I know we could have it all."

Sawyer frowned. "Everything you're telling me sounds good. Except I get the feeling there's a lot you're not telling me. What's going on, little brother?"

"That's just it. I can't figure it out. Laurel seems happy with me and I know she loves Tommy. But tonight, after the whole scare of Tommy running away, I brought up the possibility of adopting him and of Laurel and I getting married. And Laurel freaked out. She clammed up and out-and-out rejected the whole package. Except I'm sure she wants to adopt Tommy, too."

"Strange," Sawyer said, listening intently. "Is she still hung up on her ex?"

"Hardly. In fact, he's probably the reason she's against getting married again. I don't think she still loves him. She told me she's afraid if we got married it would be for the wrong reasons. She thinks because she married Scott because everyone expected it and told her it was a good idea that she'd be making a mistake if she married me just because Tommy wants us both as parents and it would be easier for me to adopt him if we were married."

"Is that the reason you want to marry her?"

"Of course not. I love her. I want to spend the rest of my life with her."

"Does she know that?"

"She should. I've been sending that message for a while now."

"Sending the message or actually telling her?"

Before Cort could answer, Nova came over to them, wearing a sleek, elegant black dress and looking a lot more sophisticated than Cort had ever seen her. "Hey, Cort, welcome back. Just don't touch anything, okay?"

"Very funny. You sure have taken to your new role. You look great."

"Thanks," she said, smiling at the compliment. "I think being a restaurant manager suits me pretty darned well."

Sawyer glanced at his watch. "Is Josh ever going to get that woman to come out here?"

Nova laughed. "I was just back in the kitchen and I think she's softening up. Give him a few more minutes. Is there anything I can get for either of you? Chips and salsa with your beers?"

Cort nodded. "Sounds great, thanks."

When she'd left to give the order to a waitress, Sawyer leaned in over the bar and asked Cort, "Have you told Laurel you love her? Maybe she's feeling pressured because you brought up the adoption first. Does she really know you want her because she's who she is and Tommy is a separate bonus who may or may not become part of your lives?"

Cort had to stop and think about that one. "I assumed I'd shown her how much she means to me. I've made it pretty clear I'm ready to give her everything. I thought that she knew that."

"One thing I've learned," Sawyer said, slapping a hand to his brother's back, "is when it comes to women, never assume anything."

Josh, all smile and swagger, a young, pretty waitress with a stubborn set to her mouth two steps behind, sauntered up to the bar interrupting whatever reply Cort might have made.

"Hey, Cort, I didn't know you'd be here, too," Josh said. "This is perfect. Now both of my brothers can tell Rita here what a great guy I am."

Sawyer and Cort exchanged a look. "Josh is a great guy," Sawyer said with a mischievous smile.

"That's right." Equally enthusiastic, Cort seconded the compliment then added, "Just ask any woman in town."

The next afternoon Cort was on the basketball court before Laurel. He had a new plan he couldn't wait to try out. He ran down the length of the court, dribbling, waiting what seemed ages for her to show up. Finally, flanked by a dozen giggling preteens, Laurel, gym bag in hand, blew her whistle to signal the start of practice.

"Three laps to warm up," she called, then stepped to the sidelines to get the basketball gear out of her bag.

Cort made his way back up the oak floor. He resisted the urge to tug at the collar of his sweatshirt. "Hi, I was hoping I'd catch you today."

She glanced up at him without so much as a twitch of a smile in greeting. "I'm usually here."

Okay, not a good start. "Looks like you're missing a couple of girls today," he said.

"Flu season." Pausing, she ran the tip of her tongue over her lips, her eyes never quite meeting his. "I didn't expect you to be here today. You usually only coach Mondays and Wednesdays."

"I decided to pick up an extra day. Now that I'm no longer in the restaurant business, I can manage a few extra hours a week here."

Laurel tightened her scrunchie, looked out at her team, blew her whistle again and tossed a ball out to one of the girls. "I'm sorry, but I really can't talk now, you know, it's hard enough to keep up with them."

"Sure. I need to get over to the boys, too. But after practice, I was wondering if you had some time?"

Hesitant, she hedged, "I— Maybe. Why?"

"I need some advice. I've set up a couple of appointments to look at houses. I need something bigger for Tommy and me."

"Okay, but what does that have to do with me?"

The resentment in her voice bit. Cort put on his most charming smile. "I was hoping you would give me your opinion. I don't quite know what I'm looking for and I'd like to hear your suggestions."

"Me, why?" she asked bluntly.

"You know more about what children need. Besides, even if adopting Tommy doesn't work out for some reason, with all the changes I'm making in my life, I need more space."

"Oh." Her body language remained guarded and Cort mentally crossed his fingers and hoped his luck would hold this time. "I might have an hour or two, but I'm not so sure it's a good idea for me to go with you. You know how I feel about things right now."

"Look, I'm not trying to talk you into anything. I won't even mention the *M* word. I know I was an insensitive jerk the other day and I've been suffering for it ever since. But now, I really just want your ideas and thoughts. Anything remotely domestic is out of my scope of experience. You saw me in the kitchen and it wasn't pretty, was it?"

Finally, she cracked a smile, relenting. "No, it wasn't. Okay, sure, we can go right after practice." With that she turned and took off down the sidelines, then stopped to look back at him. "I'll forget about yesterday, if you will."

"Gladly." Cort let go the breath he'd been holding. Sawyer had been right. She was scared, feeling pressured by his decision to adopt Tommy and by his sudden leap from being friends to marriage. He'd been clumsy and less than romantic in his approach to the subject. He needed to take a few steps back, lay some groundwork, spend time wooing her over to the idea of them together, as friends, lovers, a family.

He'd managed to coax her this far. Now all he had to do was convince her to go the distance of a lifetime with him.

"This is really nice," Laurel murmured when the Realtor had gone into another room to turn on lights. "And it's huge. How many bedrooms?"

"Four bedrooms and an office/study that could be converted if you need another," the Realtor answered, coming up behind them. "Are you planning to have a large family?"

"We're not married," Laurel said, her stomach already in knots. She should have trusted her first instinct. This wasn't a good idea. Staying completely away from Cort was the best idea. But she couldn't even stick to that for a whole day. Just seeing him today at practice had toppled her shaky resolve with frightening ease.

"I like space," Cort added with a shrug. "I have a lot of

stuff stored at my grandparents that I'd like to finally put in my own place."

The Realtor, an older, well-groomed woman, lifted a brow. "I know your grandparents well. We go to the same church."

"Practically everyone in Luna Hermosa goes to the same church," Cort said, a touch of light sarcasm in his tone.

"That's probably right," she admitted with a small smile. "So, back to the house. What do you think of it? You could move in pretty quickly. The owners had to relocate to Denver and they're making two house payments right now. They're anxious to sell."

Cort glanced at Laurel then back to the Realtor. "We'd like to walk through it again and take another look at everything. Do you mind?"

"Take your time. I'll go make some phone calls in the breakfast room."

Turning Laurel with an arm around her shoulder, Cort said, "Come on, I want to see the master suite again. That bathroom is big enough to live in."

In the next instant, she found herself letting him take her hand. His palm felt large and warm and safe around hers as he led her down a wide hallway. "You sound like an excited little boy, do you know that?"

"I am excited. I never realized how fun house hunting could be." As they entered the master suite, he paused and took her in his arms. "It's fun because you're here with me. You give me inspiration to take a leap like this."

He lowered his lips tenderly to hers and she sighed, kissing him back, what little resolve she had left to keep him at arm's length melting away as if it had never been. "Oh, Cort, if only I knew that were true."

He nuzzled her neck and whispered, "Listen to your heart and you'll know it's true."

Laurel let herself wallow in the feeling of his arms around her, his warmth and windblown scent. She'd missed this, so much. It seemed ridiculous, after less than a day apart, yet she'd become addicted to being close to him, in heart, mind and body so even a day seemed like forever. But after another long kiss she pulled back. "We should get moving or we'll miss the next appointment."

It was an excuse, but she hoped he didn't realize it. She was struggling not to let herself be seduced into believing any of this could last. Despite agreeing to forget their argument the other day, she had to keep in mind that this was all about giving Tommy a home. She was just along for the ride.

The idea crossed her mind that it might be Cort's way of showing her how much more he could offer Tommy than she could. She immediately felt ashamed for even having the thought. Cort would never throw money in her face as a tactic to convince her he'd be the better parent.

Still, Tommy deserved the best. But facing that stung as she began to accept that for Tommy's sake, she should give up any thought of adopting him. She could never offer Tommy the lifestyle Cort could. She had only love and the basics to give him, which would be enough, except that Cort could give him love and a whole lot more than a simple rented roof over his head.

"It's called a spa bathroom," Cort was saying while climbing into a fancy marble shower with separate showerheads. Launching into a lively Spanish song, he pretended to wash.

She couldn't help but laugh, even more so when he suddenly reached out and tugged her in with him underneath an imaginary flow of water. "Isn't this nice?" He mimed taking soap and rubbing her arms, shoulders and back. Then he moved to her hair, gently sliding her scrunchie out and massaging her scalp as though shampooing her loosely falling hair. "See how much fun we could have with all this space?"

Laurel felt her knees weaken and she leaned back against his chest. "That feels delicious," she murmured.

Bending, he lifted her hair to kiss her neck as he slid his arms around her waist and held her against him. "Now imagine this with warm water and candlelight. A long night, with no interruptions." His warm breath brushed against her ear as he added in a sultry whisper, "Nothing between us except water."

Oh, yes. The image came easily and brought with it a flush of heat. If she stayed here with him any longer, she'd be begging him to act out that fantasy, Realtor or no.

"You're making me dizzy," she said, opening her eyes and easing away from him.

He turned her around in his arms and kissed her, lingering. "I hope so," he said against her mouth. "That's exactly what I had in mind."

They toured the rest of the house and moved on to two more, Laurel taking care not to get caught alone with him in any more bathrooms. They both agreed nothing quite compared to the first house, and she could tell Cort probably wasn't going to be satisfied with anything less. After gathering up all of the information from the Realtor he offered to buy her dinner if she would do one more errand with him.

"I need to pick up some law books I ordered, would you mind stopping in there with me? It won't take long and then I promise you a cheeseburger."

Laurel checked her watch. She didn't have any grading to do tonight, and she was having so much fun with him she didn't want the day to end. "Sure, why not? I'd like to see what you'll be studying."

"Thanks, you won't regret it. Marco's got the best hot chocolate in town."

With a kiss to her forehead he helped her into the Jeep and they drove to a quaint local bookstore Laurel loved because it hadn't been bought out by the chains. It was housed in an old adobe building with seemingly endless small cubbies and rooms lined floor to ceiling with bookshelves. Local artists' work decorated the walls. Pottery, baskets and rugs from all over the state warmed every room. In some rooms kiva fireplaces blazed, big easy chairs and ottomans placed in front of them for customers to relax and read. A small coffee bar served Mexican coca, coffees and teas.

Cort had to duck his head as he opened the heavy oak door to the store. A jingle brought the attention of a short, stooped gentleman with a long gray beard and gray ponytail. "*Hola* Marco," Cort said to the man behind the front desk.

Marco looked up from a book, his glasses slipping down a narrow nose. "*Buenos tardes, mi amigo. Cómo estas?*"

"*Muy bien, gracias.* This is Laurel. Laurel meet Marco. He's read every book in this store."

"None has such tall tales as you, *mi amigo.*" Marco smiled at Laurel. "I've seen you here before, no?"

"Yes. I love this place. I come here whenever I can to read and grade papers by the fire."

"*Sí,* yes, the new teacher in town. Now I remember. Although, now not so new. *Bueno.*" He nodded to no one in particular then reached under the front desk and took out three heavy volumes. "So will you be teaching my friend here about the law? I see all of the books Cort ordered are on that subject."

"No—" Laurel laughed a little "—that's not my area. I teach middle-school children."

"Then here you have the perfect student."

"Very funny. Always the joker, aren't you, *mi amigo?*" Cort said, teasing. "I'll pay for these and then we're going to go back and have a cup of your amazing hot cocoa."

Marco took Cort's money, painstakingly putting it bill by bill into an ancient looking cash register. "Go find a comfortable place to sit and I will bring it to you."

Cort put an arm around Laurel's shoulder and they meandered through the store, browsing as they went. She couldn't remember when she'd felt more calm, more at peace being with him. They'd had so much going on around them that she realized they'd had little time simply to enjoy each other's company. Pressures, decisions, past pain and future fears had dominated their lives, especially since Cort had brought up the idea of marriage.

But when they settled into two overstuffed chairs side by side in front a of roaring fire, she found it perfectly natural to lean into him. The air held a faint trace of piñon smoke mingled with tempting hints of chocolate, cinnamon and coffee. And the world of problems outside seemed a world away.

"This is so nice, isn't it? What a good idea."

She lay her head on his shoulder and Cort pulled her closer, his hand gently stroking her hair. "It's the way it could always be between us. We need to do more of this," he whispered against her hair. "Just enjoy each other." She felt more than heard his short rueful laugh. "We get along pretty well when I'm not pushing the envelope."

Laurel smiled but didn't say anything. How could she tell him she wanted him to push the envelope, as far as it would go? She wanted him to want her, to love her, to make her his wife. She couldn't tell him that. He seemed to have turned a corner and accepted that she wasn't ready for more of a commitment and though he didn't know the reason why, he wasn't asking for any explanations.

Somehow he'd made peace with that reality. And she wasn't about to upset that delicate peace by telling him she wasn't the woman he thought she was. It couldn't last, but she intended to stay nestled inside this beautiful bubble as long as she could.

Until the truth shattered it.

Chapter Eighteen

In the darkest hours of the night, clouds crept over the mountains, chill with winter cold, so Laurel woke to a soft gray morning, brightened by a light veil of snow. Glad she didn't have to be at school, she wrapped a blanket around her shoulders and took her mug of coffee to the windows, watching as the snow and wind coupled in a swirling dance. Nothing moved outside and only the occasional faint sigh of the wind whispered through her empty house. It stirred a sense of isolation in her, a loneliness she hadn't felt in weeks.

The strident ringing of the phone broke into the quiet and Laurel's heart leaped, hoping it would be Cort. Things had been better between them during the past several weeks. But while he'd been attentive, including her in the things he did with Tommy and a couple of dinners with his family and friends, there had been a subtle restraint in the way he touched her, the things he said, and she only had herself to blame.

Without being completely honest with him, though, she couldn't see how to bring them back to where they'd been before she'd hurt him by dismissing his suggestion they work toward becoming a family with Tommy. And if she were completely honest with him, she couldn't believe it wouldn't irrevocably change things, and not for the better.

It didn't stop the jolt of pleasure and excitement she felt hearing his voice.

"If you're not doing anything tonight, I wanted to invite you to dinner," he said. "You can help me christen the new house."

"You've only had it for two days, and you're already having guests for dinner?" she said, laughing. He'd decided after only a few days' searching to buy the first house they'd looked at, the one Laurel could so easily imagine them and Tommy living in together. "You can't possibly have any furniture yet."

"Guest. Just you. And I've got enough for what I have in mind. How about I pick you up at six?"

Laurel's pulse jumped a notch faster. They hadn't been alone together for weeks. The idea of being secluded with him for the whole night was irresistible. "Do I dare ask what you've got in mind?"

"Sorry, that's my secret," Cort said. She could easily picture his wicked grin. "You'll have to trust me. See you at six."

He hung up before she could question him further and she was left with hours ahead of her to wonder what he'd planned. Happy to oblige, her imagination relentlessly teased her with fantasies and desires she hadn't allowed herself to acknowledge in the last weeks.

The day dragged by until her anticipation was stretched nearly to the breaking point. Never one to fuss much over her clothes, this time she spent an hour in the late afternoon trying to decide what to wear over her denim skirt and finally settled on a close-fitting buttoned sweater over a thin cotton camisole, in deep and light shades of rose. After a few minutes of dithering back and forth, she daringly decided to forego a bra and even let herself wonder if Cort would notice. She nearly changed her mind when she let herself wonder what he'd do if he did, then ruefully decided her less than generous curves made it unlikely he'd know to begin with.

Leaving her hair loose, she took extra time with her make-up and seeing the approval in his eyes when she opened the door to him exactly at six, Laurel was glad she'd made the extra effort.

"You must have done a lot of work in a very short time if you're already ready to entertain," Laurel commented on the drive over.

Eyes on the road, Cort smiled. "It's not gonna work. I'm not gonna tell you. Don't you like surprises?"

"Sometimes. As long as they don't involve things jumping out at me from dark corners."

"Damn," he said, snapping his fingers in mock disappointment, "there goes the best part of my plans."

He refused to say anything else and Laurel was left to deal with her overactive imagination again. The closer they got to his house, the more restless she got. She couldn't remember ever feeling this pitch of nervous excitement. She told herself she was being silly. After all, she'd been married, had a lover in Scott. She wasn't an innocent girl anticipating her first kiss. She wasn't even anticipating Cort's first kiss.

Cort made her feel that way, though, as if she was venturing into the unknown without any idea of where she was going to end up and in a way she was. Scott had never turned her inside out or made her feel giddy and alive with expectation nor unsettled by disturbing, intense needs and desires the way Cort did. Despite everything unresolved and uncertain between them, she wanted—no, she ached—to act on those desires.

When he took her hand and led her into his living room, she began to believe he wanted the same thing.

The room was bare of anything except a thick blanket spread in front of the fireplace and a single lamp and a portable CD player in one corner. Night spread shadows through the house, save for the golden nimbus of light cast by the lamp.

With an amused glance around the room she asked, "This is your furniture?" She let him guide her to kneel on the blanket, watching him as he coaxed the embers in the fireplace into licks of flame and then flicked on the CD player, filling the quiet with the soft, sensual flow of a Spanish ballad.

"Not all of it. I'll show you the rest later. Besides, I've got all the necessities—a blanket, a fire, food and a decent bottle of wine. Give me five minutes in the kitchen and I'll prove it to you."

"You cooked?"

"Would you believe me if I said yes?"

"Would it hurt your feelings if I said no?"

Cort laughed. "Not to that. I confess, Nova took pity on me and let me raid the restaurant. I even remembered the forks."

He'd remembered much more than that, Laurel decided, when a few minutes later he came back from the kitchen carrying an enormous hamper and two wineglasses. Sitting opposite her on the blanket, he produced more than dozen different containers from the basket, grinning sheepishly as she bit her lip to keep from smiling at the huge array of food. "I couldn't decide what you'd like best, so I grabbed one of everything."

Laurel laughed and let herself relax and enjoy the effort he'd taken to make the evening something special and to enjoy just being with him. When they'd finished, he came back from stowing the leftovers in the kitchen and sat down next to her.

"Thank you," she said, meaning it more than he probably knew. "This was fun."

"Who says we're finished?" Leaning forward, he bent and brushed a lingering kiss across her mouth. "Let's make this a celebration." He retrieved the half-empty wine bottle and refilled their glasses. "A toast, to being together."

Laurel lifted her glass, relaxed contentment ebbing slowly in the coming tide of a new, stronger sensation. "To being together."

They had hardly sipped the wine when Cort eased the glass from her hand and drew her close. "We are together. Aren't we?"

"Yes," she admitted softly, "I want to be."

His eyes smoldered with desire, reflecting a fire hotter than the one burning beside them. "Yeah, I want to be with you," he murmured, lacing his fingers through her hair. He angled his head to kiss her again, this time not satisfied with just a light touch, a small taste.

Laurel made a small sound, somewhere between a moan and a soft cry, opening to him, letting her tongue slide and tangle with his. She wanted this. She needed him. Except for the few intimate moments she'd had with Cort, it had been so long, so long since she'd even let herself think of being this close to a man.

And tonight she didn't want to think. She didn't want Cort to give her time to think because if he did, doubt and fear and all the reasons why this was a bad idea would creep in, making her question whether loving him was wise, right. Here and now, it felt right and the feeling was everything. For weeks he'd been storming her defenses, wearing away her fears, replacing them with what had become an almost constant craving to fully experience everything he silently promised with every glance, every touch, every kiss. And somehow she knew in the deepest part of her that only Cort could, or would ever make her feel this way.

Because she did love him, despite herself and her fears and all her efforts not to let herself care too much, she'd lost herself to him, heart and soul.

He dragged his mouth from hers and Laurel gave a protesting moan. "Don't stop. Please," she said.

Cort took her face in his hands and Laurel felt the tremor in his touch. "Are you sure?" As if he couldn't help himself, he kissed her again, hard and long so when he pulled back he was breathing fast. "Because the only thing I can think of right now is touching you, tasting you, being inside you. But I want this to be right for you."

"It is," Laurel said, knowing, feeling it was true, "because all I can think about is how it feels when you touch me."

"Touch you like this?" Slipping his hand under the edge of her sweater and camisole, he cupped her breast, rubbing his thumb over her nipple in a maddening rhythm.

"Do you have any idea what you're doing to me? What you've been doing to me all night?" Cort muttered hoarsely. His free hand fumbled at the buttons of her sweater. Finally, frustrated by the tiny fastenings, he stopped his caress long enough to pull apart the final buttons and strip it off her. His hands slid under her camisole again, edging it up. "Knowing you weren't wearing anything under this. Imagining what I could do to make you want me as much as I want you."

"I do…only you," she gasped as he pulled off her camisole in one swift tug.

A moment of self-doubt nagged at her and she wondered if what he saw disappointed him. He made the notion ridiculous just by the expression on his face, intent and needy, clearly aroused by looking at her. The way he looked at her made her hot; then he touched her with his hands and his mouth instead of his eyes and the heat shuddered through her. Eagerly, she answered his kiss, feeling her own almost frantic urgency to be even closer echoed in him as he shifted her back on the blanket until she was half lying under him, her legs tangled with his.

"If you don't want this to go where it's going," Cort rumbled against her ear, "you'd better stop it now."

"No, don't stop. Not tonight."

If she'd said no, Cort thought it probably would have killed him. He tried to keep a hold on his self-control but it was slipping faster by the second. Warm and eager under him, her hands clutching his shoulders, urging him to touch and taste, she made it almost impossible for him to slow things down or even remember about why it mattered.

She kicked off her shoes and he slid his hand up her thigh, drawing her leg up over his hip at the same time he kissed her deeply. The intimate press of their bodies had them both breathless. Laurel began fumbling with the buttons of his shirt and her urgency fed his own, threatening to drive away all common sense.

She pushed his shirt off his shoulders and he levered up to strip it off and toss it aside, using the advantage of position to drag down the zipper of her skirt and slowly slide it over her hips and off. He nearly lost it then, seeing her lying underneath him, clad only in thigh-high stockings and low cut panties, her hair tangled, her skin flushed.

"You're unbelievable," he murmured. Slowly, he ran his hand over her flushed skin, watching her face fill with pleasure and passion as he caressed the soft curve of her breasts and lower to tease at the edge of her panties. "Unbelievably beautiful. I've always thought so."

She shook her head as if to deny him and he smiled. "Yes. Oh, yes."

He began drawing her stockings down one long leg, then the other, savoring the soft caress of her skin against his. "The first time I saw you, I wanted to hold you. You don't know how many fantasies I've had about seeing you like this, touching you…"

Taking his time, he eased her panties off, following the path of his hands with his mouth. "I don't know what you've done to me."

Laurel breathed his name on a trembling sigh, her hands clutching his shoulders as he touched her intimately, stroking, suckling, tasting, his restraint fraying as she cried out softly, begging him with her hands and her kiss to finish what they'd started.

"I thought I was strong," Cort muttered against her throat. "But I'm not. All I want is this—" He kissed her, their tongues mating, bodies rubbing sensuously together, already finding the rhythm of passion.

All these weeks, he'd tried to keep his distance, tried to avoid even thinking about feelings this potent, this heady because he wasn't sure what she wanted. She'd twisted him up, turned him around, made him question why he continued to pursue her after all the times she'd shied away when he got too close.

The answer was this—because he'd known, without understanding why and despite everything wrong between them, that if he could just get past the barriers she kept throwing up, she would realize as he did that they belonged together.

Unable to wait any longer, Cort pushed up and away from her long enough to strip off the rest of his clothes.

"Make love to me, Cort," she whispered as he came back to her, nothing between them but heat. "I've never wanted anyone like I want you."

He wanted to love her, completely, blindly, his eyes closed to everything except the feeling. Except he couldn't, not like this. For the first time in his life, he was about to make love to a woman without protection.

Gritting his teeth against the fierce need to say to hell with it, he forced himself to pull back. He rubbed his thumb over her mouth, nearly losing it when she ran her tongue over it in invitation. "Laurel, I need to—" He groaned as her fingers tentatively stroked him where he was hottest and hardest for her.

"I need you, too," she murmured, kissing his throat, continuing her tormenting touch that became bolder as she began to realize the power she had to bring him to his knees. "Please, Cort."

"I forgot about—I can't protect you like this."

She looked at him with passion-drugged eyes then impatiently shook her head. "No, don't," she insisted almost fiercely. "Don't leave me now. It doesn't matter."

"It matters to me." Reaching over for the jeans he'd kicked aside, he fumbled in the pocket until he found what he wanted. "I want this to be right for you," he murmured, coming back to her.

She brushed her fingers over his face and the firelight caught the tears in her eyes. "It is right. I've never felt anything more right."

A wave of tenderness washed over him and he suddenly

wanted to love her so thoroughly that he drove away all the sad and lonely memories of the past years. Hers and his, so there would be nothing there but warmth and passion and a promise they would never be separated, in body, heart or soul, again.

Kissing her deeply, he slowly pushed inside her, setting the deliberate stroking rhythm, holding back his own need to thrust hard and fast until he pushed her to the edge and over. She cried out his name, shuddering in his arms and his control finally cracked and he lost himself in her.

Minutes later, spent and breathless, he shifted so she lay atop him, cradled against him and wondered what he'd just done.

All these weeks he'd been teasing, daring, coaxing her to confront the feelings she'd been afraid to admit. He'd carefully, patiently laid the bait only to find he was the one caught.

Making love with Laurel had been more than just a physical reaction to the tension that had been building between them. It had been inextricably woven with emotion in patterns deeper and more complex than mere desire, and he knew, without a doubt, his feelings for her were much more than passion and friendship, had known it for weeks, months now.

His arms tightened around her and she made a contented sound, snuggling closer. "Are you okay?" he asked.

"How can you ask me that?" Laurel murmured. She kissed his jaw then raised her head to look into his eyes, frowning slightly at whatever she saw there. "I think I should be asking you instead. Do you wish it hadn't happened?"

She wasn't looking at him anymore and he slipped his fingertips under her chin and lifted her face to his again. "I did want you, I do. And, no, I don't wish it hadn't happened. I wish it had happened sooner." He hesitated, struck by the sudden sensation of being on shaky ground, although he wasn't quite sure why. "I'm just worried I pushed you into something you weren't ready for. Maybe something you didn't really want."

"I know what I wanted," she said lightly, still avoiding looking directly at him.

"And now?"

"Now?"

"You said *wanted*. That sounds like you've got regrets."

"It's not that." She stopped, drawing out the silence until Cort had just about given up her answering. "It just makes things more—complicated," she said finally. "I imagined… I mean, I didn't exactly expect it to be— I thought…"

Cort stopped her fumbling explanation by deftly twisting so she lay under him again. He didn't need to hear it because he had a good sense of what she was feeling. She'd never been sure of herself and the power she wielded over him. He was ready to spend the rest of the night, the rest of his life, proving to her that she was more to him than a woman he'd seduced into his bed for the pleasure and challenge of it, that she was the one who'd seduced him without even trying.

"I imagined I was going to take my time and make this perfect for you," he said softly. He stroked the hair back from her face, gently shaping the curve of her cheek, her mouth, with his fingertips. "I didn't plan on you throwing yourself at me and making me so crazy—"

That had her looking at him as he'd hoped it would. "I did not throw myself at you," she began indignantly.

He went on, ignoring her sputtering. "Making me so crazy that I acted like a teenager worried about making it before your mom and dad came home."

"Are you trying to tell me you can do better?" Laurel asked, her lips twitching now with the smile she was holding back.

"Definitely."

"Sorry, I don't believe that."

"I'll just have to do my best to convince you." Levering off her, he got to his feet and then bent and scooped her into his arms, kissing away her surprised squeak. "Not here, though. Can't achieve perfection on a lumpy blanket."

Laurel wound her arms around his neck as he carried her to his bedroom. "That's a matter of opinion," she said, a soft, tremulous note in her voice that grabbed Cort's heart and made him wonder how he could have ever doubted they belonged together.

"I want to show you the rest of my furniture." She smiled, as he gently lowered her to the only real furniture he did have, an antique brass bed, and followed her down. "And I promise you, it only gets better," he said before he gathered her into his arms and slowly, lovingly, passionately, proved it to her.

Past midnight, sitting with him in front of the fire again, Laurel murmured, "I didn't get a chance to tell you, but I love what you've done to the place."

"I've always appreciated the bare-naked look myself," he said against her ear, sliding his hand up her thigh.

They'd stirred from bed after Laurel had confessed that although she loved his new bed, he'd fulfilled one of her fantasies on the blanket by the fire. More than willing to indulge her again and hoping to hear about a few more of those fantasies, Cort had easily coaxed her back onto the rumpled blanket, where they'd finished the last of the wine. Now, wearing his shirt, she lay curled up beside him, watching the fire while he idly ran his hand over her skin, unable to stop touching her.

The aura of happiness and contentment she radiated prompted him to wonder if now was the time to do what he'd intended for days now. Since she'd accused him of only wanting to push forward their relationship for Tommy's sake, he'd been biding his time, slowly trying to woo her over to believing that he wanted so much more than that.

No matter what the future held, no matter whether she felt the same or whether he was headed for emotional suicide, he couldn't hide what he felt. Saying it aloud, though, was harder than he expected. He felt like a kid, unsure of the right words, afraid of her reaction. But he didn't want to wait any longer and sitting up, he pulled her with him so she faced him.

The abrupt action confused her and she frowned a little, questioning. "Cort? Is something wrong?"

"No, nothing's wrong." *At least, I hope this isn't wrong.* "There's something I want, I need to tell you. I've been waiting for the right time, but I don't want to wait any longer." He looked into her eyes, holding her gaze steadily to convince her of the truth. "I love you, Laurel."

She caught her breath, tears shining in her eyes.

"I don't know if it's what you want or not. But I do. I've never felt anything this right with anyone else. Only you. I love your smile, especially when I know it's just for me. I love how your face lights up anytime you're around kids and your stubbornness when something's important to you. I love going to bed with you and waking up with you, being with you." He touched her face, the shape and curves he knew by heart. "I need you. Always. So much it scares me."

Taking her into his arms, he put all the promise, desire and love he didn't have words for into his kiss, hoping—praying— that it would be enough to keep her here with him forever.

She returned his kiss with an almost desperate urgency and in the back of Cort's mind, a warning whispered, telling him something wasn't right. Caught up in the sweet, fierce feeling of her in his arms, he ignored it, shifting back just enough to take her hands in his.

"Marry me, Laurel. We'll be so good together. We can be that family you want, you, me and Tommy."

Cort wasn't sure what reaction he expected, but it wasn't her suddenly pulling away from him, the happiness in her eyes dissolving into tears. Hugging her arms around her body as if she were suddenly cold, she shook her head, tears running unheeded down her face.

"No," she whispered, her voice breaking on a sob. "I can't."

Chapter Nineteen

Cort stared at her, momentarily dumbstruck. The feeling reminded him of being hit by the truck all those months ago: a blinding pain at impact followed by a black nothing. And when the numbness wore off, the pain would be double and this time there wouldn't be a cure.

He forced himself to react and said the first thing that came into his head. "At least tell me why." When she didn't answer right away, he pushed harder. "If you don't feel the same way, then tell me now."

"No, that's not it." Lurching to her feet, she took a few steps away then turned back to look at him and he could see her heart in her eyes. "I love you."

"Then why?" Cort wanted to tell her that as long as they loved each other, whatever it was didn't matter but he knew it wouldn't make any difference to her. He stood up to face her but kept the distance she'd put between them.

"Because I can't give you what you want."

"I want you."

"You want a family," she said. He could almost see her bracing herself for what she had to say; pushing at the tears on her face before hugging herself more tightly than before. "You know I lost my baby, but that's not everything. Things went wrong after that." She bit at her lower lip, briefly closing her eyes.

"Laurel," he started. He could almost touch the pain in her. "You don't have to tell me this."

"I do. You have to know. After my miscarriage, I found out—" She stopped then pushed the words out hard and quick, "I can't have any more children. It's one of the reasons Scott left me. He said—he said I couldn't give him the real family he wanted. He told me I'd never been enough of a woman for him."

Conflicting feelings assaulted Cort all at once, mixing up into a tangled mess so he didn't know which was the stronger. "Why didn't you tell me?"

"I wanted to. But I was afraid. I know how much you want a family of your own. I didn't think we had a chance of staying together if you knew I could never give that to you."

"So, let me get this straight," he ground out. He heard himself, angry and harsh, like it was someone else. "You think I'm the kind of guy who would dump you because you can't get pregnant? That I'd think you were less of a woman and I'd care more about having a *real* family, as you put it, than you? That I'd walk out on you like that jerk you were married to because I'm too self-centered to ever give up anything I want for you?"

"It's not like that."

"I think it's just like that. You don't trust me. You never have."

"No, I—"

"Don't." He spat out the word so forcefully she took a step back. "You've been lying to me from the beginning. I don't want to hear it anymore." Shoving his hands through his hair, he paced a few steps away from her, struggling for control. "Tell me," he said tightly, "all this time, what was I to you? Another one of your projects? And what was tonight? Curiosity? Or one helluva goodbye?"

"I didn't want to lose you," she said, almost pleading with him now. "I love you."

"So that's why you keep pushing me away, running every time I got too close? Because you *love* me?"

"I do! I just didn't think you would stay if you knew the truth."

"The *truth* is I don't give a damn whether or not you can have children. We could have been a family, you, me and Tommy. And there are plenty of kids like Tommy who need a home. But that doesn't happen to fit in with your idea of a *real* family. You weren't willing to give up that old dream you had with Scott to have something new with me."

"I didn't think I could have anything," she cried. She reached out a hand to him, entreating or asking for comfort, forgiveness he couldn't give right now. "I'm sorry. You don't know how sorry. I can only tell you I do trust you, and I do love you. I just didn't trust that it could be real. I wanted to. I still want to."

"But you don't," he said bluntly. "You don't trust me."

"Cort—"

"No, I can't do this. I was ready to fight for us but I lost a long time ago because you weren't even willing to try."

Laurel looked at him mutely and the grief etched in her eyes hurt him almost as much as her rejection. Part of him wanted her to argue with him, to defend herself, to say something that would make the pain she'd inflicted go away. Part of him didn't want to hear any more, because it could only prolong the hurting and make it worse.

"I should go," she finally whispered.

Not trusting himself to answer, he nodded curtly. They dressed in silence and neither of them said anything the entire drive to her house until he was standing on her doorstep, making sure she got safely inside.

"I don't want to leave it this way," she said quietly.

"What do you want then? Because I sure as hell don't know anymore."

"I want what we had before."

"Which was what, exactly? I thought I knew but it was based on lies. I'm sorry, but I don't want that back."

She drew in a tremulous breath and in the hazy light from the door lamp, tears glistened on her lashes. "I love you."

"I want to believe that. You don't know how much." The look on her face nearly broke him. "I'm sorry, but I just can't right now."

Turning from her before he let her crush his remaining defenses, he left her standing there, alone, in the cold darkness.

Leaning on the corral fence at Rancho Piñtada, Cort watched as Josh showed Tommy how to use his hands and legs to nudge the small mare in the right direction. Cort, keeping his promise to Tommy to teach him how to ride, had brought Tommy here at Rafe's suggestion. He could have gone to his grandparents' place, but he figured Tommy had enough to deal with right now without adding his grandparents to the mix and so Cort accepted Rafe's invitation without hesitation.

They'd run into Josh on their way to the barns and his brother surprised him by helping to find Tommy a suitable mount and then volunteering to give him a few pointers. Cort initially had his doubts about Josh as a teacher, but Josh proved unexpectedly patient and good at getting Tommy to relax and enjoy the lesson.

Tommy laughed at something Josh said, and Cort smiled. He was glad to see Tommy happy because the last few weeks had been rough for both of them.

He'd started the adoption process and was working on getting certified as a foster parent so Tommy could live with him while the adoption was being finalized. Tommy, excited about the prospect of finally having a real home and family, had been equally upset when Cort said the family wouldn't include Laurel. He'd done his best to reassure Tommy that just because Laurel didn't want to be Cort's wife, it didn't mean she'd stopped caring about Tommy and he'd promised Tommy that he could see Laurel any time he wanted.

Cort himself hadn't seen her in over two weeks. Tommy told him she'd missed several days at school and she hadn't been at basketball practice. He'd thought about calling her, but he didn't know what to say that would change anything. She hadn't tried to contact him, either, leaving him to believe she didn't want to even try to fix things.

"Looks like Josh found a new calling." Cort straightened as Rafe and Jule came walking up to him. Rafe nodded to where Josh was leading the mare in a circle around the corral, encouraging Tommy when the boy looked a bit uncertain and winning himself a smile. "I never would've thought Josh had the patience to work with a kid."

"Me, either, but he's actually pretty good," Cort said.

Jule shook her head at them. "Tommy looks like he's getting the hang of it, anyway." Without taking her eyes off Tommy and Josh, she said, "I thought Laurel might have been here, too. We haven't seen her in a while. Is everything okay?"

Rafe shot her a warning glance but Cort waved him off, resigned to having to explain things, at least to his brothers and their wives.

"I haven't seen her in a while, either. We aren't...things didn't work out."

"Really?" Jule asked. "I thought you seemed so good for each other."

"Yeah, well, apparently she didn't think so. I asked her to marry me and she turned me down." Cort felt a resurgence of all the angry, painful feelings he'd tried to reconcile with in the past weeks and realized he was strangling the railing in a white-knuckled grip. He forced himself to let go, to smile. "I'm going to gain a son, though. I've started adoption proceedings for Tommy."

"Cort, that's wonderful," Jule said warmly. "I'm sure Tommy's happy about it. And I know you'll be a great father."

Rafe nodded his approval, but he studied Cort with a slight frown, as if he saw behind the wall Cort was throwing up to keep from spilling out his feelings. Considering Rafe's experience at building walls before Jule had started tearing them down, Cort decided his brother probably understood better than most what he was trying to cope with.

"Cort…" Jule began. She stopped, chewed at her lower lip for a moment, then offered, "I could talk to Laurel. Maybe there's something I can do to help."

"Thanks, but you'd be wasting your time. Laurel made up her mind about us a long time ago."

He could see Jule marshaling an argument but her cell phone buzzed and she pursed her mouth in exasperation when she saw the number. "Sorry, I have to take this. Mrs. Sanchez's parrot is dying again."

She walked a little away from them and Rafe moved to lean against the fence next to Cort, arms crossed over his chest. "You sure it's over?"

"Real sure. She gave up on us before we even got started. I was just the last to know."

"Maybe. But when I was ready to give up on making things right with Jule, Sawyer asked me whether everything else really mattered without her. Maybe you should ask yourself the same thing."

Cort turned away from Rafe's steady gaze and looked at Tommy, reminded of everything he'd lost and gained in the last eighteen months, everything he wanted and couldn't have. "Something else has to matter without her. I have to make it matter," he said at last, "because she hasn't given me a choice."

"Jule, what a nice surprise," Laurel said, opening the door. It was a surprise all right, but she wasn't sure how nice it was going to be. There was only one reason Jule would show up on her doorstep unannounced. And that reason was Cort. Nervous and dreading whatever it was Jule had come to say, Laurel invited her in as graciously as possible.

"I'm sorry for not calling first," Jule said gently, "but I was afraid you wouldn't see me if I did."

Laurel gestured to her couch. "Please sit down. You're

probably right. Not that I wouldn't love to talk—normally—but right now…well, I'm sure I don't have to tell you about Cort and me."

"I wanted to see if you are okay. Cort's, well, he's trying to adjust, although it's obvious he's upset. But I hadn't heard anything from anyone about you. Tommy said you hadn't even been at school."

"I took some vacation time." Laurel looked away, felt tears threatening again. "Things are just…things are difficult right now."

"Oh, Laurel, I'm so sorry. If it's any comfort, Cort's as miserable as you are," Jule said with a sympathetic smile.

Laurel shook her head. If anything, that made it worse. "This is all my fault."

"I doubt that. Is there anything I can do to help? We love Cort and we're awfully fond of you and all of us hate seeing the both of you so unhappy."

Reaching for a tissue, Laurel twisted it in her hand. She'd been keeping them handy night and day lately. "I wish there were but I'm afraid I've ruined any possibility to get back together."

"Are you sure? I don't know what happened between you two, but—"

"What happened is I lied to him," Laurel said flatly. This time, she could tell all of the truth. She had nothing more to lose. "I had a miscarriage a few years ago and there were complications. I can't have children."

"Oh, Laurel…" Jule reached out to take her hand, giving it a squeeze.

"I never told anyone until recently, not even my family. All the time Cort talked about wanting a family of his own, I should have said something. I hurt him so badly by not telling him early on. But I was terrified. My ex-husband abandoned me when he found out and I couldn't let myself trust that Cort wouldn't do the same thing, especially when I knew how important having children was to him." She paused, shaking her head. "It seems ridiculous, I know. But I couldn't get out of that frame of mind and past the pain. Until it was too late."

"It's not ridiculous at all," Jule said firmly. "You were devastated. Pain like that takes a long time to heal after such a cruel rejection."

Laurel sniffed and rubbed at her nose with her tissue. "It's nice of you to be so understanding, but I can't expect Cort to feel the same. He was so angry and upset when he found out I'd been hiding this from him. I don't think he'll ever feel the same about me again."

"I wouldn't be so sure about that. Cort doesn't fall in love easily. And I can't believe he'll fall out of love any easier."

"But how can I possibly convince him I was wrong not to trust him? That I do love him and I want to spend the rest of my life with him and Tommy? Who, by the way, may not feel the same about me anymore, either. He's been so distant and aloof since Cort and I broke up. I feel doubly rotten about that. He needs stability and consistency and he had his hopes up that the three of us would make a family, and then…" She broke off, her voice catching on a surge of emotion.

Jule gave her hand another squeeze. "Maybe you need a little less of beating yourself up and a little more determination to put things right," she said quietly. "Never give up, Laurel. If I'd given up on Rafe—and believe me many people told me I should have—we wouldn't be together today."

"I didn't know. You two seem so perfect together."

"Now, but Rafe was difficult, to put it mildly. He had so many reasons not to trust that our love for each other was strong enough to overcome anything that he kept rejecting me over and over again."

"Why didn't you just give up and move on?" Laurel asked. She had a hard time convincing herself Cort wouldn't do just that.

"Because I knew in my heart that he loved me and that we were meant for each other," Jule said with a smile. "And, I knew *he* knew he loved me, too, but it took a long time for him to work through his problems enough to be able to see that and admit it both to himself and to me."

"I think Cort loves me. He told me he did—" The memory of it was enough to touch warmth to the chill that had been living inside her for the past miserable weeks. "He's done everything to show me he does."

"I know he does. Listen, I forgave Rafe, and believe me back then he could be pretty awful." She laughed a little, obviously remembering a past she might rather forget. "But I knew I had to let all of that go and trust he would come around. I believe Cort would forgive you, too, if you can find the courage to give him a chance to try."

Laurel's heart began to beat faster and despite herself, she began to hope. "Would he, after what I did to him?"

"If he doesn't, then everything I know about Cort and everything I've learned about love is a lie."

"That's right, put the nail dead center on the board and tap it a little until it takes hold." Cort and Tommy had gone looking for the perfect tree in their new backyard to build a tree house in and yesterday they'd found it. It was a giant old cottonwood with an endless tangle of sturdy limbs that seemed to call to them to bring children and laughter into its grandfatherly arms.

And so they'd listened, making a quick trip to the lumber store to get supplies then starting bright and early the next day. It was cold, but sunny and warm enough to work. Besides, Tommy was anxious to have it finished by spring so he could have friends over to play in it.

Now Tommy sat on the first plank, ready to hammer the next. Curled over a hammer and nail he tapped lightly on the metal head. "Am I doing it right?"

"Perfect," Cort said, guiding Tommy's hands, "now give it a good whack."

With a quick hit, Tommy drove the nail into the pine plank and then looked up at Cort, beaming. "It's not so hard."

Cort ruffled his hair. "Not when you know what you're doing."

"This is fun." Tommy grabbed another nail from a nearby box. "How long til it's built?"

"Well, it'll take a while. We've gotta get some work done on the other house, too." Thanks to the contacts he'd made while working for the sheriff's department, Cort had been able to pull a few strings and get the paperwork expedited, giving him custody of Tommy while the adoption went through. Tommy had moved in a couple of days ago and the big house was starting to feel a little more like a home. "We've got a lot of boxes to unpack yet and we still need to get a desk for your room."

"And one of those climbing things for Ben and Jerry," Tommy said, calling the cats by the names he'd decided on. He'd named them after Cort's favorite ice cream after he found out that Cort, despite Jule's reprimands, had a habit of treating the cats to a few spoonfuls every now and then.

"That, too," Cort agreed.

Tommy fidgeted with the nail, then sighed. "I wish…"

"What?"

Darting a glance at Cort, Tommy said, "I wish Mrs. Tanner would change her mind."

Cort's heart constricted, but he tried not to let Tommy see the renewed wash of pain. "Me, too, buddy. But it isn't gonna happen." It was still a challenge to keep his voice steady whenever he mentioned Laurel, yet he couldn't let Tommy see how much losing her still hurt. "We'll do okay, you and me. Right?"

The boy nodded and Cort put an arm around him. "I know you want things to be different but there are some things I can't fix. This is one of them." Tommy didn't answer and after a few moments, Cort nudged the hammer toward him again. "Come on, let's see if we can get a little further before lunch."

They'd only been at it a few minutes when a familiar voice stopped them both.

"Anyone up there?" Laurel called up to them.

Cort forgot to breathe as he and Tommy exchanged a glance. Tommy waited, looking expectantly at him, and then, apparently deciding Cort wasn't going to say anything, leaned over and said, "We're both up here. Cort and me are building a tree house."

"That's exciting. I rang the doorbell several times because the Jeep was in the yard. When I saw all of the wood sticking out of the back of it, I thought you two might be building something."

"Wanna climb up and see it?"

"Well, I would but I'm wearing a skirt."

Tommy scrunched up his nose. "Girls." He turned back to Cort. "Can we go down and see her?"

"Uh, yeah," Cort managed. He cleared his throat. "Sure." Shimmying down in front of Tommy so he could catch the boy if he fell, Cort landed lightly on his feet, lifting Tommy down the last stretch.

On the ground the threesome faced each other, Cort and Laurel for the first time in weeks. Cort found himself feeling a miserable mix of uncomfortable, hurt, happy, scared, hopeful and curious. He took a deep breath. *Say something, anything,* he prodded himself. "How about some hot cocoa?"

"That sounds great," Laurel said, her eyes never leaving his. "I wanted to talk to you. If it's okay."

Cort's stomach knotted and he turned away from her to lead the way back to the house. "Sure, yeah." *Talk, why not? She can't hurt me any more. Unless she's come to say she's leaving Luna Hermosa...* That, he didn't want to think about.

They walked inside to the kitchen, the silence between them awkward and heavy. Even Tommy seemed subdued. "We don't have much to offer, but we do have cocoa."

"Fine, that's fine," Laurel said. "Can I help?"

"No, thanks. Even Tommy and I can do this by ourselves. Right?"

"Yeah, we do it all the time."

When the cocoa was ready, Laurel turned to Tommy.

"Would you mind if Cort and I went into the other room and talked for a few minutes alone? It's grown-up stuff. I won't keep him long, promise."

"That's okay." Tommy said. He looked from Laurel to Cort with a hopefulness that made Cort wish she hadn't shown up if all she wanted was to put the Rest In Peace marker on their relationship. "I'm hungry anyhow. I'll make a peanut-butter sandwich."

"Thanks, buddy," Cort said, opening the swinging kitchen door for Laurel. "We won't be long."

How long can it take to say goodbye?

Standing facing him in the living room, Laurel gathered her courage and prayed she could make him understand. "Cort, I don't know how to put this and I'll probably bungle it, so I'm just going to say it."

He tensed, as if expecting a blow. "I'm listening."

"I'm so sorry I didn't trust you. I wanted to, you don't know how much I wanted to. And I don't expect you to understand, but I was terrified of losing you because I know how much you want a family of your own." A tear slid down her face. Laurel ignored it, determined to finish what she'd begun. "I let my past get in the way of you and me. But I was wrong." Her breath caught. "So very wrong."

"Laurel," he said, and made a move in her direction, then stopped himself. "I do understand. I shouldn't have pushed you toward something you weren't ready for. I just convinced myself we wanted the same things at the same time. But I've thought a lot about it and tried to put myself in your position. It's okay, really."

"No, it's not okay. Nothing's been okay for weeks."

"You're right," he said quietly, "it hasn't."

She was shaking, inside and out, afraid at any minute to hear him say it really was over. She couldn't let him walk away though without giving everything she had to convince him to stay.

"I love you," she said. "I hope you can forgive me because I want to spend the rest of my life proving just how much I love you." Closing the distance between them, Laurel touched a trembling hand to his face and echoed his own words, the words she'd held so close to her heart even when she despaired of them ever being her reality. "Marry me, Cort. I know we'll be so good together. We can be that family you want, you, me and Tommy."

For a moment, the world stopped and Laurel balanced on the edge of falling until, slowly, Cort brought his hand up to cover hers and caught her. Closing his eyes, he pressed a kiss into her palm. When he looked at her again, Laurel knew his answer. "Laurel, I—"

"Yes! Say yes!" Tommy burst into the room. "See," the boy said, and tugged at Cort's arm. "She just made a mistake, that's all. She does want you." He turned to Laurel. "And me?"

Tears flowing freely, she swept Tommy into her arms. "Of course, I want you. I love you, too. I want you to be my son forever." She ruffled Tommy's hair as she raised her eyes to Cort's. "If it's okay with your dad."

"More than okay," Cort said with a smile that healed Laurel's heart and filled her with a light that banished yesterday's shadows to places where they couldn't hurt her again.

"So does that mean yes?" Tommy asked.

Cort's smile broadened. "Give me a minute. I'll be right back."

He disappeared for several moments, leaving Laurel and Tommy looking at each other in confusion. When he returned, Cort took Laurel's hand and slid the ring he'd brought back onto her finger. Through her tears, the diamond seemed a brilliant rainbow.

Cort curved her hand in his and in one word, promised her everything. "Yes."

She was in his arms then, laughing and crying, and returning his kiss with all the love and passion she could put into it. It might have gone on forever if Tommy's groan hadn't reminded them they weren't alone.

"You guys aren't gonna do that all the time now, are you?" he muttered, scrunching his face up at them.

Cort smiled into Laurel's eyes. "Oh, yeah," he murmured, "all the time."

"And then some," she agreed.

Tommy groaned again and Cort and Laurel laughed, pulling him into their circle, and making it complete.

* * * * *

For a sneak preview of Marie Ferrarella's
DOCTOR IN THE HOUSE,
coming to NEXT in September,
please turn the page.

He didn't look like an unholy terror.

But maybe that reputation was exaggerated, Bailey Del-Monico thought as she turned in her chair to look toward the doorway.

The man didn't seem scary at all.

Dr. Munro, or Ivan the Terrible, was tall, with an athletic build and wide shoulders. The cheekbones beneath what she estimated to be day-old stubble were prominent. His hair was light brown and just this side of unruly. Munro's hair looked as if he used his fingers for a comb and didn't care who knew it.

The eyes were brown, almost black as they were aimed at her. There was no other word for it. *Aimed.* As if he was debating whether or not to fire at point-blank range.

Somewhere in the back of her mind, a line from a B movie, "Be afraid—be very afraid…" whispered along the perimeter of her brain. Warning her. Almost against her will, it caused her to brace her shoulders. Bailey had to remind herself to breathe in and out like a normal person.

The chief of staff, Dr. Bennett, had tried his level best to put her at ease and had almost succeeded. But an air of tension had entered with Munro. She wondered if Dr. Bennett was bracing himself, as well, bracing for some kind of disaster or explosion.

"Ah, here he is now," Harold Bennett announced needlessly. The smile on his lips was slightly forced, and the look in his gray, kindly eyes held a warning as he looked at his chief neurosurgeon. "We were just talking about you, Dr. Munro."

"Can't imagine why," Ivan replied dryly.

Harold cleared his throat, as if that would cover the less-than-friendly tone of voice Ivan had just displayed. "Dr. Munro, this is the young woman I was telling you about yesterday."

Now his eyes dissected her. Bailey felt as if she was undergoing a scalpel-less autopsy right then and there. "Ah, yes, the Stanford Special."

He made her sound like something that was listed at the top of a third-rate diner menu. There was enough contempt in his voice to offend an entire delegation from the UN.

Summoning the bravado that her parents always claimed had been infused in her since the moment she first drew breath, Bailey put out her hand. "Hello. I'm Dr. Bailey DelMonico."

Ivan made no effort to take the hand offered to him. Instead, he slid his long, lanky form bonelessly into the chair beside her. He proceeded to move the chair ever so slightly so that there was even more space between them. Ivan faced the chief of staff, but the words he spoke were addressed to her.

"You're a doctor, DelMonico, when I say you're a doctor," he informed her coldly, sparing her only one frosty glance to punctuate the end of his statement.

Harold stifled a sigh. "Dr. Munro is going to take over your education. Dr. Munro—" he fixed Ivan with a steely gaze that had been known to send lesser doctors running for their antacids, but, as always, seemed to have no effect on the chief neurosurgeon "—I want you to award her every consideration.

From now on, Dr. DelMonico is to be your shadow, your sponge and your assistant." He emphasized the last word as his eyes locked with Ivan's. "Do I make myself clear?"

For his part, Ivan seemed completely unfazed. He merely nodded, his eyes and expression unreadable. "Perfectly."

His hand was on the doorknob. Bailey sprang to her feet. Her chair made a scraping noise as she moved it back and then quickly joined the neurosurgeon before he could leave the office.

Closing the door behind him, Ivan leaned over and whispered into her ear, "Just so you know, I'm going to be your worst nightmare."

Bailey DelMonico has finally
gotten her life on track, and is
passionate about her recent career
change. Nothing will stand in the way
of her becoming a doctor...that is,
until she's paired with the sharp-tongued
Dr. Ivan Munro.

Watch the sparks fly in

Doctor in
the House

by *USA TODAY* Bestselling Author
Marie Ferrarella

Available September 2007

Intrigued? Read more at
TheNextNovel.com

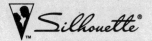

Silhouette®

Romantic
SUSPENSE

Sparked by Danger,
Fueled by Passion.

When evidence is found that Mallory Dawes
intends to sell the personal financial information
of government employees to "the Russian,"
OMEGA engages undercover agent Cutter Smith.
Tailing her all the way to France, Cutter is
fighting a growing attraction to Mallory while at
the same time having to determine her connection
to "the Russian." Is Mallory really the mouse in
this game of cat and mouse?

Look for

Stranded with a Spy

by *USA TODAY* bestselling author

Merline Lovelace

October 2007.

Also available October wherever you buy books:

BULLETPROOF MARRIAGE *(Mission: Impassioned)*
by Karen Whiddon

A HERO'S REDEMPTION *(Haven)* by Suzanne McMinn

TOUCHED BY FIRE by Elizabeth Sinclair

REQUEST YOUR FREE BOOKS!
2 FREE NOVELS PLUS 2 FREE GIFTS!

SPECIAL EDITION®
Life, Love and Family!

YES! Please send me 2 FREE Silhouette Special Edition® novels and my 2 FREE gifts. After receiving them, if I don't wish to receive any more books, I can return the shipping statement marked "cancel." If I don't cancel, I will receive 6 brand-new novels every month and be billed just $4.24 per book in the U.S., or $4.99 per book in Canada, plus 25¢ shipping and handling per book and applicable taxes, if any*. That's a savings of at least 15% off the cover price! I understand that accepting the 2 free books and gifts places me under no obligation to buy anything. I can always return a shipment and cancel at any time. Even if I never buy another book from Silhouette, the two free books and gifts are mine to keep forever.   235 SDN EEYU 335 SDN EEY6

Name	(PLEASE PRINT)	
Address		Apt.
City	State/Prov.	Zip/Postal Code

Signature (if under 18, a parent or guardian must sign)

Mail to the Silhouette Reader Service™:
IN U.S.A.: P.O. Box 1867, Buffalo, NY 14240-1867
IN CANADA: P.O. Box 609, Fort Erie, Ontario L2A 5X3

Not valid to current Silhouette Special Edition subscribers.

Want to try two free books from another line?
Call 1-800-873-8635 or visit www.morefreebooks.com.

* Terms and prices subject to change without notice. NY residents add applicable sales tax. Canadian residents will be charged applicable provincial taxes and GST. This offer is limited to one order per household. All orders subject to approval. Credit or debit balances in a customer's account(s) may be offset by any other outstanding balance owed by or to the customer. Please allow 4 to 6 weeks for delivery.

Your Privacy: Silhouette is committed to protecting your privacy. Our Privacy Policy is available online at www.eHarlequin.com or upon request from the Reader Service. From time to time we make our lists of customers available to reputable firms who may have a product or service of interest to you. If you would prefer we not share your name and address, please check here. ☐

SSE07

HARLEQUIN®

NeXt™

GET $1.⁰⁰ OFF

your purchase of any Harlequin NEXT novel.

Receive $1.⁰⁰ off

any Harlequin NEXT novel.

Available wherever books are sold, including most bookstores, supermarkets, drugstores and discount stores.

Coupon expires February 28, 2008.
Redeemable at participating retail outlets
in the U.S. only. Limit one coupon per customer.

5 65373 00076 2 (8100) 0 11436

HNCPNSSEUS09

HARLEQUIN®

NeXt™

GET $1.⁰⁰ OFF

your purchase of any Harlequin NEXT novel.

Receive $1.⁰⁰ off

any Harlequin NEXT novel.

Available wherever books are sold, including most bookstores, supermarkets, drugstores and discount stores.

Coupon expires February 28, 2008.
Redeemable at participating retail outlets
in Canada only. Limit one coupon per customer.

RETAILER: Harlequin Enterprises Ltd. will pay the face value of this coupon plus 10.25 cents if submitted by customer for this specified product only. Any other use constitutes fraud. Coupon is nonassignable. Void if taxed, prohibited or restricted by law. Consumer must pay any government taxes. Mail to Harlequin Enterprises Ltd., P.O. Box 3000, Saint John, New Brunswick E2L 4L3, Canada. Limit one coupon per customer. Valid in Canada only.

52608041

HARLEQUIN®

Mediterranean NIGHTS™

Sail aboard the luxurious Alexandra's Dream and experience glamour, romance, mystery and revenge!

Coming in October 2007...

AN AFFAIR TO REMEMBER

by

Karen Kendall

When Captain Nikolas Pappas first fell in love with Helena Stamos, he was a penniless deckhand and she was the daughter of a shipping magnate. But he's never forgiven himself for the way he left her—and fifteen years later, he's determined to win her back.

Though the attraction is still there, Helena is hesitant to get involved. Nick left her once...what's to stop him from doing it again?

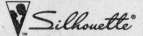 Silhouette®

COMING NEXT MONTH